Angel's Share

a&b

Angel's Share

MIKE RIPLEY

First published in Great Britain in 2006 by
Allison & Busby Limited
13 Charlotte Mews
London W1T 4EJ
www.allisonandbusby.com

Copyright © 2006 by MIKE RIPLEY

The moral right of the author has been asserted.

A catalogue record for this book is available from
the British Library.

10 9 8 7 6 5 4 3 2 1

ISBN 0 7490 8157 0
978-0-7490-8157-7

Printed and bound in Wales by
Creative Print and Design, Ebbw Vale

MIKE RIPLEY is the author of thirteen previous novels in the 'Angel' series, which have twice won the Crime Writers' Last Laugh Award for comedy. He was also a scriptwriter for the BBC's *Lovejoy* series and served as the *Daily Telegraph*'s crime fiction critic for ten years. He currently writes a monthly crime column for the *Birmingham Post* and regularly talks on crime fiction at libraries and festivals. His crime fiction gossip column 'Getting away with Murder' can be found at *www.shotsmag.co.uk*.

After twenty years of working in London, he decamped to East Anglia and became an archaeologist. He could thus claim to be one of the very few crime writers who actually did investigate dead bodies.

At the age of fifty, he suffered a stroke and has written about his experience and recovery in *Surviving a Stroke*. He has been appointed to the government's Stroke Strategy Steering Group and now works to promote the Blood Pressure Association.

Also by Mike Ripley

'I am of the police, no. I am a private detective. Confidential.'

– Raymond Chandler, *Farewell, My Lovely*.

To Philip Oakes (1928-2005).
Poet, novelist, biographer, journalist,
scriptwriter, critic, scholar and gentleman.

*

Special thanks are due to Alec Walters
for help in navigating the Dorset coast
and blowing up boats.

Chapter One

It is quite true that I wasn't doing anything that morning except looking at a blank computer screen and thinking about writing an email. It is also quite true that I don't have a great deal to do any morning. But that is no reason why I should have to go out hunting for old Mr Ellrington's missing girlfriend. I don't happen to be a policeman.

'Angel! Will you put down that frigging book and at least *pretend* to be doing some work.'

'But of course, Veronica,' I said with my best smile. 'Are we expecting visitors?'

'They're called *clients*,' she snapped, teetering on the edge of one of her hissy fits. 'And they like it if we look as if we're busy, not lounging around reading a paperback. What is it anyway?'

'*Pearls Are A Nuisance*,' I said proudly.

Veronica said nothing.

'By Chandler,' I enthused.

She looked at me with a sort of sadness in her grey eyes.

'Chandler who?'

I shook my head slowly, mostly to try and unclench my teeth, and thought, not for the first time: was this any way to run a private detective agency?

I slotted the book in among the others of my growing collection on the window sill. Veronica, it seemed, was noticing them for the first time.

'Where did all those books come from?'

'Now that is one of the great benefits of living out in the country,' I said. 'You get to go to things they call bring and buy sales at church halls and vicarages and they always have loads of really interesting second-hand books going dirt cheap. Even the old green Penguin editions...'

'Are they all *stories*?' she said, almost gagging on the word.

'Well, novels, yes. I've got almost all the Chandlers – that's Raymond Chandler by the way. The obligatory MacDonalds – Ross and John D., of course, plus a sampling of Crumley, Parker, Grafton and Paretsky. Oh, and a fair number of Nero Wolfes by Rex Stout, because I'm an old-fashioned romantic at heart.'

'But...they're all...*stories*...right?' she said slowly.

'I look on them as training manuals,' I said.

And I did. Which was why I was claiming them as legitimate expenses against income tax.

I had only been a private detective for a month and I was still learning the ropes, some of which had proved quite a shock to the system I don't mind admitting. Like the crazy notion that if you have a job, they expect you to come in to the office and do it *every day* with only the weekends off for good behaviour. I mean, nobody had said anything about that. Where were the tablets of stone *that* was written on?

Actually, it would have been in the very small print of my contract of employment if I had one, but me being me and Amy being Amy, it hadn't quite worked out that way.

My fate had been sealed the minute Amy had realised she was pregnant. Now, fair play, that probably was my fault, but there was no need to over-react the way she did and insist that, because she might have to retire from public life for a few months, I had to get a job. Plus, she had pointed out that *her* house in Hampstead was obviously unsuitable for the raising of children, though obvious to whom I wasn't quite sure.

Her solution to both these problems came to her in an adrenalin rush probably sparked off by her hormones. She found me a job and told me to find us a house in the country. Failure on either count was not an option; or rather it was an option which would result in me sleeping alone, and alone on the street.

Fortunately living with Amy had taught me that multi-tasking involves more than having a cigarette with a drink and I surprised everybody, myself included, by completing a successful house-hunt, barring the paperwork and actually handing over shedloads of cash. I left all that mortgage business to Amy, not that she would have trusted me with any of it, or allowed me to deal with all the solicitors, surveyors, insurance assessors, valuers, damp proofers, woodworm specialists, electricians and plumbers who were sniffing round after a piece of the action.

After all, I had done the difficult bit. I had found us a charming, seventeenth-century, four-bedroomed country house in a picturesque hamlet in rural Cambridgeshire called Toft End which was close enough to a motorway and a rail line to allow commuting into London, but isolated and peaceful enough to impress the hell out of Amy's friends and colleagues in the fashion business, especially the female ones of similar age who, during every high-powered board room meeting, were fretting over the battery levels in their biological clocks and secretly daydreaming about thatched roofs, roses round the door, Range Rovers and owning 2.4 Labradors.

I admit that the fact that The Old Rosemary Branch had been a former pub (and was rumoured to be haunted) was what had attracted me to it in the first place. That and the fact that I knew something about the estate agent handling the initial sale that he wouldn't want made public. The inevitable £50,000 reduction in the asking price, even before Amy had viewed the property, merely sweetened the deal. I had been confident, though, that Amy would love the place when she saw it and for once my judgement of women had proved dead accurate. After her first tour of inspection she was on her mobile to a very posh firm of interior designers even as she was fastening the seat belt around the blooming bump over her stomach.

All she had to do was sign on the dotted line and pick a removals firm from the Yellow Pages; apart from the small matter of raising the finance, that is. But that wasn't a problem for her. After all, she had a house in very desirable Hampstead to sell which she did with such speed and efficiency that I suspected she had been considering offers for some time. I never knew how much she got for the place, except that it was more than enough to pay for The Old Rosemary Branch, and I never even got to know who bought it as I was never allowed to show around a prospective buyer. My only contribution to that side of things was to make sure that Armstrong II, my trusty Austin Fairway London black cab (though not technically a taxi any more), was kept well out of sight for the duration of the sale. Amy had insisted that Armstrong wasn't 'cluttering up' the driveway when potential purchasers turned up. It simply wouldn't have done to give the impression that London cab drivers lived in Hampstead, even if some of them did. Amy had also taken the view that it might be better if I wasn't around cluttering up the place during the day and so she had got me a job.

As I couldn't remember having done anything specific to upset her and as I hadn't broken a mirror, walked under a ladder or kicked a black cat recently, I put *that* down to her hormones.

'How on earth can you call those *stories* "training manuals"?' Veronica spluttered, not willing to let the matter lie.

I didn't think it the appropriate moment to tell her that it had been a dodgy, possibly disbarred, accountant in a pub in Wandsworth who had advised me. The same guy who told me I could claim for 'work clothes' but then looked slightly dubious when I asked if that covered a new suit from Hugo Boss.

'It's all part of the lifelong learning culture, Vonnie, dear,' I waffled. 'The government's very keen on that, as long as it doesn't have to provide any of it. If you don't embrace it, they call you a NEET – Not in Employment, Education or Training – and they slap an Anti-Social Behaviour Order on you. Still, for some of the youngsters these days, ASBO will be the only letters they get to put after their names.'

'What the *frick* are you talking about?'

I knew she was getting cross. When she started inventing swear words, it was a sure sign.

'I'm talking about me taking my responsibilities seriously, Veronica, and as my boss, you really should be supportive. I didn't ask to come and work here, but now I'm here I'm willing to give it my best shot, even if that means extensive retraining and having to read these...' I waved a hand over the row of paperbacks on the window sill '...over and over again.'

She rocked back on her kitten heels and peered at me over the tops of her glasses.

'Retrain?' she said cuttingly. *'From what?'*

I had to admit she had a point. I hadn't exactly been doing much when Amy had come up with the idea that I should become a private detective. In fact my last proper job had been...well, I'm sure I'd had one sometime and if she had only given me time to think, I would have come up with something. She insisted I had all the necessary skills but when I had asked her what those were, she said vaguely:

'Oh, you know, people skills.'

'You mean I'm a good man-manager?' I had prompted.

'No, I mean you're good at spotting nasty people. You have a natural affinity for low-lifes, scumbags, pervs, drunks, chauvinists, conmen, scam-artists, bobbers and weavers.'

'You mean musicians?'

'Them too. You get on with just the sort of people private detectives protect us from – and then there's that Rule of Life you have, you know, the one that says if you ask somebody the right way, they'll tell you anything. That could be a private eye's motto, that could.'

I hated it when someone quoted my own platitudes back at me, but I didn't let it show.

'Plus...plus...' Amy had said, holding up her fingers one, two, three, like she'd just had even more ideas. 'You drive around in a black London cab, so nobody will notice you. That's another skill.'

This was turning out to be quite a character résumé: I hung out with pond life and nobody noticed me doing it.

'You can – on occasion and with a bit of help – scrub up quite presentably if you wanted to mix with real people, or you could pass for one of those sad bastards who pretend to be a *Big Issue* seller. That must be a talent,' she added.

It was me who had told her about the scam where you stand looking forlorn at a tube station entrance with just a single copy of last week's *Big Issue*, rescued from a litter bin, and when somebody eventually offers to buy it (as they always do on the 'there but for the grace of God' principle), you look up plaintively and tell them that you're very sorry but you don't have any change and that you've only one copy left because somebody nicked your allocation whilst you were in the Gents. Nine out of ten punters would give you a quid and tell you to sell the magazine to someone else. You might even get a fiver and be told to keep the change if you tried it on a Thursday (pay day) and hit on a bunch of secretaries off to the wine bar after work. I've often found the younger, professional, regularly-employed female to be the most generous breed of London's teeming populus, especially when flush with cash and out on the lash. Amy puts it down to no domestic responsibilities and feeling guilty about spending so much money on the clothes she designs and markets at them.

'And another thing,' she had said, as if reaching a logical conclusion, 'you wouldn't be the slightest bit interested in hanging around a new house while I redesigned the kitchen and supervised the decorators, now would you?'

'So, basically, you're saying I have to get a job to get me out of your way?'

'Oh don't be such a big girl's blouse, it was a rhetorical question,' she had snapped.

'Do I not know what rhetorical means?' I had said haughtily, sweeping out of the room.

I had started work the next day, as the new boy at Rudgard & Blugden Confidential Investigations of Shepherd's Bush Green, London W12.

Except I wasn't just the new boy, I was the only boy, as it was supposed to be an all-female firm of private eyes.

R & B Investigations, which I had once thought had an air of snappy street-cred about it, was formed by an unholy alliance between Stella Rudgard and Veronica Blugden, two unlikely soul mates separated by deep chasms when it came to class, sophistication, education and business skill. Not to mention looks, intelligence, fashion sense and capacity to handle alcohol. Veronica had come down to London from somewhere up north seeking her fortune and had more or less stumbled into the detective business, with Stella being the object of her first case. Stella, who hailed from a family of landed gentry in Hertfordshire (which they called the Northern Home Counties), was thought to have run away from the bosom of said family, but Stella had her own agenda and came out of hiding to end up running the show. Amazingly the partnership had held together and had actually prospered, trading on the fact that it was an all-female agency.

Until now.

Or until a cataclysmic series of events had coincided, the like of which could not possibly have been foretold by ancient prophecy, a casting of runes, the examination of a pigeon's entrails or half a dozen planets being in line. Even I might have noticed given warning signs like that.

R & B Investigations had blipped on the Angel radar again when one of their operatives had started investigating Amy's past, much to her annoyance and mine when I discovered there were large chunks of it I didn't know existed. To sort things out I had gone straight to the top to see Stella Rudgard, only to find her on the brink of an ideal husband of substantial wealth and excellent tailoring. Naturally, I didn't get much sense out of Stella, who went off on an extended honeymoon to the Caribbean as Mrs Stella Wemyss-Wilkins, and I had to sort things out, as usual, for myself. The end result was R & B Investigations were one operative down and their co-founder and senior partner was getting a taste for the Caribbean high-life and not exactly looking forward to coming back to the office grind in Shepherd's Bush.

At this point, Amy, with her own agenda, had stepped in and bought up a sizeable portion of Stella's share of the business. I was never told the details, only that a crucial part of the deal was that I was taken on and given gainful employment to keep me out of mischief and especially Amy's hair, so she could enjoy her pregnancy in peace. And if it all worked out and I kept my nose clean during what seemed to be an elastic period of probation, then I might even get paid a salary.

'…because whatever you did in a previous existence, it couldn't have been anything which involved keeping accurate records.' Veronica was getting into her stride now. 'And obviously not a dress code.'

Ouch! That was one of her favourite ones. Why couldn't I wear a suit and look professional? I had given up pointing out that solicitors, estate agents and accountants all wore suits but that was no guarantee they knew what they were doing.

'Now come on, Vonnie, do I ever criticise your sense of dress?' I said, attempting to take the moral high ground.

'All the time,' she said without a flicker of a smile and, to be fair, she had a point.

'I suppose you're referring to my report on the Zaborski case,' I offered, changing the subject rapidly.

'Well I would refer to it if I'd seen it,' she laid on the sarcasm with a trowel. 'I mean, I've finished my library book and I'm just dying for something new to read. Something light, perhaps, with not too many long words and a happy ending. All I've seen so far are your expense claims, and *by the way...*'

Here it came. Veronica was famous for her 'by the way...' lectures to the extent that no one in the office could use the phrase and keep a straight face anymore.

'...you are supposed to submit your expenses on an Excel spreadsheet, not on the back of a menu from a Chinese take-away.'

'I didn't claim for the meal,' I said in my defence, knowing it sounded lame.

My one and only case, officially, for R & B Confidential Investigations so far had involved plugging a leak from a pharmaceutical company run by rich kid/whiz kid entrepreneur Olivier Zaborski. He had seemed pleased with the result and, as he was absolutely loaded, I wouldn't have thought he would blink twice at my expenses. I also regarded my expenses claim as one of the finest pieces of creative writing I had ever done.

'I wasn't sure it was wise to commit too many details to paper, Veronica,' I offered. 'After all, Mr Zaborski had a problem, we made the problem go away. Nobody got hurt: end of. Why complicate things and give away trade secrets?'

'*What* trade secrets?'

I wasn't sure and maybe I was pushing it a tad there. The bit about nobody getting hurt hadn't exactly been accurate either.

'Our methods and systems,' I waffled. 'Surely too much detail would only confuse the client, not to mention providing a few hostages to fortune. I mean, if you got a detailed bill from your solicitor saying *Picked up phone £25, Number engaged £25, Tried later £25*, you'd go ballistic, wouldn't you?'

'Which brings us nicely back to your expenses claim,' she

gloated. 'Just how do you justify £2,000 for a car? Not the hire of a car but the actual car itself?'

'It wasn't worth more than two grand.'

'You are deliberately avoiding the issue. How do you justify buying an entire car for frick's sake?'

'Well, originally, it was loaned to me, like a courtesy car from a garage. When I couldn't give it back, I was charged for it.'

'And why couldn't you give it back?'

'It sort of caught fire.'

'So we can claim on the insurance then?'

'Probably not,' I admitted.

'Why not? And where is the car now?'

'Last I saw it was on the deck of a Russian freighter headed for the Baltic, but I suspect it fell overboard somewhere along the way and is now sleeping with the fishes at the bottom of the North Sea.'

Veronica's mouth had sagged into a perfect O.

'Would it be better if I put all this in a written report to Mr Zaborski?'

She shook her head slowly and began to back towards the door frame.

'No, never mind. Amazingly, he's already approved your expenses. We got his cheque this morning.'

'Now that,' I said sweetly, 'is what is known as a result. Got another case for me? Bring it on.'

Unfortunately, she had and she did.

'There's a Mr Ellrington coming here at five this afternoon. He wants help finding a missing girlfriend.'

'But Veronica,' I said reasonably, 'I don't happen to be a policeman.'

Chapter Two

On first sight I estimated James Ellrington to be in his early sixties and put him down as a civil servant.

'I'm a retired civil servant,' he said as soon as we had shaken hands, which just went to prove there was nothing to this detective lark, 'and I'm afraid I have absolutely no experience of private detective work.'

That made two of us, I thought, but I said:

'We are here to help in any way we can.'

'As long as it's legal, decent and honest?'

'Well, if you insist.'

He wrinkled his nose rather than smiled at that, but he didn't get up and storm out, so my client relationship skills must be improving. I must remember to tell Veronica so she could tick another box on my staff appraisal.

'I had grave reservations about consulting a firm of *private eyes* as I believe you're called, but I admit my only knowledge is from films – or *paperback* detective novels.'

He said 'paperback' with almost as much disdain as he had said 'private eyes' but then he caught sight of the row of books on the window ledge and had the decency to look embarrassed when he noticed I was following his gaze.

'I'm sorry,' he stumbled, 'I didn't mean to belittle you.'

'You didn't,' I said truthfully. I mean, I had been belittled by experts like Amy, who could probably belittle for Britain at the Olympics. Mr Ellrington was nowhere near her league. 'I read them,' I said, nodding towards my makeshift bookshelf, 'purely for enjoyment, but I tell my boss they're training manuals.'

Mr Ellrington risked a smile and warmed to the subject.

'I suppose you pick up lots of tips from them, like how to put a tail on people and how to tell when the dames are lying to you and how you should always keep a bottle of Bourbon in the second drawer down in your desk.'

This was getting weird. How did he know about the bottle of Ezra Brooks' Ninety Proof Sour Mash? And did he know that the real private eye always drinks a whiskey that comes in a square bottle, so that it doesn't roll around noisily in the desk drawer? I'm told that's what alcoholics do too.

'I'm afraid real life enquiry work is usually unspectacular and unexciting in the main,' I said, repeating part of Veronica's company mantra. 'The majority of our work is not solving crimes, it's finding solutions to problems.'

James Ellrington sat back in his chair and crossed his legs, picking an imaginary piece of lint off his suit trousers and flicking it towards the floor. His body language said it all. He was relaxing, thinking that here was an oik he could do business with, because as a civil servant he had enjoyed an entire career of dealing with oiks like me. Whereas I was thinking I could easily afford a suit as good as that; or at least, Amy could.

'I find it interesting that you call it enquiry work and you link it to problems and not crimes, because my business here does not involve any sort of crime. That should be made clear from the outset and as to the particular problem involved, on the normal scale of things, it probably doesn't amount to a hill of beans.' He flicked a finger towards my library. 'As Raymond Chandler would have said.'

'Right hero, wrong film,' I corrected him, but I don't think he noticed. He'd probably been quite a senior civil servant. I could tell from the way he assumed he couldn't be wrong.

'I want you to find someone for me,' he announced boldly. 'I suppose it's what they call a missing person case.'

'The police do them,' I said reasonably. 'I'm not a policeman.' Come to think of it, no one in Rudgard & Blugden Confidential Investigations was, or ever had been, a police person, although the founder of the firm had been. A slightly dodgy ex-Met copper by the name of Albert Block had established the agency in Shepherd's Bush as a way of eking out his pension. It was he who had taken on a youthful Veronica Blugden, fresh off the overnight coach from Nottingham or Leeds or one of those other places north of Sainsbury's, initially as someone to make the tea, mislay the filing and type up the invoices.

Once Vonnie had met Stella and the two had decided to pair up as a double act, old Albert's days were numbered and he retired for real and the women took over. From the off they only hired women and preferred cases brought to them by women. It was, as Amy was fond of saying, their 'USP' – Unique Selling Point. How ironic then that it was Amy who was to tarnish that image by buying into the company and insisting on desegregation by employing me, even though, as I said time and time again, I had no qualifications, aptitude or enthusiasm for the work. Any work, come to think of it.

My honest pleadings went unheard and so I found myself sleeping with the senior, and only, non-executive director of the firm (Amy), whilst reporting to the managing director (Veronica) and the absentee chairman (Stella – still on honeymoon) and working with two 'graduate trainees' (Lorna and Laura – virtually indistinguishable, so I called them The Thompson Twins, though nobody else in the office got it) and, the one bright spot, the redoubtable Mrs Delacourt, a Jamaican matriarch of the old school, the mother of an old mate of mine, Crimson, and R & B's most successful and cost-effective undercover operative.

Before she had bought into the firm, Amy had, as always, done her homework and must have gone over the books as it was she who had told me that about thirty per cent of R & B's income was generated by 'staff infiltration' where a firm recruited a detective to pose as a worker in order to uncover the various fiddles going on. Mrs Delacourt had proved a natural at it and even her son Crimson (though not the sharpest blade in the knife drawer) didn't suspect a thing. He was firmly convinced she really was a cleaner at Heathrow's Terminal 4. Amy had also identified a fairly healthy 'profit stream' from advising on, and selling with a hefty mark-up, security and surveillance equipment for homes and businesses. There were some modernised town houses in Islington which now had more cameras covering them than Hollywood needed for the crowd scenes in *Ben Hur* and all the ones supplied or sub-contracted through R & B did actually work, unlike the DIY 'deterrent' ones you can buy which are battery powered and have a flashing red light on top but otherwise serve no useful purpose. They're not even worth nicking, as they have no resale value and you see hundreds of them at car boot sales.

Although I was the new boy, I was aware that we did certain types of job, but as far as I knew we didn't do missing persons, so I was only being honest with my client. Like I said, I was new at this game.

'I've tried the police,' said James Ellrington. 'They sent me here.'

'*Here?*'

It came out louder and an octave higher than I had planned.

'Well not to this agency specifically, but they advised I should consult a private detective. The police are really only interested if it is a minor or a vulnerable adult who has gone missing or where a crime is thought to have been committed. This is a private matter – hence, a private detective is called for.'

He sounded as if he had thought it through, but I was sure there was something in the Association of British Investigators' code of practice which said I was duty-bound to discourage him, if only on the grounds that he didn't look an interesting enough client.

'Somewhere between ten and one hundred thousand people go missing in this country every year, Mr Ellrington,' I said, putting on my sympathetic-but-powerless face, the one I usually got from civil servants. 'No one knows exactly how many. I suppose if we did, they wouldn't be missing. Tracing them, or pretending to, is a big business. There are nearly 2,000 tracing agents offering to find people for you, but no matter what they offer, they can't really do very much. The Information Commissioner's Office and the Data Protection Act make sure of that.'

I was hoping he would say he didn't know we had an Information Commissioner in Britain; then I could have said that I wasn't surprised as that information is a closely guarded secret. But he didn't rise to the bait.

'Since the Data Protection Act came in, for example, we estimate we can trace less than half of known debtors or loan defaulters, whereas before the DPA it was about eighty per cent of them. If someone has a criminal record, then the Police National Computer should have them, but everyone knows it's at least six months behind with its data inputting. Otherwise, if you want to find someone, the people who probably *know* are the Inland Revenue or the National Insurance department or the Benefits Agency, but they don't open their files to anyone.'

And they didn't talk to each other – thank God.

'I'm sorry I haven't made this clear enough for you,' he said, making it my fault that I didn't understand. A typical senior civil servant's trick; they are, after all, specially trained to talk down to people like me. 'There is no question of a crime having been committed and the person I am trying to find is not 'missing' in the sense that other people may go missing. It's just that I don't know where she is living at the moment and I want to find her.'

'Her?' I queried, just to show I had been listening and

picking up the clues he had given me.

'Yes, I want you to find an old female friend of mine. In fact it is because it involves a woman that I chose what I thought was an all-female agency.'

'It mostly is,' I said, 'but there was some problem with sex discrimination legislation and they thought they had better employ a token male. Me.'

It didn't seem to reassure him.

'Actually,' I soothed, 'the all-female angle is to reassure female clients. If you had been a woman you would have been seen by one of our female operatives and, if you wish, I can easily get one to come in and take this meeting.'

I had only just thought of it, but if paying clients insisted on dealing with a female detective, that surely was good for the reputation of the firm – and less work for me.

'That will not be necessary. To be honest, I hadn't really thought the matter through,' he said, but I had already formed the impression that there were few things James Ellrington didn't think through.

He uncrossed and crossed his legs, trying to get comfortable in the office's client chair. I wrote a mental memo to Veronica: why not invest in a leather recliner or a Lay-z-boy to put clients more at ease? And an office TV to fill in those dead afternoons between clients, perhaps?

'So you're looking for a girlfriend?' I asked to get him back on track.

'A *former* girlfriend,' he replied, a tad tetchily.

'And may I ask why?'

'I suppose you have to ask that.'

Did I? I was winging this.

'To establish my honourable intentions, if that's not too old-fashioned a concept.'

'Our code of practice states we have to be open and honest with our clients, and we should expect our clients to be the same with us,' I said.

'Very laudable. I had no idea your profession had a code of practice.'

I was pretty sure we did. Perhaps I ought to get something framed and hung on the wall so I could point to it with a sober and trustworthy expression. Another memo to self: work on sober and trustworthy expression; or at least trustworthy.

'But whether you have or not, I do believe transparency is the only way to progress a business relationship and so, if confidentiality is in place, I am willing to infill my position.'

'I can assure you, Mr Ellrington, that anything you tell me in this office, stays in this office,' I said pompously.

I wasn't likely to tell tales out of school when I could hardly follow what he was going on about. That's the trouble with transparent management-speak. It's about as transparent as wallpaper paste.

'As I would have expected,' he said with a polite nod of his head. 'Yours must be a fascinating job, part priest in the confessional, part defending barrister fighting his client's case.'

'I tend to think of it being more like a job for a good cab driver,' I said, having only just thought of that.

'Excuse me?'

'Once the client is on board and the meter's running, we like to take you straight where you want to go by the most direct route possible.'

'That's very reassuring, I've never thought of hailing a detective as you would hail a cab,' said James Ellrington, 'not that I've ever needed a private detective before.'

'Until now,' I prompted, resisting the urge to look pointedly at my watch in a the-pubs-are-open-and-I-don't-get-overtime sort of way. 'And you need one to find this girlfriend you've mislaid.'

That actually creased his mouth into a fair impersonation of a smile.

'You could put it that way, I suppose. It makes me sound rather careless, though in a way that's exactly what I was.'

'Ah, the one that got away,' I said easing back in my chair. I didn't put my feet up on the desk because that would have had him storming out in a huff, but if I had smoked a pipe I would have been pulling on it thoughtfully.

'Why do you say that, Mr Angel?'

'It's an observation, not a judgement. So much enquiry work these days involves tracing, shall we say, faces from the past. People we missed, lost touch with, let go, before we could understand them or get to know them better. Or perhaps we slighted them and it's been worrying us ever since. Why do you suppose things like *Friends Reunited* are so wildly successful?'

'I always assumed that sort of thing was so that you could flaunt your success in front of your old school friends,' he said.

'Well, yes, that's always a bonus,' I admitted.

'But I've never been one for school reunions,' he said thoughtfully.

Neither was I. I had never been to one on the grounds that they still might have a warrant out.

'Though my story does go back to my school days. Do you remember the Sixties, Mr Angel?'

The Sixties? I had trouble remembering Tuesday.

'Of course you wouldn't, you're too young. How stupid, please forgive me. Your parents will, though.'

He didn't know my parents. My father would deny point blank being old enough to remember a decade when neither Claudia Schiffer nor Uma Thurman had been born and my mother still thought it *was* the 1960s in a tie-dyed natural cotton and knit-your-own-yoghurt sort of way.

'So you are the generation that invented sex? Should I thank you?'

He looked slightly shocked at that, but only slightly. I didn't really care if he didn't like my attitude. I wasn't trying to sell it.

'I wouldn't presume to say that, but I do think we were the first generation to be free to experiment with it, and it is only very late in life that one realises that with that freedom should have come some responsibility. Oh I don't mean responsibility for an unwanted pregnancy or anything like that, I mean *emotional* responsibility. We were young and we could have sex, relatively safely. So we did; without thinking. We lived for the moment and never thought enough about the future.'

I got the feeling this was a speech he had rehearsed, so it was best not to interrupt.

'And now, of course, we look back and think what might have been. Did we make mistakes back then which could have altered the course of our lives? Were we too young and given too much freedom to see what was best for us? What did we miss out on in terms of lifelong satisfaction because we had the opportunity of instant satisfaction? *What might have been?*'

What might have been. When strung together, four of the most dangerous words in the English language and a sure-fire recipe for trouble.

But then, nowadays, trouble was my business.

Chapter Three

Toft End is an old village, a lost village, a shabby village, hardly a village at all. Once, very long ago, it had been the centre or focus of something even if only the confluence of several droveways down which shepherds prodded their flocks to market. Such was the passing trade, though, that it was worth opening a pub for, and they called it The Old Rosemary Branch and no doubt it did good business. But those days have, like the shepherds, long gone and now the pub is mine, except that it hasn't actually been a pub since it was delicensed in 1933 and replaced by The New Rosemary Branch about a mile up the road, and strictly speaking, it's Amy's as it was her dosh which paid for it.

Before she became pregnant, I could never imagine Amy living anywhere other than London and even then not outside Zone 1 and only with an 0207 phone number (0208 prefixes she regarded as 'the outer limits'). But the hormones had won and she had succumbed to the nesting instinct, which in her case involved slightly more than painting the spare room and Blu-tacking some highly coloured mobiles to the ceiling.

You didn't build a safe family nest in the city, she argued. A bunker, perhaps, but not a nest. That had to be somewhere snug out in the country, although within daily commuting range of the shops in the West End. Once The Old Rosemary Branch had been identified as a potential nest site (for which I never really got the credit), purchasing it and selling the house in Hampstead had gone through with commendable promptitude, partly due to Amy paying top dollar for a team of female solicitors who knew her work as a fashion designer, but mostly down to the fact that I had nothing whatsoever to do with any of it. I was quite relaxed about that. After all, I now had a job to go to, and as someone who had tripped and fallen before ever reaching the bottom rung of the property ladder, I was beginning to wonder what all the fuss was about. How come people said that moving house was the second most stressful thing you ever did?

I was thinking there wasn't much to it at all until, that is, the actual *move* started. To say that it required the same amount of organisation as the D-Day invasion of Normandy might be pushing it, but it was probably the equivalent of an Anzio landing or a Berlin airlift. I made the mistake of remarking to Amy that when I had moved into her Hampstead house, I brought two Sainsbury's carrier bags with me – and I'd had trouble filling them. She hadn't been amused and had me packing boxes of books for three evenings running.

Most of the serious heavy lifting was, of course, done by a professional firm of 'relocators' in a truck which could have handled about a third of the equipment of a heavy metal band on tour. The relocation crew of four fit young men and two very fit girls were smartly dressed in company overalls with logos on their backs, and exuded calm professionalism, but Amy had them moving at the double for most of the day, working up a real sweat for the first time since they'd left the Jobcentre. When they had turned up an hour late at Toft End to unload, Amy had pointed out that the amount she was paying them was enough to expect a decent SatNav system in the truck, or, failing that, an AA Book of the Road, and they had all avoided eye contact and buckled down to unloading, not one of them daring to propose the traditional removal man's prayer of 'Is the kettle unpacked and is there a chance of a cuppa, darling?'

Truly, a pregnant woman armed with bags of attitude and a substantial cheque-book is universally acknowledged to be a force to be reckoned with.

Our departure from Hampstead went unmarked by street parties or firework displays. No neighbours had come to wish us well, help us pack or offer to make sandwiches for the journey. If I'd known any of their names I would have rung them and told them they were miserable swine.

Not that there was a welcome wagon waiting for us at Toft End, though I pointed out to Amy that as there wasn't a dead crow nailed to the door, that meant the locals probably accepted us. For that, I got put on unpacking duties where surprisingly almost everything I touched had to be carried upstairs, washed before it could be used, or plumbed in.

She had already found a Chinese take-away in Cambridge which delivered (and had SatNav) and her mobile got a signal in Toft End (she'd checked before signing anything) so we weren't going to starve. I had realised that I could walk to The New Rosemary Branch at the other end of the village for beer, wines, spirits and some crafty passive smoking and be back almost before Amy had thought of something else for me to do, so we weren't going to die of thirst either.

That first evening we ate Ma Po bean curd, Mongolian aromatic lamb and egg noodles off plates balanced on packing cases whilst listening to *Bogalusa Boogie* by Clifton Chenier, one of my favourite CDs of Louisiana zydeco music (to be honest, my *only* CD of zydeco but the first album I had managed to find among the packing). Amy was drinking mineral water and I had opened a bottle of Chardonnay just to make sure that the new fridge was working properly. We had food, drink, music and there were beds made up in at least two of the bedrooms, so to take her mind off the hundred and one other jobs which needed doing, not to mention the Herculean task of organising her wardrobe at some point, I began to tell her about James Ellrington.

'Oh, bless. That's really rather sweet, an old man searching for his long-lost love,' she said, which hadn't been the reaction I'd been expecting.

'Of course,' she added, chewing noodles, 'he could be a bitter and twisted old psycho stalker preying on younger women.'

That was more the Amy I knew, but she hadn't finished: 'Which reminds me, how's your father?'

In the hurly-burly of the move I had almost forgotten my father, mentally packing him in a tea-chest, nailing the lid down and marking it 'Not Wanted On Voyage'. Was that Freudian or what?

'I thought the whole idea was to move house without leaving a forwarding address,' I said brightly. 'He'll never find us out here in the village that time forgot.'

'Don't be mean to our new neighbours,' said Amy, 'not until you've at least met some of them.'

'I've not met any because I've not *seen* any. When's the next full moon?'

'Don't disrespect the countryside, Angel. We agreed it was time to move out of London.'

We did? But before I could say anything she played her trump card and patted her stomach.

'Best thing for all of us,' she murmured. 'Anyway, I left our new address with the hospital in case your father needed it and I said you'd call him.'

'I'll get around to it,' I muttered into my noodles.

It was typical of my family. Amy and I were going through a major life-changing experience: she was blooming into pregnancy, restructuring her business interests, selling a house in Hampstead and relocating to the country in less than six weeks, and I was expected to go to work *every* day. At this crucial point in our lives, my father had gone and had a stroke. How selfish can you get?

Amy had growled something about 'Now that's three kids I have to look after', which I didn't really understand but, fair play, she had taken charge of the situation with her decisiveness, her flair for organisation and her credit cards. Dear old Dad had been transferred from the Stroke Unit in Colchester hospital to a private room in the Devonshire in London, which turned out to be a hospital not a pub, where he would be closer to home – his flat in Morpeth Terrace in Westminster – and had the best medical attention Amy's money could buy. It had to be her money as my father didn't have any and I just knew his will would say something like: 'I, being of sound mind and body, have spent the bloody lot.'

He had been lucky with his stroke, or so all the doctors told him though I always thought the luckiest thing would be not to have one at all. His was a blood clot on the right side of the brain, which affected the left side of his body and we were assured that a haemorrhage, or bleed, on the left side of the brain would have been far more serious. So in one sense he had avoided the *very* bad bullet, but his brain attack had still left him with a limp in the left leg, a left arm which acted like one of Dr Strangelove's, slurred speech and the short-term memory of a goldfish with Alzheimer's or a barman in a Wetherspoon's on a Friday night. Not to mention unemployed. As he constantly pointed out, members of the House of Lords (he was a life peer, nothing posh) get an attendance allowance. If they don't attend, they don't get the allowance. I had suggested that now he'd had a stroke, he might blend in better with the House of Lords, maybe even get a government job, but that had gone down like a lead balloon and he had snapped that I wasn't helping his recovery.

What he meant was that I wasn't helping him sort out his tangled personal life.

The stroke had hit him whilst he had been on his way to Suffolk to tell his former wife, and my mother, that he was thinking of remarrying. He thought it wiser to tell her before she read it in the tabloid press, as his fiancée was page three girl Kim McIntosh, nineteen-year-old topless model spinster of this parish. Amy had always said that it wasn't as bad as it sounded, as Kim was actually 25, although she had done her first topless shoot at nineteen and the tag had stuck. Perhaps she had a point, for the tabloids, if they knew of the rumoured nuptials, paid them not the slightest bit of attention. The truth was that my father was not an important enough life peer to bother with and, to be honest, at 25, Kim McIntosh was past it in tabloid journalism terms, the current preference being for 'up skirt' shots of E-list celebrities.

We had negotiated a compromise in that I would break his bad news to Kim if he would break the good news to my mother that she was about to become a grandmother. I had seen pictures of Kim McIntosh in the tabloids and I also knew how my mother would react to being called Granny, so I was fairly confident that I'd got the better half of the deal and, despite her reservations, Amy had finally agreed that I should go and see young Kim in person rather than just leave a message on her answerphone or send her a text with a smiley face logo.

To be honest, I had gone to see her expecting to get an eyeful and instead got a real eye-opener.

The address my father gave me for her, a faded 1960s terraced house in Basildon, was not easy to find, being just off the edge of my new Big Scale A–Z map (a legitimate expense for tax purposes), but in Basildon no one gave a cruising black London cab a second look. Not even the spotty youth sitting in the driving seat of a beat-up old Honda with a camera with telephoto lens round his neck. An oik like that, with a camera like that, in a street like this at this time of the morning, meant only one thing: an amateur *paparazzo* desperate for a shot of something interesting happening to nineteen-year-old topless model Kim McIntosh.

Except she wasn't nineteen anymore and as far as I knew didn't do topless, at least not publicly, anymore. But the sad little voyeur-by-proxy had got the right street and Kim McIntosh was at home with her mother as I discovered when I rang the doorbell, but only after being scrutinised through an eye-level peep-hole which hadn't been in the original builder's specification.

I heard a lock snap back, then two dead bolts and then the door opened about three inches on a chain.

'We didn't ring for a cab,' said a female voice.

I had parked Armstrong at the kerb at the bottom of the front garden path so that if they saw me arrive they would think I was a cabby, not a photographer; and everybody trusts a cabby.

'The cab's mine,' I said, telling the absolute truth. 'I need to see Kim; I've got a message for her.'

'So have half a million other men,' said the voice quite calmly.

'Only half a million? What's happened to the men in this country?'

'That's been on my mind for the last twenty years,' said the voice and I could tell there was a smile there, but the chain didn't move.

'Mrs McIntosh? My name's Angel,' I said.

'Oh,' said the voice faintly.

Now the chain came off and the door opened so I could see I was talking to a woman who shared a fair proportion of DNA with the Kim McIntosh I had seen in photographs and who could easily pass for being in her late thirties. I could have done something cheesy like asking if her sister was in, but thankfully she didn't give me the chance.

'You must be the son,' she said, 'you'd better come in off the street. There's too many prying eyes round here.'

'He's down the street in a blue Honda,' I said and she looked quite impressed as she held the door for me.

'So you've spotted the little prick, have you? He doesn't even bother to hide in the bushes any more. Upstairs, first on the right.' She indicated the staircase just in case I'd never seen one before. 'Kim's in her study.'

I thought I had misheard at first, thinking she said 'studio' which made a mental connection with all the images of 'models' I carried round in my head.

'I take it you've brought bad news,' Mrs McIntosh said when I was on the second step.

I froze and looked down at her, putting on my serious-but-concerned face.

'I'm afraid it is.'

'Thought as much. He's dumping her, isn't he? And he hasn't got the guts to tell her face to face. That girl has no luck with men.'

'No, it's not that at all,' I soothed. 'My father's in hospital. He's had a stroke and he wanted Kim to hear it from someone in the family.'

'Oh my God!' Mrs McIntosh put the back of a hand to her mouth. 'I told her she ought to go easy on him or she might break him, but I was only joking, honest. I'll come up with you. Kim's not good with sickness. She really doesn't do "ill".'

The McIntosh house seemed to have three bedrooms and a bathroom upstairs and the standard of decoration was good throughout. I wondered why I was thinking like an estate agent. Perhaps having to deal with them recently had rubbed off on me – or infected me?

'Kim!' Mrs McIntosh shouted from behind me. 'You've got a visitor!'

Then, reducing the volume, she said: 'She'll have her ears on, just go in.'

It was a study, not a studio and Kim McIntosh was sitting at a desk by the window, a roller blind painted with Van Gogh's *Sunflowers* pulled down to stop the light reflecting off a computer flat screen. From her ears trailed two white wires ending in a pink iPod parked on the desk next to a black wireless keyboard. She was wearing stonewashed black jeans and a short-sleeved silver TALtop designed, wouldn't you know it, by a certain Amy May when she was footloose, fancy-free and unpregnant. In fact the TALtop had been the making of Amy's career as an über-*fashionista*, so I would never knock it, especially when the old design looked as good in the flesh, or rather on the flesh of someone like Kim McIntosh.

She was concentrating on a display of spreadsheets on the screen through small, square, frameless glasses, her tongue protruding about a centimetre from between pursed lips.

'You could chuck a bomb in here when she's got her ears on and she wouldn't notice,' said her mother from behind me. 'We could stand here all day and she wouldn't twig we were in the room.'

On many another day, that would sound like a plan, but I was here on a mission, not to gawp at the scenery, though of course gawp is exactly what I did.

Even dressed in straightforward student casual, with no make-up on and unaware that I was even in the house, Kim was strikingly pretty. It was easy to see why the camera loved her, even with her clothes on.

'You don't recognise her with her clothes on,' said her mother in my ear like the Jiminy Cricket voice of conscience.

'I wasn't going to say that,' I hissed at her, though I didn't know why I was whispering.

'You were thinking it,' Mrs McIntosh said wisely. 'Kim! Visitor!'

She was close enough to my ear when she shouted to make me jump, but Kim calmly pulled out her earpieces and turned her swivel chair to face me, looking up over her glasses.

'Oh, hello,' she said. 'Sorry, I was miles away.'

And then she smiled a smile which lit up her face and the only thing I could think was how on earth I was supposed to call this woman 'Mother'.

'This is Kit's son,' said Mrs McIntosh, trying to rescue me, but it didn't help as Kim's smile simply grew wider and brighter and she sprang to her feet to give me a hug.

'So you're Finbar,' she said with a squeak. 'I've heard all about you.'

It was just what I needed to break the spell, though I waited until the hug had landed.

'Actually, I'm Fitzroy.'

The hug melted away and her brow creased in puzzlement.

'The younger son; much younger. Finbar's my older brother.'

'Oh. Kit hasn't actually ever mentioned you.'

Now why was I not surprised at that?

'You're not a journalist are you?' Mrs McIntosh said in a voice verging on a growl.

'Good God, no,' I said, though I thought it better not to brag about being a private detective. 'I'm a musician.'

Well I was, or had been, though these days it seemed like it was in a previous life.

'I thought he was a cab driver,' said her mother. Whoever's side she was on it probably wasn't mine. 'He arrived driving a black cab. It's parked outside the front door.'

Kim's brow uncreased and her shiny blue eyes seemed to grow behind the rectangular lenses of her glasses.

'It's Roy, right? Yes, that's it. Black cab, plays the trumpet – yes?'

I nodded enthusiastically as if my life depended upon it. Thinking of Mrs McIntosh standing behind me, it probably did.

'I'm so sorry. Of course he's mentioned you. Didn't you marry a designer or something?'

'You're wearing one of her tops.'

'Amy May? Wow, wicked! I've loved her stuff since I was a teenager.'

'I'll make a point of telling her that,' I said, and I would, especially the 'teenager' bit, though I was thankful, once again, that Amy had a name worth dropping.

'Should have known he was straight-up with a name like Fitzroy,' said Kim's mum. 'First Finbar, now Fitzroy – and isn't there a daughter?'

'Finnoula,' said Kim with a giggle.

'Mind you, Kit himself got lumbered with a right royal monicker, didn't he?'

'Yes he did,' I agreed with Mrs McIntosh, not sure whether she was testing me or not. 'If your given name is Christopher Carlton Cleves Angel, then naturally you take it out on your kids.'

'Too right,' she laughed. 'There's a couple down this street, they've named their boy Euryn. What sort of a name's that?'

'I think it's Welsh, or Celtic,' I said. 'There's an Iron Age hill fort in Wales called Bryn Euryn.'

'Be that as it may, the poor little sod's going to have a hard time when he gets to secondary school.'

'Fitzroy's not as bad as Euryn, Mum,' said Kim, 'so don't go on about it. It's nice to meet you at last, Roy, even if I gave the impression I didn't know you existed.'

She held out a hand for me to shake. The hand was soft, the grip wasn't.

'I didn't know you were a student,' I observed, taking in the bookshelves in the room for the first time, most of which groaned under the weight of over-sized academic textbooks which seemed, at a glance, to be mostly about bio-chemistry.

'Not many people do. It doesn't go with the usual CV they put in the paragraph under my picture.'

She took a pace back from me and struck a pose, her back arched, bust out, one hand at the back of her neck, one on her hip.

'Kissable Kim,' she mimicked. 'That's what they like calling me. Kissable Kim uses all her 38-inch charms to work for world peace, as well as trying to impress her lecturers whilst studying for her Masters in Biological Science at the Department of Animal and Plant Sciences, University of Sheffield.'

She dropped the pose.

'Doesn't really work, does it?' she asked, putting her head on one side.

'Oh I don't know. It proves things aren't all grim "up north".'

'You little smoothy. Now I see the family resemblance,' said Mrs McIntosh, thankfully breaking the spell.

'Ah yes, I'm here on a family matter. I'm here on behalf of my Dad...er...Kit.'

'I guess it's bad news,' Kim said with a sigh as she pulled off her glasses and tossed them casually on to the desk. 'Should I sit down, reach for the Kleenex or get Mum to crack open the Bacardi Breezers?'

'Maybe all three. It is bad news, but it could have been worse.' I took a deep breath and ploughed on. 'Kit has had a stroke, he's in hospital. They tell me it wasn't the worst kind of stroke and he has a good chance of making a full recovery.'

Nobody had actually told me that, but it sounded better that way, as did referring to 'Kit' rather than 'my father'.

'Jeesus!' said Kim, sitting down with a thump on her swivel chair, 'that's a bit of a stunner.'

She sucked in air for about five seconds and then hit overdrive.

'How is he? Where is he? Can I see him? Does he want to see me? A stroke you said, that's not like a heart attack is it?'

Mrs McIntosh eased me out of the way and put an arm around her daughter's shoulders to comfort her before I could think of it.

'He's doing fine,' I said, 'and you're quite right, a stroke is a brain attack, not a heart attack. And yes, he will want to see you but give us a few days to get him settled back in London.'

'Where was he?'

'In a hospital in Colchester. He was on his way to Suffolk when it happened. He drove himself into the hospital.'

'Why didn't he send for me?' Kim asked in a semi-sob, fighting back the tears.

'Because he's what *my* mother would have called a proper gent,' said Mrs McIntosh, tightening her grip on her daughter's shoulders until her knuckles whitened. 'He didn't want the press to know, did he?'

'He didn't even tell them he was a peer at the hospital,' I said, which was true though I wasn't sure if my father's motives had been entirely altruistic.

'There you are, then,' Mrs McIntosh soothed. 'I bet he went

on to some National Health general ward and didn't use his title so that no guttersnipe journalist would hear about it.'

I shrugged and nodded, agreeing with whatever she said.

'You think he did that for me?' Kim said, almost childlike. If it was an act, it was a bloody good one, and her mother pulled her closer, smothering her head to her bosom.

In my experience, mothers can't usually be fooled that easily and I realised with absolute clarity that I was dealing with something very dangerous here: love.

'You of all people know what the press is like, babe. Journalists are almost always reptiles. Somebody famous said that once and it's true. Who was it said that?'

They both looked at me as if an answer was really important.

'I've no idea,' I said.

I had. I knew it was one of Josef Goebbels' most insightful comments (his only one) but it somehow didn't seem right to let him into the room.

'We've kept it out of the newspapers so far and we've had him transferred to the Devonshire hospital. He's OK, honest. He can walk, talk and make passes at the nurses but, obviously, it has knocked him back a bit.'

'But strokes only happen to old people!' Kim fumed.

There was a time when I would have said 'And your point is…?' but now was not the time.

'That was my first reaction,' I admitted, 'but I'm on a steep learning curve. Strokes are equal opportunity attackers, they can happen to anyone at any age.'

'You said he was driving to Suffolk. That was to see Beth, wasn't it? To tell her about us.' The tears were coming now; unstoppable, *tsunami* style.

'Yes, he was on his way to see my mother…his ex-wife, but don't even think it. I checked with the doctors in the hospital and they told me the stroke could have happened at any time.'

'There, there, babe,' Mrs McIntosh comforted her. 'You see, it wasn't your fault.'

'Absolutely not,' I agreed. 'That's a stupid idea.'

'But he was under a lot of stress worrying about how she would react,' said Kim pathetically.

'Listen to me,' I said, waving a finger at her. 'I checked with the doctors and they said that whatever brought on the stroke, it wasn't stress. Got that? Stress can't cause a stroke.'

Of course, the doctors didn't know my mother.

Anyhow, that was how I had broken the news to young Kim, though my father had yet to come good on his half of the deal and tell my mother about her impending grandchild.

When I had told Amy how Kim had taken it, the first thing she had asked was: 'What was the engagement ring like?' and when I had, truthfully, said I hadn't noticed one, she'd said, 'Huh! Some detective you are.'

But then, after some reflection, she offered the following advice: 'Be very careful how you go from here, for you are dealing with absolutely true love and that's dangerous territory to go blundering into.'

Funnily enough, when I told her about James Ellrington's visit to the office, over the Chinese take-away that first night in our new house, she said exactly the same thing.

Chapter Four

James Ellrington had met Margaret Anne Hayes at school in Yorkshire. Not the same school, but neighbouring single-sex ones, he at Queen Elizabeth's Grammar School and she at the Girls' High School in the small cathedral town of Wakefield. Both were posh schools, or thought they were, at the bottom end of the public school league table. Margaret Anne, the daughter of the sales director of a local textile mill, was a fee-paying pupil; James, the son of a miner, was a scholarship boy and, if not exactly from the wrong side of the tracks, his family thought of themselves as two streets down past the level crossing from Margaret Anne's.

The young lovebirds had met during an inter-school drama club production. Following long tradition, female parts in drama productions at the boys' Grammar had always been played by gangling fifth formers. The Girls' High, however, took the much more practical and modern view that male roles in their productions should be played by males. That was over fifty years ago and Ellrington could not for the life of him remember what play the young, star-crossed lovers starred in. It wasn't, he was sure, *Romeo and Juliet* though, which was a pity but maybe that would have been just too neat.

James was sixteen, Margaret Anne had just had her fifteenth birthday but, as is always the case, was the more mature and sexually more inquisitive of the pair. Not that there was much opportunity for sexual inquisitiveness, as this was 1950s Yorkshire, which is a bit like saying fourteenth-century Yorkshire but with Bill Haley and the Comets doing the soundtrack. The Swinging Sixties and the Summer of (Free) Love were still in the future, so innocence was the order of the day as the love-struck young pair went 'steady' as they said in those days, or 'were courting' as they said in Yorkshire then – and probably still did.

The courtship received the tacit approval of both sets of parents. James's mother was secretly proud that her son was mixing with a better class of people such as Margaret Anne and her family and if his mother was happy, so too was his father who had no inverted snobbery when it came to his son deserting his working-class roots. Once James had shown his scholarship-winning academic abilities, there was never any question of him following his father and both grandfathers down the pit; and in those days there really were working coal mines where men went down and coal came up. Mines were then a crucial part of British industrial production, not the life-size museum re-enactments of the tourist trade as they are now.

On Margaret Anne's side, both her parents warmed to the polite, well-mannered, academically gifted young James, especially when the possibility of a place at Cambridge beckoned, for neither the Hayes nor Ellrington families had ever sent anyone to university.

Cambridge was the making of James Ellrington and the breaking of his relationship with Margaret Anne. Late in the summer before his first term as an undergraduate, they took each other's virginities around midnight, lying in the long grass of a field at the rear of Sandal Rugby Club. Sandal was the upmarket suburb where Margaret Anne lived, so upmarket they played Rugby Union there, not Rugby League, and the Club's monthly dances were a popular draw for local teenagers in those pre-disco days.

The young lovers, for now they really were, swore undying

loyalty to each other and even considered getting engaged for the duration of James's university degree course. Margaret Anne discouraged the idea, knowing that to her mother an official engagement would involve an announcement in the local newspapers and not just the *Wakefield Express*, but the holy *Yorkshire Post* and such a step was not to be taken lightly.

And so their pledge to stay faithful to each other was all there was to sustain the relationship as they faced the next three years 150 miles apart. It was not enough.

For James, the temptations were extensive and immediate. Cambridge at the dawn of the Sixties was a world and a half away from James's small West Riding one-pit village where the social life centred on two small pubs, a huge Working Men's Club (CIU affiliated), one Anglo-Catholic church, five Methodist chapels and a lending library based in the village school two nights a week.

Within a month, he had discovered the concept of dining out in Indian (exotic) or Italian restaurants (and discovering that spaghetti didn't only come in a tin in sweet tomato sauce), the pleasures of drinking wine rather than big-headed Yorkshire bitter and heated political debates long into the night with his fellow students. He met rich undergraduates from titled families who drove their own sports cars (kept at secret addresses in the town if their college disapproved, as most did); the boisterous and over-loud sporty brigade, only interested in a rowing or rugger 'blue'; the flamboyant, theatrical types who haunted the wings of The Footlights Club; the openly homosexual (a character not allowed in Yorkshire, James was sure, under several by-laws). Within two months he had taken steps to lose his Yorkshire accent, lengthening his A and shortening his E vowels and practising the letter AITCH.

With male undergraduates outnumbering females by eight-to-one, there was little scope for dalliance there and in one respect, James remained absolutely faithful to Margaret Anne. He simply allowed her to fade from his heart.

He began to skip the regular weekend reverse-charge phone calls from a telephone box on Magdalene Street (strange as it may seem, in the time before mobile phones people often went days without speaking to each other) and his letters became shorter and infrequent. There was simply too much else to do.

For Margaret Anne's part, she probably ached whenever the telephone failed to ring and she would devote herself to ten-page love letters written in her best handwriting on her mother's Basildon Bond stationery, never mentioning the times when she had stayed in waiting for a call when she could have been out with her friends. She also planned for the future as practically as she could.

Going to university herself never occurred to her; she was, after all, a girl and this was Yorkshire, but she was aware that one of them ought to start earning as soon as possible if they were to have an idyllic life together. The perfect solution seemed to be to get a qualification as a secretary and her parents were happy to pay for her to enrol in the prestigious Oxford and County secretarial college.

Although physically nearer in Oxford for the duration of James's second year and despite James braving the interminable bus journey via Aylesbury for weekends in Margaret Anne's digs just off the Banbury Road (where he was rewarded with ever more experimental sex), the couple grew more distant; talking less, especially about their future.

It was, he would admit, entirely his fault. Cambridge had opened his eyes to new worlds, both intellectual and social. His tutor was a celebrity pundit on the BBC's Home Service, all his lecturers were published authors, his fellow undergraduates knew musicians, film directors and actors and went on holiday to places like St Moritz in the winter and Greece in the summer. Two of the gauche young men on his staircase were 'Honourables' and would eventually inherit more substantial titles.

James had come a long way from his Yorkshire mining village and had no inclination to return there. He was reading Law but had no illusions as to his capabilities. At best, his degree (a Third as it turned out) could have seen him joining any firm of solicitors in Wakefield (it was a Cambridge Third after all) but by now that seemed far too *provincial*. He had, in short, become a snob.

It was the woman, naturally, who first realised that the relationship was in terminal decline, and was the first to do something about it.

At the end of her one-year secretarial course at the 'Ox and Cow', as it was known locally, Margaret Anne applied for her first job back in the Yorkshire James now despised. It was a good job as personal secretary to the managing director of a middling-sized company manufacturing self-assembly office furniture. For an inexperienced 20-year-old, it was an amazing opportunity and one which she grasped fully, determined to shape a life in which she could, if necessary, exist without James.

Being relatively innocent, having had only one boyfriend and now back living with her parents, it probably never crossed her mind that she got the job ahead of a dozen other candidates because of her youth, her charm, her natural good looks and her figure, qualities which she had in abundance.

By the end of James's third year at Cambridge and Margaret Anne's first year with Calder Grove Interiors in Wakefield, the once inseparable pair were communicating by letter once a month. With finals over, James had to find some way to tell Margaret Anne that he had no intention of going back up north for the summer – he was instead planning an expedition to the vineyards of Bordeaux in a Morris Minor Traveller along with three fellow students – nor, indeed, ever if he could avoid it.

He never had to tell her, for she beat him to it. The clues had been there in her letters – the promotion to personal assistant to her company's managing director; how her boss, Mr Pennington, was encouraging her to learn to drive as there could be the possibility of a company car; her first invitation to a weekend company sales conference (in Harrogate); her first sales trip, accompanying her boss to Ireland; and suddenly, in her letters, 'Mr Pennington' had become 'Simon'. But James blissfully ignored the signs and it came as a genuine surprise to read Margaret Anne's last letter, the one which told him she was breaking off their 'understanding' as she felt they had 'drifted into separate lives'. And yes, she had met someone else, and, yes, it was her boss at Calder Grove Interiors. And the bottom line was that she and Simon had decided to get married that August.

Later that summer James's mother sent him a cutting from the Births, Marriages and Deaths page of the *Wakefield Express* (the page usually referred to as "Hatches, Matches and Despatches") which contained a picture of the happy couple standing in the porch of a church.

'And he's kept it all these years,' said Laura with a sigh, clutching one of the photocopies of the cutting I had handed out. 'Bless. That's really quite romantic.'

Veronica made a noise which sounded like 'Pfui!' and Lorna muttered 'Whatever' under her breath.

'Funnily enough,' I said, 'that was Amy's reaction exactly.'

'Really?' Laura's face lit up. Amy May the fashion designer was one of her heroines.

'You haven't been discussing an active case outside the office, have you, Angel?' growled Veronica.

We were having something called a Workload Agenda Meeting in Veronica's office, 'we' being the entire staff of R & B Investigations including Mrs Delacourt on her day off from her counterfeit cleaning job at Thiefrow. I hadn't seen Mrs D for ages and thought this staff get-together was a really good idea, possibly leading to an extended lunch down the pub. Then I realised that we were only expected to talk about work and that these damned meetings happened regularly every week, it was just that I had never made it to one before.

'When a major shareholder in the firm asks me about the ongoing workload of the company, I have to respond, don't I?'

I said haughtily. 'I do if I want to go on sleeping with her.'

Veronica and Lorna both frowned at me. Laura flashed me a smile when she was sure the others weren't looking. Mrs Delacourt burst out laughing.

'Get it while you can, my lad,' she roared. 'There'll come a time when she's so big you won't get in the bed, and after the baby arrives you won't get near her.'

'How long have you been an antenatal counsellor, Mrs D?'

'Since I felt the first contraction when I had my Crimson,' she said, folding her arms across her bosom.

'It didn't stop you going on to give Crimson three sisters and a little brother,' I observed.

'I'm not saying your Amy won't come round, we all do in the end, but once the baby arrives, things change. You'll see.'

Veronica was tap-tapping on her desk with a pencil.

'Can we get on?' she said and I was grateful to her for once for the rescue.

'Sure, sure, let's crack on and crack this case. Let's go to work,' I enthused.

'And what exactly is this James Ellrington hiring us to do?' asked Lorna and because it was her I automatically suspected some sort of sub-text.

'Find his one true love, of course.' She looked at me blankly; so did Veronica. 'He wants us to trace Margaret Anne Hayes, or rather Margaret Anne Pennington as she became. Unless she's divorced, of course, and reverted to her maiden name. Or she's dead, that would be tricky too.'

'And why does he want to find her after all this time?'

'Because she was the love of his life. His first girlfriend, his first lover.'

'And was *he* the love of *her* life?' asked Mrs Delacourt.

'I think he thinks he was,' I said carefully.

'Just because he took her virginity?' Lorna pressed.

'Oh, come on,' grinned Laura, 'you always remember your first, don't you?'

Lorna ignored her so she turned to Veronica for support. Veronica looked down at the surface of her desk and refused to make eye-contact. Mrs Delacourt simply closed her eyes and smiled.

Now I had to rescue Laura.

'There's definitely a deep feeling there. Ellrington told me he has had a good life. He was a high-level career civil servant, he had married and they'd had children, but when his wife died of cancer two years ago, he embarked on what he calls a "whole-life appraisal". Only a civil servant could call it something like that, but anyway, the conclusion he came to was that he had missed a bit – a little piece of his life had escaped him. It was almost as if something had slipped from his grasp. A piece of happiness had evaporated; he called it his "angel's share". It was something he had lost, almost through carelessness, without which he feels incomplete.'

I had four pairs of eyes on me now, but I couldn't see a glint of kindness in any of them.

'What the *frick* is an angel's share when it's at home?' blurted Veronica.

'I think the term comes from the whisky industry.'

'It's Scottish?'

'Japanese, actually.' Now they really thought I had lost it. 'No, seriously, the Japanese blend huge amounts of whisky. When they mature it in oak casks or whatever it is they do, about ten per cent is lost to evaporation and they call that the "angel's share". That's how James Ellrington feels about his old girlfriend. She is the angel's share of his life, the bit that evaporated. It's not that the other ninety per cent of his life has been bad, he just has this yearning for the whole hundred per cent.'

'And what does this Ellrington intend to do if he finds his long-lost love after all this time? Will you be there to play the violin in the background?'

Trust Lorna to set up camp on the moral low ground.

'Perhaps he really has loved her all along, but only just realised it,' murmured Mrs Delacourt dreamily.

'And maybe he's a stalker who's been biding his time.'

'After 42 years? Per-leese!' Laura waved the cutting from the *Wakefield Express* under Lorna's upturned nose, then turned on me. 'This date is accurate, right?'

'As far as I know. Somebody had written 23rd August '63 on the original and it was yellow enough and crumbly enough to be an original.'

'*Forty-two years*,' breathed Mrs Delacourt softly. 'Even the Train Robbers didn't get that long.'

'And how do you think Miss Hayes, or Mrs Pennington if she still is, will react if her childhood sweetheart turns up on her doorstep as an old age pensioner?'

'I don't know, Lorna,' I said patiently. 'She'll probably make him a cup of tea and get out the coconut macaroons and they'll chat about old times, maybe even listen to *their* song.'

Lorna blanked me. She was good at that.

'They had a song, their own special song,' I floundered. 'It was *Let It Be* by The Beatles.' Still blank. 'They were a rather well-known beat combo in the Sixties, so I'm told.'

'That's not right,' said Laura, which surprised me as I thought she was on my side.

'I'm not making it up. Ellrington told me himself.'

'No, I meant that if this press cutting is correctly dated to 1963, and Ellrington hasn't seen Margaret Anne since, then they couldn't have had *Let It Be* as their song. It didn't come out until 1970.'

'I doubt your mother was born then, let alone you. How do you know that?'

'My specialist subject,' Laura said with a smile. A very nice smile.

'She's in a pub quiz team,' Lorna hissed and Laura's smile turned sheepish as she nodded in agreement.

'Well, maybe he got that wrong...'

'He forgot their special song? Typical man!' Mrs Delacourt waded in. 'I bet you and Amy have a special song.'

'Ian Dury: *Sex and Drugs and Rock and Roll,*' I said without hesitation. 'And I'd say yours was Bob Marley's *Lively Up Yourself.*'

'You're not far wrong, there, Angel. In my younger days...'

'Can we get on, please?' Veronica scowled at us. 'I don't think this is relevant or important. What steps have you taken to find this Margaret Anne Hayes or Pennington?'

'Well, I've made photocopies of the press clipping for everyone.'

You could have cut the silence with the knife that was pressing between my shoulder blades.

'She's from Yorkshire, yes?'

'That's right,' I said, eager to be helpful. 'She lived in Wakefield. Ellrington comes from a little village out in the sticks, called Flockton or something like that, but they went to school in Wakefield and that's where she got married. I would have thought the newspaper being called the *Wakefield Express* might have given that away.'

'So first we find out what happened to this Margaret Anne after she got married.'

'That's exactly what the customer wants,' I said cheerily and then the thought struck me. 'Does this mean I have to go to Yorkshire?'

'Surely they've suffered enough, haven't they?' This from Lorna, but I ignored her and made sure she knew she was being ignored.

'You don't have to go anywhere,' Veronica pronounced. 'This is a job for Double-O-Seven.'

'Bloody hell, Von, that's a bit extreme isn't it?'

Chapter Five

'He's sort of our man "oop north" in flat-cap and whippet country,' Laura told me as I put the kettle on in R & B's office kitchen. 'In case we have an enquiry which needs an operative on-the-ground north of...'

'Sainsbury's?' I suggested.

'I was going to say Birmingham, but you might have a point. It's a sort of reciprocal agreement.'

'So your 007 is a private eye?'

'A confidential enquiry agent, yes. His name is Ossie Oesterlein and he runs a one-man agency in Huddersfield. He does a job for us; we do one for him down here in the big bad city for the same number of billable hours.'

'I suppose the sound of his clogs and him complaining about beer with no head on it would give him away down here.'

'Something like that,' she giggled.

'So Double-O stands for Ossie Oesterlein. Where does the "seven" come from?'

'Lorna says it's his IQ, but she's really, really mean when she wants to be. It's what he calls himself when he answers the phone, except he says it "Hoh-Hoh-Seven" which is both kinda cute and kinda sad.'

'And they said the audiences up north were tough.'

'Ossie's a sweetie, so you be nice to him.'

'Me?'

'When you ring him. It is your case.'

I knew that, but did I have to do everything around here?

I tried to imagine what his office was like as I talked to him.

There would be a pebbled glass door on which would be lettered in flaked black paint: *'Ossie Oesterlein...Investigations'*. It would be a reasonably shabby door at the end of a reasonably shabby corridor in the sort of building that was new when it was a mill and orphaned children dived between the chomping machinery to rescue the scraps of waste wool known as 'shoddy'. The address would almost certainly be something like No. 3, The Dark Satanic Mills, Huddersfield.

'Ossie Oesterlein?'

'Double-Hoh Enquiries. Oesterlein speaking.'

'This is Rudgard and Blugden Confidential Investigations in London—'

'No it isn't.'

'It isn't?' I said stupidly.

'R & B's an all-girl agency. Is this a wind-up?'

If I hadn't been able to tell by the accent, the use of 'all-*girl*' was confirmation that I'd got the right man, or at least the right part of the country.

'It used to be an all-*female* agency, Mr Oesterlein, but there have been a few changes recently. I'm the new boy. My name's Angel.'

'Oh, aye. Fitzroy Maclean Angel isn't it?'

'Yes it is. I'm very impressed.' Impressed? I was horrified. 'How did you know that?'

'Ahm a detective aren't I?'

Silly me.

'Of course you are, that's why I'm calling. Obviously you're a detective with psychic powers.'

'Nay, lad,' the voice chuckled. 'Just a good memory. That lass Veronica, sent me a hemail last month saying you were on their

books. Couldn't forget a name as convoluted as Fitzroy
Maclean Angel, could yer? What did you ever do to upset your
Dad that much?'

So, gender equality hadn't reached Yorkshire yet, but email
had. Interesting.

'I'll think of something, Mr Oesterlein.'

'Call me Ossie, lad.'

'OK, Ossie Lad, I'm not sure how we do this but we need a
good leg man in Yorkshire...'

I regretted it immediately.

'I'm more of a tit man myself. We like 'em busty up 'ere,
generally with a bit more meat on 'em than you get down in
London.'

'You ever met Veronica Blugden, Ossie?'

'Can't say I 'ave, lad. We've done all our business over the
phone. I don't get down to London much. Don't see the call for
it; got everything we need 'ere.'

'You may very well have something up there I want.'

'Oh aye? What'd that be?'

'I want you to find me a girl.'

'Now you're talking, young Fitzroy, blonde or brunette?'

'I'm not sure, and she's not so much a girl as an old-age
pensioner.'

I gave 'Double-O' Oesterlein as many details as I could and he
asked me a dozen or more questions, some of which I could
answer.

I spelled out the names in question – Ellrington, Margaret
Anne Hayes and Simon Pennington – and offered to fax him the
cutting from the *Wakefield Express*. He asked if I had a
photograph of her and I said not apart from the picture in the
press cutting. I hadn't even asked Ellrington for one, reasoning
that it wouldn't be much use after all these years.

'You never know, lad. People round here have long
memories.'

And no, I didn't have home addresses for the former Miss Hayes or James Ellrington, except he'd mentioned a village called Flockton. I didn't see the relevance of them forty or more years on. Again, I got the 'You never know' treatment and a lot of tut-tutting down the line, implying that he thought the standard of soft southern detective work was pretty low.

'I suppose the best way to find Margaret Anne is through her married name, or maybe her employers,' I suggested.

'No kidding, Sherlock?' he said, which I thought a tad harsh.

'But I don't suppose...' I glanced at my notes '...that Calder Grove Interiors still exists.'

'Oh it does, lad. My office is kitted out with all their gear. Desk, chairs, filing cabinets, bookshelves. I've even got one of those spinning globes of the world which opens into a drinks cabinet from their catalogue.'

Why did I just know he would have one of those?

''Course I've got that at home. I'm not allowed drink in the office.'

'I know,' I said, sympathising with a fellow private eye, 'it's a terrible temptation, isn't it?'

'Nay, it's in the terms of my lease. I'm not allowed to have alcohol on the premises.'

'Wow, that's strict, who's your landlord? The Rechabites?'

I was showing off by mentioning the International Order of Rechabites, named after the Old Testament tribe of Recab, who had set up teetotal friendly societies in the north of England in the nineteenth century, local branches being known, in suitable Biblical fashion, as 'Tents'. But Oh-Oh Oesterlein had the perfect last word on the subject.

'Actually, it's the brewery's doing.'

'Pardon?'

'My office is above a pub, lad, so if I fancy a brew I have to walk all the way down one flight of stairs.'

So much for my dark Satanic mills image. Double-O-Seven was going up in my estimation.

'Anyhow, like I said, Calder Grove Interiors is still trading, though I think it's been bought out by some Swedish flat-pack company. I can check out this Simon Pennington chap with their personnel people, or human resources as they like to call it these days.'

'You can't think he'd still be working for the same company after forty years.'

'Depends how young he was when he started. People are very loyal around here.'

Loyal, and they had long memories up there; no wonder I lived down south.

'When you get the press clipping, you'll see from the report of the wedding that he was 32 and that would make him about 74 now,' I pointed out.

'So he could have been retired for eight or nine years, but he'll be getting a pension from the firm.'

'If he stayed there until he was 65,' I scoffed. 'That would be, like, for forty years.'

'People do, lad, people do.'

I was trembling as I put the phone down.

This working for a living business went on until you were 65? Nobody had ever said anything about that.

I called in to the Devonshire hospital to see my father that evening, having phoned ahead to see that he was not already 'receiving visitors'. This was a code I had established with the staff there after the time I had walked into his room and discovered that he already had a visitor, Kim McIntosh, and she was giving him the sort of physiotherapy that you only ever see in Swedish films of a bluish hue, and you never – ever – get on the National Health.

Still, I suppose she'd got over the shock of my father's stroke and it seemed, if anything, to have cemented their relationship. Cemented it so well you couldn't actually get a cigarette paper between them. I made a mental note to remind my father that this was probably due to the diplomatic skill with which I had broken the news to Kim. And at the same time remind him that he still had news to break to my mother.

At the Devonshire, he was something of a star pupil, or perfect patient as the jargon went. With stroke survivors, if you were mobile enough to go missing for several hours on end, and coherent enough to complain about the food, you weren't a nuisance, you were well on the way to recovery. Except, of course, a stroke is a 'brain attack' and where a heart attack damages the body, a stroke damages the brain, short-circuiting or burning out brain cells which don't grow back and can't, as yet, be bought like replacement bulbs on the Christmas tree lights.

My father had shown remarkable early stage recovery, particularly in the main motor functions of his arms and legs, though he was still prone to flailing about like a windmill when stressed. His speech had come back more slowly and when he talked it sounded as if he was both drunk and drowning in treacle, but it had come back. What was still missing in action was his memory or the logic to unlock it. He could remember who Kim was and, indeed, what to do with her when she climbed into bed with him, but on some occasions he was clearly bemused as to where he was and why he was there; though you'd have thought membership of the House of Lords as a life peer would have prepared him for that.

Still, the fact that he 'knew his own mind' and was willing to take part in any physiotherapy, occupational therapy or speech therapy on offer, made the hospital staff quite bullish about his recovery. Which was all very well until the afternoon when they got the call from the Chez Gerard restaurant in Charlotte Street saying that a man in pyjamas, dressing gown and slippers was ordering steak and *frites*. The fact that he had no way of paying for it didn't seem to bother them, but when he said he *didn't know* if he liked his steak rare or medium, they had suspected something was amiss. And when they had (politely) asked if he was all right, he had responded as if he was making a speech in the Lords, getting to his slippered feet and addressing the whole restaurant:

'I am not drunk. I am not mad. I have had a stroke, that is all.'

The story goes that several of the lunchtime crowd actually applauded him, though he probably couldn't work out why. It gave a quick-thinking maître d' the chance to grab a phone and call the Devonshire. I suspect they may have had the number on speed-dial.

The staff had confirmed that his stroke had been triggered by high blood pressure – 'some of his readings have been off the scale!' one nurse told me enthusiastically – and to avoid a second, more serious stroke, he would have to get his blood pressure down using a combination of drugs and 'lifestyle changes'.

I didn't like the sound of 'lifestyle changes' so I asked for details and they seemed reasonable enough: cut out salt and quadruple the amount of fruit in his diet; stop smoking (he was only on the occasional cigar anyhow); and take at least forty minutes strenuous exercise every day, though they didn't say whether that should involve Kim or not. All those were do-able and blood tests had shown his cholesterol level to be fine so he didn't have to do anything on that score. Best of all, no one mentioned alcohol.

He was lying on his bed, propped up by a yard-high wall of crisp white pillows, trying to read a hardback edition of Gore Vidal's *The Golden Age* I had given to him about five Christmases ago through his bifocals with the Armani frames.

'Kim brought me this from the flat. I never had the time to get around to it before,' he said, waving the book at me. 'It's bloody heavy.'

'You mean hard going?'

'No, bloody heavy! Couldn't you have waited for the paper-back?'

'I didn't know you were going to have time on your hands,

did I? Are you having any trouble reading it?'

He made to put the book down on the edge of the bed but missed entirely and it smacked onto the floor.

'Once I get my eyes focused on the pages, I can *see* the words, but they don't really make much sense.'

'It'll come, give it time,' I said as I picked the book up and placed it on the small chest of drawers by his bed.

'I hope so, be a bugger if it doesn't. I've read all the other books by...by...?'

'Gore Vidal.'

'Who? And how is Amy?'

'She's absolutely fine,' I said, going with the flow, 'and settling into country life like she was auditioning for the remake of *To The Manor Born*. She'll be riding to hounds before you know it.'

'I thought we'd banned fox-hunting,' he said, thinking about it seriously. 'Yes I'm sure we did. There was a bit of a fuss about it. Anyway, she shouldn't be riding in her condition.'

So he could remember that his daughter-in-law was pregnant but not the legislation he had voted for. That was a good sign in my book.

'Speaking of her condition, Amy was wondering if you'd had a chance to tell Mother the good news yet?'

'With my blood pressure?' he shouted, so loudly a crisp white nurse looked in through the doorway. 'I've got to take it easy from now on and confronting your mother is up there with bungee-jumping and wrestling alligators as things to avoid.'

'Don't try to con me, Dad. I've been reading up on stroke and hypertension.'

'What's that?'

'High blood pressure, and stress only affects your blood pressure temporarily.'

'I could have a heart attack.'

'Your heart is fine. They did tests and they found one. And your cholesterol level is spot-on. The staff here all agree that you are making a disgustingly good recovery and pretty soon you'll be here under false pretences.'

'I can't drive,' he said, his voice cracking.

'I'll drive you.'

'I'm not up to it…I get confused…I forget things.'

'You remember our deal? I tell Kim about you; you tell Mother she's about to become a grandmother.'

He looked up at the ceiling.

'I'm not sure I do.'

'Oh well, never mind. By the way, the hospital Registrar wants to know how you plan to settle the bill here.'

'I thought Amy said…'

He couldn't stop himself in time; maybe the stroke really had slowed him down.

'So we can remember some things, can we?'

'I can remember why I'm scared of your mother,' he sighed, shrinking back into his pile of pillows.

'She might be really pleased at the news,' I offered.

He glared at me over the top of his bifocals.

'Yeah, right. You want me to tell a woman who won't admit to being *forty*, or accept that The Beatles have split up, that she's going to be a grandmother and that she should stop tie-dying my old shirts and burning incense and start knitting bootees? Her face would go a colour unknown to nature.'

That would almost be worth seeing but I wasn't going to fall into his trap.

'A deal's a deal.'

'Very well,' he sighed, admitting defeat. 'I'll ring her, how about that? I mean I can't go to Suffolk in my condition. Though I suppose she could come down here. I'm sure she'd love to see your new house in the country…'

'Telephone will be fine,' I said quickly, feeling myself being flanked. 'But before the weekend. Amy's clock is ticking.'

'I promise, but you have to do something for me.'

'Something *else*?'

He pretended to look hurt, then put a finger to his lips and leaned forward, as if he suspected his private room was bugged.

'I want you to get me some drugs,' he whispered.

'Do you think that's wise in your condition?'

'Prescription drugs, you idiot. I've got a private prescription – in the top drawer there – I just want you to go to a pharmacy and get it for me.'

'What's it for?' I was already reaching.

'I have a condition called ED,' he said quickly.

'Erectile Dysfunction? What they put you on, Viagra? You can buy that on eBay, you know,' I said loudly, not that there was anybody in the building likely to be shocked by the fact that a stroke patient was having trouble getting an erection.

There again, there couldn't be many patients in the Devonshire who had a former page-three topless model as an incentive, so maybe the situation was serious.

'You've looked this up, haven't you?'

'Yes,' I admitted. 'It's fairly common among stroke patients, so I'm told, so I thought I'd brief myself in case you wanted any advice. What can I tell you? That the Viagra factory in Kent now covers 340 acres and the workforce is over 3,600? That it was invented by a woman and is the fastest selling drug in the world?'

I opened the drawer and removed the single thing in there, a small green prescription form from a doctor's pad.

'It's not for Viagra,' my father said through gritted teeth.

'No, it's Cialis,' I read, 'that's even better. It takes effect quicker and remains active for up to 36 hours, so somebody, probably the French, have nicknamed it "Le Weekend" and some call it the "Albert Finney" after the film *Saturday Night and Sunday Morning*. You're lucky, they could have prescribed Alprostadil, which is *injected* into the penis. Talk about the cure being worse than the disease, eh?'

My father held up a shaky hand in a gesture of surrender.

'Spare me the lecture, just get the prescription filled. Don't buy anything off the Internet, it's usually sub-standard or downright fake.'

'Did one of your fellow peers tell you that?'

'All of them.'

'Fair enough, don't worry, I'll score some love pills for you, but you only get them once you've rung the grandmother-to-be.'

'Very well,' he sighed. 'I'll do it tomorrow; trust me, I will.'

'Any time before "Le Weekend" will do,' I smiled.

On the way out I nobbled one of the administrative staff and asked if I could have a daily print-out of calls from the phone in my father's room. Amy was paying for them after all, but I said I was worried about his memory. He had some important calls to make to anxious friends and family and I wanted to make sure that he'd made them.

If a certain number in Suffolk didn't show up soon, he and Kim McIntosh would be watching television all Saturday night and Sunday morning.

Chapter Six

In the office the next morning, Laura asked me how I had got on with Double-O Oesterlein and what *quid pro quo* he was demanding.

'He didn't say, though he talked a lot,' I told her as I changed the filter in the new office coffee machine. (A reluctant investment by Veronica; to stop me nipping out to the Costa Coffee Green Room kiosk at the BBC just up the road.) 'Have you ever met him?'

'No, nobody has. He usually communicates by email.'

'I thought "Eee, mail" was what they said in Huddersfield when the postman arrived.'

'Don't be cruel, Angel. Ossie is very helpful usually, even if he does insist on calling anyone who supports Chelsea a "hairdresser" and he did ring up once and told Veronica to put the kettle on the hob and the boss on the phone.'

'I bet that went down well.'

'Veronica doesn't speak to him anymore.'

'I'll try and remember his technique.'

'I think your own blend of fake innocence and sarcasm is grinding her down quite nicely. How are you getting on with your case database?'

'My what?'

'Every active case should be logged into a database on our Intranet system, so that all staff can keep fully up to date on developments.'

'So Veronica can keep tabs on me, you mean,' I said with fake innocence and just a hint of sarcasm.

'And Lorna. She does the invoices for clients based on an operative's time, expenses and whatever actions they initiate. It's a sort of home-grown version of the Holmes program the police use.'

Now I might not have recognised a database if I saw one, but I knew what the HOLMES program was. The acronym stood for Home Office Large Major Enquiry System, which was a bit of a fudge but somebody had obviously thought it a wizard wheeze to spell out Sherlock's surname for a computer program which ran murder and serious crime enquiries. Technically it was Holmes 2 as the original, Holmes 1, was abandoned five or six years ago when it became clear that Britain's 43 police forces had not cooperated or even swapped Christmas cards on which computer system they were investing in. (A rather vital flaw in the plan, as any fifteen-year-old computer geek could have told them.) Holmes 2 was supposed to be a program which all forces could access and the object was to cut out the Byzantine card-index system which had bogged down murder hunts such as the infamous one for the Yorkshire Ripper. Every interview, statement, person involved, DNA test, car registration and phone call actioned by a detective on the case would be entered into the Holmes 2 program, probably by a civilian 'Indexer' these days, and would in theory become instantly cross-referenced and accessible to any officer on the enquiry. The one thing the Holmes program lacked was a button you could press marked 'Who Done It?'.

The Rudgard & Blugden system was far less sophisticated, just an Access database where you could sort information by queries, if, that was, you knew what on earth you were talking about. Fortunately Laura did and offered to set it up for me on the office computer. After ten minutes of listening to my breathtaking ignorance when it came to computers and my offering to make her another coffee, she relented and offered to input what meagre data I had on the Ellrington case herself.

It seemed to take her about thirty seconds to type in everything I knew about James Ellrington's quest to find Margaret Anne Pennington, née Hayes. I was only halfway through Chapter One of a Ross Macdonald I had plucked from my window sill bookshelf when she started bugging me with questions.

'So we know that Margaret got married in August 1963.'

'From the press cutting, yeah,' I agreed, trying to concentrate on my book.

'She was pretty, judging by the picture,' Laura was rambling.

'It's a bit difficult to tell from a faded black and white wedding photo printed on newsprint forty-two years ago.'

'That sort of bone structure doesn't fade, nor does that smile.'

I put a finger in my book to keep my place.

'Hey, come on; don't go all dreamy on me. We're supposed to be professionals, aren't we?'

'But she was so *young*. I mean, twenty is no age to get married, is it? And *he* was so much older.'

'It's a simple case of a young secretary falling for her older boss. Still happens these days, I suspect.'

I tried to say it as Lew Archer would have said it.

'Does it? I'm not sure about that. A 20-year-old girl marrying a 32-year-old man? That's quite an age gap.'

'No it's not,' I said thinking of my father and Kim McIntosh. Now *that* was a gap.

'It is if the older guy isn't a Hollywood superstar or an oil tycoon,' she countered.

'I'm glad you said that and not me. I wouldn't want dear little Veronica worrying her pretty little head about my political incorrectness.'

Laura narrowed her eyes and tried to laser me at that.

'What's the age gap between you and Amy?' she asked.

'Actually, she's older than me.' She was too, by about five weeks. 'So I suppose that makes me her toy boy.'

Laura looked back at the computer screen, studying it intently.

'When you're an attractive, successful woman like that, you're allowed one. Or two.'

I ignored her and went back to my book. I got about halfway down the page before she started up again.

'I wonder if she felt the same way as he did? I mean, does she keep a candle burning for him?'

'If we find her, we can ask her,' I muttered, trying to read.

'I mean, she might not have given him a second thought since 1963 and gone on to be a happily married woman with children and grandchildren.'

'Grandchildren' rang a warning bell with me somewhere at the back of my mind, but I was more intent on discovering how Lew Archer was doing finding *The Wycherly Woman*.

'Does Ellrington have any children?'

I realised Laura was talking to me.

'A son, I think. Yes, I'm sure he mentioned a son.'

'And his wife?'

'I don't know if the son's married.'

'Not the son, Ellrington's wife. What happened to her? It ought to be in the database.'

'What on earth for?'

'Family relationships are often crucial. What if Ellrington is digging up some old girlfriend as a pretext for a divorce?'

'What are you on about, woman? Ellrington's a widower. His wife died a couple of years ago from breast cancer he said. And even if she hadn't, why go to all the expense of hiring us? There are easier ways of getting a divorce these days. No, the way I see it is the guy is suddenly free and clear.'

'Free and clear? You think he murdered his wife?'

'Oh for God's sake, you've been reading...' And then I realised I was the one holding the paperback detective story and corrected myself '...those trashy magazines again, haven't you? No, I do not think for a minute James Ellrington murdered his wife, or anybody else. He's 65 years old, his son has presumably flown the nest, he has an excellent civil service pension and for the first time in years he is without a wife and he has time on his hands. He's doing what most men would do in that situation.'

'What's that, then?' she said with a curled lip. 'Drinking heavily and pestering little schoolgirls at the bus stop with packets of chocolate buttons?'

I felt the hairs on the back of my neck go up and the office temperature drop a few degrees. Carefully, I folded down the corner of the page I was reading and slowly, without any sudden movements, placed it back in my window sill library.

'What I meant was he's reviewing his life; he's looking back. He's thinking *what might have been.* His wife has died and he's lonely and he thinks back to his first girlfriend and realises that maybe she was his one true love, but he lost her.'

'He let her go.'

'Yes, all right, he did. But he's thinking here I am, free and clear of responsibilities, I still have my health and I've got plenty of cash, or at least enough to hire a private detective. And I might just find my long-lost true love and maybe, just maybe, she's also *free and clear* now.'

Laura looked shocked.

'Oh come on, if she's still married to this Simon Pennington, he must be 75 by now. Maybe she's a widow, I mean women live a lot longer than men.'

'They do?'

'No, it just seems like it sometimes. But the point is she may be a merry widow or a gay divorcee and at a loose end. She might wake up every morning wondering what happened to her first love and thinking what might have been herself. You never know, we might be reuniting lovebirds who haven't seen each other for 42 years.'

'It can't be that long. Maybe 35 years; I told you.'

'Told me what?'

'That if *their* song was *Let It Be*, they must have been together in 1970, not 1963. Ellrington either got it wrong or is lying.'

'Or you're wrong.'

'1970,' she raised her eyes to the ceiling, 'The Monkees disbanded, so of course did The Beatles. Hendrix played Seattle, and then later the same year he died, as did Janis Joplin.'

'And Johnny Hodges,' I interrupted without thinking.

'Who?'

'He was nicknamed "The Rabbit". He played saxophone for Duke Ellington.'

'Who?'

'Never mind.'

'The Kinks released *Lola*, Smokey Robinson did *Tears of a Clown*, Simon and Garfunkel did *Bridge Over Troubled Water*. It was also the year of *Let It Be*. I don't remember any of them, I wasn't born then, but it is my specialist subject on the pub quiz team, and my pub quiz team wins prizes.'

I gave in and allowed her the victory.

'OK, so he made a mistake, or he forgot.'

'Forgot? Forgot *their song*?' Laura was glowing pink around the neck and cleavage. 'What sort of a man forgets a couple's favourite song?'

'All of them?' I suggested.

With Laura busy inputting my data, no word from Double-O Oesterlein, and both Lorna and Veronica out of the office for the rest of the afternoon, I decided that the best use of my time would be to head off home to Cambridgeshire, missing the rush hour traffic. When Laura started to object, I told her I needed thinking time and she agreed, rather too quickly, that I did.

Commuting back and forth to Toft End in my trusty black cab Armstrong certainly gave me plenty of time to think, mostly about why I was spending so much time on the M25.

Since they had started publishing street maps which showed where the speed cameras were situated on the North Circular Road, the traffic flow on the M25 had congealed even more as frustrated drivers with nine points on their licences sought an alternative route east.

As I was heading in roughly the right direction, I tried to think of a way of getting my father up to Suffolk for a face-off with my mother. He had actually been driving up there to see her to break the news that he and Kim McIntosh were planning on getting married when he had experienced his 'brain attack', as he was beginning to call his stroke. He had turned off the A12 and with great presence of mind, all things considered, had driven to Colchester Hospital and booked himself into Casualty. It was a pretty extreme way of getting out of fronting my mother with his good news, but I had good news to break to her and my sympathies were with Dad.

When their marriage had hit the rocks, with the inevitability of a super-tanker trying to negotiate its way around a coral island of outstanding environmental importance, my father had pursued younger women and the sort of business career which the obituary writers call 'chequered'. A catalogue of bad business decisions and an absolute knack for being in the wrong place at the wrong time, had somehow left him with several non-executive directorships, even more trusteeships of small charities, and absolutely no money. There was something almost Dickensian about the way he could live beyond his means, not actually be good at anything and yet remain so witty, charming and urbane that all who came into contact with him simply assumed he was a good chap. I had always suspected that he got his life peerage from a naïve incoming Labour government, by mistake. Somebody had presented somebody with a list of candidates and somebody must have said 'Lord Angel, that sounds nice, doesn't it?' but the official reason had been service to pensions' arbitration, whatever that meant. He had apparently sat on some sort of review body for ten years, sorting out small disputes between companies and employees. Ironic, really, considering he had never put a penny into a pension fund of his own, always assuming that something would turn up, probably on the other side of the mythical fence where the grass was greener.

There was no doubt that having House of Lords, London SW1 as his address boosted his free lunch quotient and increased geometrically the number of receptions and parties he was invited to. Indeed, it was at one such 'official' party that he met Kim McIntosh. But it never did very much for his earning power. He had been hoping for a couple of non-executive directorships which would allow him to pull down thirty grand a year each for no more than two days a month work, but none had materialised. Maybe there were just too many new New Labour peers with time on their hands and the non-executive director market was flooded.

The one good business deal he had done in his life was to buy his tiny flat in Morpeth Terrace in Westminster, originally as a hideaway love-nest for one of the many mistresses he had 'in town' while my mother was left at home in Suffolk. As he was always telling me, the flat was all he had. That and his daily attendance allowance at the House of Lords; and he stressed, it was an attendance allowance. If you didn't attend, you didn't get the dosh and somewhere in the House there was an ancient clerk, no doubt wearing tights and buckles on his shoes, who made a pencil mark against a list of peers' names every day, like they used to take the register at school.

Since his stroke, my father had not been to the House and was consequently denied his only regular source of income. Amy was covering his hospital and physiotherapy bills, but as far as I knew he was strapped for cash – not an unknown condition for him. Therefore, I reasoned, as Armstrong chugged up the M11, I might be able to bribe him into going to see my mother and breaking the news that she was going to be a grandmother.

I would probably have to drive him there as it would be months before he was allowed back behind a wheel and Amy no longer had months to spare. I could wait until he was fit, but then my mother's wrath at hearing the news after the event would be truly awesome. The lesser evil was squaring up to her now and reminding her that she was no longer in her mid-twenties, the age to which she had regressed following the divorce. Yes, that was definitely the lesser of two evils and hardly frightening at all if you got somebody else to do it.

When they had split up, my mother had actually taken a small ad in *The Times* to inform the world that she was setting herself up as a professional artist, open to commissions, under the name Bethany Angel; retaining her married name but dumping the more formal 'Elizabeth'. She used her chunk of the divorce settlement to set herself up with a small terraced house and an old butcher's shop turned into a gallery, in a small former fishing village called Romanhoe, which she told everyone was in Suffolk, because it sounded better, though it was actually just inside the Essex border. The village attracted her because of its flourishing, if self-styled, artistic community into which, cash-rich, she was welcomed. In fact, for a time she was called 'the piss-artist formerly known as Betty'. The trouble was she loved living the life of an artist, but wasn't that keen on producing the actual art, though God knows there wasn't a medium she hadn't tried, with most of her experiments ending in tears. Her gallery shop burned to the ground during her oxy-acetylene welding phase, but the insurance money financed her move into hand-thrown (and I do mean 'thrown') pottery for which she had found a small market on the Craft Fair circuit.

She didn't seem to miss married life at all and as a 'free woman' she had decided to catch up a life perceived as missed, although always just that one beat out of time. She took up smoking, drugs (Class B), casual sex, white wine spritzers and listening to Oasis (though never once admitting it was because they reminded her of The Beatles) and dressing in large-block primary colours and ever-shorter skirts.

Still, she was happy, or seemed to be, and didn't seem to be hurting anyone. No one in their right mind would want to interrupt her regression into a youth she was working so hard at mis-spending. The one thing that was likely to do that was reminding her of her real age. At least two people, that we knew of, had tried and suffered. One was a local lady magistrate before whom my mother appeared on a drunk-and-disorderly charge after deciding on a naked swimming session in the mud flats of Romanhoe one Sunday after a particularly liquid lunch in a busy riverside pub. It had been such a good lunch that Mummy Dearest had forgotten to check whether or not the tide was in. It wasn't, and her floundering in the mud in front of a pub full of otherwise happy customers could hardly go unnoticed. She was hauled out, hosed down and bundled into a police car but really hit the local headlines when she appeared in court and the presiding magistrate, with all the blue-rinsed disdain she could muster, told my mother to pay her fine, behave herself in future and try to act her age. Whatever my mother said as she was hurried out of the courtroom by her solicitor (versions differ) it almost certainly included the words 'shrivelled', 'old' and 'kipper' in some order or other, and although no further legal action was taken, the lady magistrate only lived with her new nickname for about two months before resigning from the local bench.

The other incident, which these days would have guaranteed her an Anti-Social Behaviour Order, something she would have worn with pride, involved one of her boyfriends of a similar age, but more mature outlook. When he had told her he was whisking her off for an Aegean cruise on a luxury liner, she had been thrilled. When she had looked at the brochure and found it was a holiday organised by SAGA, she had hit him with a bottle of Bacardi Breezer.

My father was well aware of these stories. The MP for

Romanhoe had even sought him out in one of the House of
Lords' dining rooms to pass on a number of complaints about
noise and raucous behaviour from several of his constituents, at
which my father had laughed and reminded the MP that as a
divorcee, he didn't have anything to do with his ex-wife, and as
a life peer, *he* didn't have to worry about voters.

I could understand why he was scared of going to see her.
Like me, he put little faith in the cry 'Don't shoot the
messenger', but I really did think it was time he showed a bit of
backbone.

By the time I was off the M11 and threading through the
back lanes to Toft End, I was no closer to thinking up a fool-
proof incentive which would get him out of London and up to
Romanhoe.

And then, suddenly, the answer was staring me in the face.

Down the sunken lane leading to The Old Rosemary Branch,
in fact parked right outside, was a beautiful Aston Martin DB7
in British racing green.

As Armstrong chugged up behind it, I rehearsed my opening
line:

'The name's Bond...'

Chapter Seven

Of course, I never got to say it; Amy did.

As soon as I got the front door open, she just couldn't resist shouting:

'Hey, Angel, we have a visitor. The name's Bond, Jane Bond.'

'I know,' I said airily. 'I saw her car in the lane. Where is she?'

Amy's eyes flashed towards what we had decided was probably going to be the lounge when we had everything unpacked, although ironically it had been the public bar, not the lounge, when the house had been a pub.

Jane Bond was standing by the inglenook fireplace nursing a mug of something, hopefully for her sake not the sage tea Amy had become addicted to.

'So, Mrs Bond, we meet at last,' I announced, putting my arms out for a hug.

She frowned, but kissed me on both cheeks.

'We have met before, Mr Angel. If you remember, we sold you this house.'

'Of course you did. How is everybody at Symington & Sedgeley?'

Symington & Sedgeley was a firm of upmarket estate agents covering Cambridge and the surrounding shires, whose name Amy had picked out of *Country Life* when she had decided that we should move out of London. Of course I was the one who had to do the legwork and go to see them, but I'd been working near Cambridge anyway, so I combined a bit of firm's business with a bit of personal business. Jane worked for the boss and patriarch of the firm, Julius Symington, and I had turned up right on cue for once, not only looking for a country property which fitted most of Amy's criteria but also able to rid the firm of an annoying little shit called Devon Sedgeley, who had been getting on Jane Bond's tits for years.

'Everyone at the office is fine,' she said politely, 'and we were all very impressed with how quickly the sale went through.'

'That's entirely down to Amy here,' I said.

'That's absolutely right,' said Amy, placing a hand on her stomach. 'But then I didn't have the time for lengthy negotiations.'

'I'm so impressed,' said Mrs Bond. 'When I was expecting my first, just the thought of moving house as well would have done my head in. They say it is as stressful as getting a divorce, but it isn't. Almost, but not quite. Anyway, I thought I would stop by and welcome you to the wilds of Cambridgeshire and see if you needed anything from the welcome wagon.'

'Well, since you're here…' I began.

Jane brought us a house warming present, a bottle of champagne. I've put it in the fridge.'

'I'm sorry,' said Mrs Bond. 'I forgot you were pregnant.'

'I won't always be,' smiled Amy. 'We'll save it until after the event.'

'Long to go now?'

'Six weeks and three days if it's on time, which will be a bloody first for anyone in this house.'

'Do you intend to do the birthing here?'

I wasn't sure I liked the way their conversation was going.

'Not an option, I'm afraid,' said Amy. 'Once you're over thirty, they insist on a hospital birth if it's your first one.'

'But only for the first?'

What was this 'first' business?

'So I understand,' Amy was saying, 'and if there are no

problems, then you can insist on a home birth in future.'

'Have you thought about joining the National Childbirth Trust?'

'I did think about it, but it might be a bit late for this one.'

What *were* they talking about?

'Well, bear it mind. I was an active member for years and once upon a time I was in great demand as a birth buddy,' said Mrs Bond.

A *what?*

'Roy knows where to find me if you ever need anything,' she added as if comforting the sick.

'Well, actually, I wanted to remind you about a favour you owe me,' I said quickly, to change the subject, although it brought a withering glare from Amy.

'Last time we met I promised you a ride, didn't I?'

Jane Bond was trying hard to keep her face straight, but couldn't quite keep the twinkle out of her eyes.

'In the Aston, of course,' she added eventually, but I couldn't let her get away with that.

'Oh I see, you meant in your car...'

But I only let her squirm for a second or two – she had hardly started to blush.

'Indeed you did, and I'd like to take you up on that, if you could spare a day from the office for a run in the country.'

'I thought this was the country.'

'A different bit. I was thinking of a day-trip from London to the Suffolk coast.'

'Angel...' Amy growled softly.

'Well, go where you want. I promised you a drive, take the beast where you like as long as you bring it back in one piece.'

'I was hoping you would drive.'

'Me?' Mrs Bond shrugged her shoulders. 'You want me to come along?'

'I think that's vital,' I said.

* * *

'Nice lady,' Amy said as we waved at the Aston disappearing down the lane, 'and in fantastic shape for a woman her age. What do you reckon? Fifty-five? Fifty-eight?'

'Somewhere around there,' I agreed. 'She's got great legs.'

'And great hair and fantastic skin tone. Did you notice her hands? It's always the hands that give a woman's age away.'

'Great legs,' I agreed again.

'And she knows how to dress. That suit might be off-the-peg but the shoes were Salvatore Ferragano gold sandals unless I'm very much mistaken.'

Amy is rarely much mistaken about shoes and if she approved of them, they would almost certainly retail at about £150 each.

'They show off her great legs,' I agreed.

'Have you got a thing about her legs?'

'No, but I hope my father has.'

When I got into the office the next morning, there was a sign taped to the edge of my desk which read, in multi-coloured lettering: 'Have we earned our fee today?'

I screwed it up and threw it roughly in the direction of the waste bin before I noticed there was another one on the back of my chair and that someone had done it as a screensaver on my computer.

'Well, have we?'

I hadn't heard Laura follow me in and when I turned around to glare at her, she held her hands up, palms outwards.

'Not my idea,' she said quickly. 'We've all been fly-posted. Veronica's been doing a management course on team-building and motivation. I think she's having Post-It notes printed up with it on.'

'Good grief.'

'Seriously, how's it going with the Ellrington case?'

'Well, I'm still waiting to hear from our friend in the north.'

'If there's anything to find, Ossie will find it,' she said. 'What else?'

'What do you mean "else"?'

'What other steps have you taken to find his old girlfriend?'

'She doesn't show up on the Internet,' I said confidently, 'either as Margaret Anne Hayes or under her married name.'

'Few people do, proportionately. I certainly don't, do you?'

'I bloody hope not.'

'In fact the Internet is fairly useless for tracing people. Any other lines of enquiry?'

'Aren't there credit checks and things we could do?'

'We've run James Ellrington. He paid his deposit with a cheque so we had his bank details. He came up clean, or at least he'd never been refused credit. What did he do for a living?'

'He's retired.'

'I know, but what did he retire from?'

'The Civil Service.'

'Which bit?'

'I haven't a clue,' I told her truthfully, somewhat bemused that it was me who was getting the third degree. 'Why would that be important?'

'I don't know, it might be it might not. It's a gap in the database.'

'Oh well, I'll get on it right away in that case.'

'Don't get sarcastic with me, it just deepens your worry lines. I only thought that if Ellrington, say, had been in MI5, that's a different sort of civil servant to somebody who'd worked down the local tax office for forty years.'

'If he'd been *that* sort of civil servant, he wouldn't need a private detective to find his old sweetheart.'

'You mean an MI5 officer?'

Laura was so innocent.

'Christ, no. MI5 can't find MI6 most days. Have you ever trawled their website?* They have a mission statement thing to try and attract new recruits under the heading "For a life less ordinary". It goes: get up, make toast, catch train, brief office managers, have team lunch, disrupt terrorist cell, go shopping,

---

* www.mi5.gov.uk

get home, go to bed. Doesn't say anything about getting pissed in wine bar and leaving your laptop on the tube. Ellrington doesn't strike me as the MI5 type. OK, so he did go to Cambridge, but he's not obviously gay. What I meant was if he'd been a tax inspector, *then* he wouldn't need a detective. The taxman knows everything about everybody.'

'I think you're a bit paranoid about the taxman.'

'You'll learn. You think the Mafia's got power? That Opus Dei runs everything? Amateurs, complete bloody amateurs compared to the Inland Revenue.'

Laura let out a low whistle and moved slowly backwards out of the office.

'It's your case...'

'And I'm on it. I'll be out most of the day.'

'Where?'

'Wimbledon, where else?'

James Ellrington didn't actually live in Wimbledon, he just told people he did the same way my mother said she lived in Suffolk rather than Essex. It just sounded better.

The address he had given me was within walking distance of Wimbledon Chase train station, but technically it was Merton or Merton Park rather than Wimbledon proper. It was one of those things where, if you were selling a house there, you'd say Wimbledon, but if you were buying on a fixed budget, you'd ask an estate agent for anything between Merton and Morden.

I made one pass down Manor Road to locate the house, part of a 1920s terrace looking out over the playing fields of a school, before parking Armstrong and walking back up the street. It was a bright late summer morning in south-west London. The dog-walkers were out on the recreation ground, complete with pooper scoopers and scrunched up Sainsbury's carrier bags. The school kids were still on holiday and the birds were singing in the municipally-maintained trees. Most of the residents of Manor Road seemed to be doing some sort of home improvement, with every second house having a skip outside on the road or a ladder propped up against the bedroom windows. In most residential areas of London an unguarded ladder meant a burglary was guaranteed within the next five minutes. In Hackney, the ladder would be pinched within two.

There were cars parked the length of the road and all of them still had four wheels. There were no broken tequila bottles in the gutter, no posse of hooded youths hanging around on the street corner on mountain bikes so small they could have come from a circus where they had made the clowns redundant.

It was amazing how even the briefest contact with an estate agent made you think like one. I had only seen Jane Bond for about twenty minutes the day before and at the time I had either been noticing her legs or thinking about her Aston Martin; and yet here I was valuing the houses in Manor Road and thinking up trite phrases for the written details or 'particulars'.

Then I stopped day-dreaming and realised I had been subjected to auto-suggestion. I had driven by it and now I was looking at it as I walked down the road: James Ellrington's house had an estate agent's For Sale sign outside it.

He hadn't mentioned anything about moving house, but then again, why should he? It wasn't as if he was doing a runner without paying his bill; he'd actually paid a retainer and, given the amount of work I had done on his behalf (if I was being honest), he was well in credit. It was just another thing that he hadn't told me.

Of course I hadn't asked him anything about his domestic arrangements, so maybe it was all my fault. I wasn't asking the right questions, but, then again, I was under the impression that we were supposed to be investigating Margaret Anne Pennington, née Hayes, not James Ellrington. But what did I know? I was new at this game and probably not very good at it.

Which was why I was walking down Manor Road on a summer's morning, about to pay an unexpected call on my client for no good reason other than I couldn't think of anything else to do.

Some days are like that, I've found. Especially the ones which involve this working for a living business.

I had no opening gambit, no snappy excuse for being there, no cheerful greeting prepared. It was probably just as well, then, that it wasn't James Ellrington who answered the door when I rang the bell.

He'd been dipped in the same gene pool, though, showing a strong family resemblance around the jaw line, the nose and the ears. If he had been wearing a hat, there would not have been the shadow of a doubt that he was James Ellrington Junior. But he wasn't wearing a hat and he was going bald – badly.

He didn't have enough hair left for a comb-over and hadn't summoned up the nerve to go to a corner shop barber and ask for a Number One, the obvious solution adopted by the vast majority of male Londoners (except me) who seem to start losing their hair by their mid-twenties these days. I've never read a convincing reason to explain this epidemic of premature baldness among those of the later twentieth-century generation. Maybe it was something they put in the alcopops or a by-product of too many pot noodles. Almost certainly it was connected to the excessive use of mobile phones. I think we should be told.

'Yes?'

'I was looking for Mr Ellrington,' I said politely, taking off my sunglasses to be less threatening.

'You found him!'

'I meant Mr James Ellrington.'

I could have added 'you father' as I was pretty sure this was the son, but these days you can't be too careful and should never assume family ties where the knot might have slipped or been cut.

'He's gone to Sunbury for the day and won't be back until

this evening. If it was the house you wanted to see, I could show you around.'

I thought about that for a moment, trying to figure out exactly how many rules of the Association of British Investigators I would be breaking, and realised it was probably all of them.

'I don't have an appointment, I'm afraid. I was just in the neighbourhood and the estate agent had mentioned...'

'That's not a problem. It's a buyer's market. Sellers can't be choosers these days. Come in, come in.'

OK, last chance.

'No, I can't really just drop in on you like this...'

'Rubbish, you're here now.' He held out a hand for me to grasp. 'I'm Peter Ellrington, James is my father.'

'Archer,' I said, 'Lewis Archer.'

His handshake was careless and his palm sweaty. I could also smell cigarette smoke deeply engrained into the fabric of his clothes. That was a skill I had developed since Amy had outlawed smoking and declared a nicotine-free zone around her person, which theoretically had a radius of about twenty miles.

Peter Ellrington had obviously not been expecting visitors, or if he was, he hadn't made much of an effort. He was dressed in an old pair of jeans which sagged badly around the arse, not in a cool 'anti-fit' way at all, a faded black T-shirt advertising Jack Daniels, blue cord-soled deck shoes and no socks. I wasn't sure about Merton Park, but I knew it wasn't a good look for Wimbledon.

It wasn't a good look anywhere for a man of his age. Perhaps a Kate Moss, four sizes down, could have got away with it. Peter Ellrington just looked like a slob, and an old one at that, which got me struggling to guess his age. I knew from what Ellrington Senior had told me that he had married a few years after he and Margaret Anne had split, which would make Peter's birth either late Sixties or early Seventies, putting him in his mid-thirties; but he sure as hell looked older than me and in a bad light I would have put him around the fifty mark, though I knew those numbers didn't compute. There was something about his skin, which had a deathly pallor, and another smell about him apart from cigarettes, a faint whiff of what could have been sweet sherry. He had either had a bad life or a very good one.

'What brings you to this neck of the woods, then?' he asked me as I followed him down the entrance hall and into what was obviously the kitchen.

I remembered what I was supposed to be doing there.

'I hear it's a peaceful area.'

'Depends what you're comparing it with,' he said. Suddenly he had a cigarette in his mouth and was flicking a lighter and he had done it so quickly I hadn't seen a packet.

'Hackney,' I said and he nodded, conceding the point.

I had said Hackney just because it always gets that reaction although its reputation is over-hyped. Everyone knows the borough of Brent has the highest murder rate in the capital.

'Well, it's certainly quiet around here. Lots of schools, plenty of parks, and that's about it.'

'So you're moving to somewhere with a bit more danger and excitement, then?'

He narrowed his eyes and exhaled smoke directly towards my face. I was shocked by his action, but only because it was such a surprising thing for anyone to do these days. Since the smoking police had assumed control, blowing smoke into someone's face was high up on the list of war crimes at the International Political Correctness Tribunal. I didn't react to Ellrington's rudeness, partly because I didn't want to give him any satisfaction and partly because I was grateful for the odd blast of secondary smoke to ease my withdrawal symptoms.

'It's my father who's moving. He's got a place in the sun lined up now he's retired. My mother died two years ago and there's nothing to keep him here anymore.'

'You're not taking on the house yourself?' I asked innocently, or what I thought was innocently.

'Christ, no! I'm not hanging around. I'm only here to give the old man a bit of company.'

I scanned the kitchen and figured that the sort of company Peter Ellrington offered his father obviously did not involve doing the washing up, or emptying a swing-bin overflowing with tinfoil cartons and their cardboard lids with numbers scrawled on them. Mind you, he would have had difficulty getting to the bin without disturbing the half dozen empty bottles of Co-Op Sweet Sherry. So I had been right about his choice of aftershave, not that that was any comfort. In my experience, which was wide and far-reaching, sherry drunks were among the worst type of drunk. Peter Ellrington was probably the Sherry Marketing Board's worst nightmare.

'The cooker, the fridge and the washing machine and dryer are all included in the deal,' he was saying and I realised I ought to be listening again.

But not the microwave I noted, which on cursory inspection seemed to be the only bit of kitchen kit to actually get some wear and tear.

'It's three bedrooms isn't it?' I asked, thinking it was the sort of question I ought to be asking.

'Yes. Two decent ones and one smallish one to be honest.' It was good of him to admit that; 'small' to a London estate agent usually meant 'cupboard'. 'But I'd rather not show you up there without my father being here.'

'That's perfectly reasonable: I don't have an appointment,' I agreed. 'I should really have rung the estate agents.'

'Pah! Bunch of vultures. They don't do much for their money.' He turned towards the kitchen sink and ran the stub of his cigarette under the mixer tap then dropped it into a cracked porcelain soap dish. He wasn't pitching for the *Country Life* market.

'Have you had much interest?'

'Plenty,' he said a little too quickly and there was a sly, foxy look about him as he said it. 'Several offers in already.'

I tried to look impressed and concerned at the same time, or at least as if I cared.

'Have you lived here long?' I tried. To my amazement, he had another cigarette in his mouth but where it had come from I hadn't spotted. He was like a magician, pulling them out of the air.

'It's my father's house. He's been here about fifteen years.'

'What did he do?'

'What's that got to do with anything?' he said suspiciously.

'I just wondered if he'd worked locally, that was all.'

'He was a civil servant, now retired. He worked in various places: Yorkshire, Manchester, Birmingham and wound up in London. So what do you do?'

'I drive a cab,' I said, keeping eye contact.

'Really?' he said with a smirk.

'Somebody has to.'

Well, I wasn't lying and he might have seen me drive up.

'I suppose so,' he said through a cloud of smoke. 'Do you want to see the rest of the house? Apart from the upstairs that is. You've probably got other places to see.'

This guy was definitely clocking up overtime on my weird-ometer. I just couldn't get a handle on him, though I had a gut feeling that his medication was nowhere near strong enough.

'A quick look,' I said politely, 'then I'll get out of your way.'

'Dining room.' He pointed with his cigarette and led the way through into a small, neat room with a small polished oval dining table that hadn't been used for a while judging by the patina of dust covering its surface.

'And then there's the lounge,' he carried on without pausing. 'We tend to live mostly in here.'

The lounge was at the front of the house and had a bay window overlooking the street and the recreation ground beyond. The fact that you could see something green instead of another building usually adds several thousands to a house price in London.

It was a room which looked lived in and one which was

cleaned regularly. It had everything you would expect in a suburban terraced house's front room: a two-seater sofa and two matching armchairs in a semi-circle around a fireplace which had been bricked up long ago; a TV and video/DVD player in one corner and a midi hi-fi system in the other. The hi-fi system had a turntable for playing vinyl records and there was a pile of old LPs stacked on the floor.

I wondered if one of them was The Beatles' *Let It Be*, but couldn't think how I might raise the subject with Ellrington Junior.

'Very nice,' I found myself saying, 'Good size and a good ...er...aspect. This is south-facing isn't it? So you get the good light.'

'Probably is, never thought about it before,' Ellrington was saying, pulling on his cigarette and gently hopping from one foot to the other, making it clear that he wanted me gone. Or another drink, or both.

I had no intention of hanging about as I had no real idea of what I was doing there, apart from admiring the framed photographs on the wall over the former fireplace.

One in particular caught my eye. It showed James Ellrington – clearly him, though about ten years younger – with his arm around a dark-haired woman of about the same age. They were standing on the prow, or the front end, of a boat.

It wasn't the *Titanic* but then it wasn't a pedalo on a park lake; it was some sort of motor-cruiser moored alongside a flock of others and wherever the photograph had been taken it had been a bright sunny day and jolly boating weather.

What had caught my eye was the name of the boat the smiling couple were on.

Margaret Anne.

Chapter Eight

As soon as I was inside Armstrong, I switched my mobile phone on and dialled the office. Lorna answered. Up until then the day had been going quite well.

'Lorna, I need you to do something for me.'

'Where are you?'

'Out in the field, following up some leads in the Ellrington case.'

'Oh yeah?'

The tone of her voice left me in no doubt that she thought I was lying through my teeth although I thought I had used all the right buzz-words.

'Got a pencil handy?' I asked cheerfully.

'Yes...' she said suspiciously as if I was going to give her instructions on where to insert it. As if I would. As if.

'Find out for me if there's a marina or a yacht club in Sunbury, that's Sunbury on Thames.'

'I know where it is,' she snapped, 'and of course there's a marina there. There are hundreds; you can see the boats from the M3. It's something to do with it being on the river. The Sunbury *on Thames* bit gives it away, don't you think?'

Now I was thinking about where she could put her pencil.

'Then see if you can find the one James Ellrington belongs to, with a boat called the *Margaret Anne*.'

'What sort of boat?'

'I don't know. It's not a battleship and it's not a racing yacht. Does that narrow it down?'

I could have said it wasn't a Russian cargo freighter either. I had been on one of them, briefly, quite recently and had no pressing desire to go to sea again.

'That's not helpful at all, but if it's somewhere like Sunbury, it's more likely to be a motor cruiser than a fishing boat. What exactly am I supposed to be finding out?'

'Which yacht club he's in, where his boat's parked and how long he's had it if you can.'

'How do I do that?'

'Oh, for goodness' sake, tell lies! Say you've got a delivery to make to the *Margaret Anne* and Mr Ellrington is there waiting for it. Say you're from a film company looking for boats to use in a film about Dunkirk and you wanted to check out one called the *Margaret Anne*. Say you're selling Internet server connections for boat owners moving between marinas and you've been told that Mr Ellrington might be willing to use his boat as a demonstration model...'

'I get the idea. I'll think of something.' At last there was a spark of enthusiasm in her voice, and then she blew it by asking: 'Why would anyone be making a film about Dunkirk?'

'Oh, just wing it. I'm sure you'll pull it off, just remember to block the phone line so they can't do a 1471 ring back check. Now the other thing I want you to do is run a Criminal Records Bureau check on a Peter Ellrington. Can you do that?'

'Yes we can. R & B Investigations is registered with CRB itself and through what they call an Umbrella Organisation. The checks cost about £50 a go, but it can take a while sometimes. They usually ask for a full name, address and date-of-birth.'

I gave her the Manor Road address for Peter Ellrington and admitted that I didn't know his date of birth, so I gave her Amy's.

'If they query that I can pretend he's applying for a job with us and maybe he's lying about his age. Do you want the standard check or the enhanced?'

Lorna really did sound if she was enjoying this detective business now I had hit upon something she knew how to do. Personally I had little faith in her getting much out of the Criminal Records Bureau whose reputation had been shaky from its inception. Being located in Liverpool hadn't helped, prompting old jokes about dodgy Scousers such as the fact that it was based in Liverpool so that all the enquiries could be charged at local rate.

'See what the standard one turns up,' I said, then had a thought. 'Hang on a second, have you done this before?'

'Of course I have.'

'Have you done one on me?'

'Our code of practice on data security prevents me from answering that question.'

'It's only employers and organisations can get a CRB check done, isn't it? Somebody who is self-employed or an individual can't run a check on themselves, to see what the CRB has got on them. That's right, isn't it?'

'I believe so,' she said primly. 'R & B Investigations request checks in their capacity as an employer, that's all I know.'

Well, as an employee I might be kept in the dark, but I could always get the results of the check out of my employer. I was, after all, sleeping with her.

'Are you on your way back to the office?' Lorna was saying.

'Not just yet. I've got...another meeting lined up.'

'Who with?'

'A contact of mine, a Mr Young. I don't think you know him.'

The Mr Young in question not only brewed excellent bitter ale at his Wandsworth brewery, but also owned The Crooked Billet pub situated on a road called Crooked Billet on the edge of Wimbledon Common. I wasn't meeting anyone called Young, just sampling his hospitality by treating myself to a quiet pub lunch where I could reflect on the Ellrington case, life, the universe and everything. Mostly, I reflected on how I had to limit myself to just one beer as I had a long drive home.

The daily commute was getting to me. Not the driving so much, although the way I was clocking up the miles would mean Armstrong would soon be round the clock for the second time – not unknown for black cabs, but the plain fact was he wasn't getting any younger and I began to wonder if Amy's finances would run to a second decent vehicle so I could keep Armstrong in London as a run-about. He was, of course, ideal for the detective business, maybe even tax-deductible, as who the hell noticed a London black cab in London?

We, or rather Amy, had a Freelander which was no doubt happy that it now had more space in which to gambol and play out in the countryside, even though it was at the smaller end of the Sports Utility Vehicle range. The big SUVs only really come into their own when they're clogging up the city streets at 8.45 a.m. and again at 2.55 p.m. on the school run picking up children who can hardly reach the passenger door handles. They tend to be driven by women who can squeeze a size 16 figure into a size 14 dress, but need a parking space the length of a Heathrow runway.

It's not their fault, the latest generation of 'Chelsea Tractor', as they're known, are almost certainly bought by men demanding bigger, heavier vehicles to give the impression they are driving a tank – an obvious signal to other road users to get the hell out of their way. The Land Rover Defender weighs 2,000 kilos; the newer, American, Ford Excursion weighs 3,500. One of the BMW Series 5 off-roaders costs more than the ton of wheat it would take to fill the back.

No, that bit of the car market was getting silly. Amy could keep the Freelander for swanning around Cambridgeshire and going to WI meetings or church socials or whatever she had in mind for after...

And there, I realised, was the problem I had to face up to. In less than two months it was going to be 'after' and everything that was 'before' and 'now' was going to change.

I looked down into my glass at the dregs of my pint and wondered if I dare risk another, but I was saved by the bell or rather the ring tone of my mobile phone, a rather subtle uno-dos-tres opening Salsa riff. In the days when an electronic ring tone could make it to the top of the charts, it was a remarkably restrained example of the art-form and not at all embarrassing in a public place, unlike most of them. I had even heard one home-made ring tone which was simply a guy's wife shouting 'Answer the bloody phone!' which was quite surreal really, as it hadn't actually rung if you thought about it.

I half-expected it to be Lorna showing off with all the information she had found out for me so far and so quickly, or maybe just to check up on me, but in fact it was the other Thompson Twin.

'Angel? You have mail,' said Laura in my ear as I held the phone close to cut out the background noise which would give it away that I was in a pub. Mobiles don't pick up much background sound these days, but old habits die hard.

'I have? It's too early for my birthday or Christmas, so it must be an invitation to something. Something good I hope.'

'No, email. You have an email.'

'Laura, my sweet, are you one of those sad creatures who sends somebody a text to tell them you've sent them an email to see if they've got the letter you wrote? The letter you told them about on the phone.'

'I'm sorry, I didn't follow that at all.'

'Don't worry, I'm not sure I did. It's from Double-O Oesterlein isn't it?'

'It is!' she squealed. 'How did you know that?'

'I'm starting to get into this detective thing. What does our friend in the north have to say for himself?'

'You're honoured; he wants to tell you himself. Personally, as in face-to-face. He's actually coming up to the big city to see you. That's a first. I wonder if he knows he doesn't need a passport?'

'Don't be cheeky, I'm hoping Ossie will provide us with some solid leads in the Ellrington case.'

Hoping? I was relying on it, as I didn't have a clue what I was supposed to do.

'I think he's just angling for an expenses-paid trip up to the big, bad city. He's staying at least one night as he's asked me to find him a hotel, so I've booked him into Duke's on Euston Road. It's really handy for the British Library.'

'Oh, I'm sure Double-O Oesterlein wouldn't want to miss that. If he's looking for something to do in the evening, you could try and get tickets for cabaret night at Madame Jo Jo's on Brewer Street in Soho.'

'What is Madame Jo Jo's?' she asked innocently.

'It's a sort of club. He may have other plans, of course. But try and get a couple of tickets just in case. When does he want to see me?'

'In the morning. He dropped a lot of hints about being taken to lunch and he wants someone to meet him off the train at King's Cross at 10.30.'

'I can do that,' I volunteered.

'But you don't even know what he looks like.'

'Do you?'

'Well, not really.'

'Don't worry, I'll find him. We private eyes can sniff each other out at a range of up to a mile. It's an instinct we have.'

Sometimes an instinct can be helped by a large cardboard sign, so next morning I was standing by the gates at King's Cross holding up 'Mr Oesterlein' writ large in blue felt tip on the side panel of a box which had once contained two dozen bottles of Budweiser.

I wasn't sure what to expect, although I didn't seriously think he would appear wearing a flat cap and clogs, with a whippet on a lead made from baling twine and a bagful of coal just in case they didn't have any down here in the soft South. (In London, a smokeless zone for more than a generation, he could probably have sold washed coal as a gemstone, so few people under thirty would recognise it.)

I had sort of toyed with the scenario that he would turn up in full Humphrey Bogart mode with trench coat, hat and cigarette glued to his lower lip, or even – if fleetingly – in cape and deerstalker and smoking a meerschaum pipe. But I dismissed both images. He probably didn't smoke at all; nobody seemed to these days, although I had heard there were pockets of resistance in the north which the smoking police had not yet bombed into submission.

The only thing I got right was that he was wearing a hat: a big, black, broad-brimmed felt fedora. It was the sort of hat usually worn by long-haired radical vicars with ankle-length overcoats, female crime novelists and flamboyant gays going bald. He was also wearing a green, spotted cravat. I didn't know anyone who wore a cravat. I'm sure members of gentlemen's clubs in Pall Mall still did, but I didn't know any of them.

The double-breasted suit in a wide pin-stripe didn't help either. He was as easy to spot as a kangaroo in a dinner jacket.

He proved he didn't need glasses for driving by reading his own name on my sign from a good thirty yards down the platform. He was carrying a folded newspaper which he raised and waved to attract my attention, but he had to get a lot closer before I could make out that it was the *Yorkshire Post* and by that time I had checked out the shiny, wide black Oxford brogues he was wearing, which you didn't see that often these days and certainly not in a size somewhere in excess of a 12. His feet were truly huge but to be fair, the rest of him was in proportion; he was a big man, though probably not taller than six foot five and no wider than a brewer's dray. Over his shoulder he carried a black leather overnight bag which bulged at the seams. From the thickness of it he had either brought his entire wardrobe or a television set so he could get the local news while he was away from Yorkshire, though I was unlikely to make such an observation out loud to a man so big.

'Rudgard and Blugden?' he boomed when he was a yard away and looking down at me.

'Mr Oesterlein? Mr O. Oesterlein?'

'That'd be me. Where's the car?'

'Just round the corner, about a minute's walk.'

'I think I can manage that but I'm gagging for a cuppa tea. Fooking buffet on the train ran out of hot water before Doncaster. You'd think, by now, wouldn't you? Two hundred and sixty quid for a fooking ticket and they can't do hot water!'

'You can get a cup of coffee there.' I pointed to a Costa Coffee which was en route to the exit. 'Or there, or there.' I pointed out a Pret A Manger and a Burger King. 'But I'm not sure if any of them make tea that's worth drinking.'

'As long as it's warm and wet.' He put down his shoulder bag and fumbled in a trouser pocket, producing a handful of change. 'Be a pal, would you? I'm gagging. Two sugars.'

I took the change from his proffered hand and counted it as I stomped across the station concourse. He had given me 95p. I made up the difference and got him a large tea to go, four sachets of white sugar and a plastic stirrer. Let him sort that lot out in the back of Armstrong as we went over the speed bumps in Cheney Road.

He was standing there reading the *Yorkshire Post* when I returned.

'Ah, just the job,' he beamed. 'Did you get a receipt by any chance?'

'Never thought to ask,' I answered innocently.

'Pity. Still, never mind, eh? Lead on – oh, you couldn't give me a hand with that could you?'

He nodded down towards his bag on the concourse, then held out his plastic cup of tea and his newspaper so I could see his hands were full.

I sighed as loudly as I could and picked up the bag by the shoulder strap. The damn thing weighed a ton, almost as if he did have a television set in there.

'Out of the station and hang a left,' I said through gritted teeth. The big ox just smiled at me.

Once outside, that damn bag grinding into my hip, he said:

'Is this York Way? I've heard of York Way.'

'No, that's round the other side of the station.'

'Bit of a red light district, isn't it? York Way.'

'You won't see any red lights there,' I wheezed, trying to keep up with his giant strides. 'Red lights need electricity and that's an overhead the girls round there don't run to.'

'So you have girls on the game do you? I thought it was all rent boys down here.'

'Oh, you want St Pancras, then. It's just across the road.'

He stopped in his tracks and gave me a killer look, trying to decide if I was winding him up or not. I held his gaze, but there was something weird going on. I was sure I could hear, yes I *could* hear, music now we were out of King's Cross and away from the background throb and the tinny tannoy announcements. If I didn't know better, I would have sworn it was coming from Oesterlein himself and if I hadn't known that I hadn't had a drink that morning, I would have said it was a brass band playing the *Floral Dance*.

'Can you hear something?' I asked him.

'Hear what?'

'You didn't bring a brass band with you on the train, did you?'

From the weight, he could have had the cornet section in his bag.

'Oh, bugger,' he said and thrust his carton of tea at me. 'Cop that.'

He undid his double-breasted suit jacket to reveal a pale pink nylon shirt stretched tightly across his bulk. In the breast pocket was an iPod with earpiece wires going up around his neck under that ghastly spotted cravat.

'Forgot I hadn't switched this off,' he said, fumbling in his shirt pocket and then pulling the earpieces from his neck.

'You're into brass bands, then?' I asked, giving a fair impression of being interested.

'Not just any brass band, pal, only the best. Brighouse and Raistrick.' He pronounced it 'Raastrict'. 'I like to take a little bit of Yorkshire with me whenever I go travelling.'

He was going to just love Madame Jo Jo's. And they were going to love him.

But he wasn't going out on the town just yet.

One look at Armstrong confirmed his first impression that I was merely a humble cab driver, pre-paid by Rudgard & Blugden and at his beck and call.

'Your hotel's just down the road, near the British Library,' I told him and got a grunt in reply. Obviously not a book person. 'But I doubt if your room's ready yet. Do you want to check in anyway and dump your bag?'

'No thanks, pal.'

I clocked him in Armstrong's mirror. He was unfolding a sheet of paper.

'Straight to the office then?'

'Not straightaway. I've got an errand to run first.'

He gripped his steaming carton of tea between his knees while he took the lid off and began to rip open the sugar sachets. He was at my mercy. I selected first gear.

'Would you happen to know Hackney at all?' he asked, stirring with one hand and passing the sheet of paper through the driver's sliding glass partition to me.

I was so surprised at this development that I forgot to slip the clutch and we pulled out into traffic quite smoothly.

On the paper was written: Ghadji's Wines and News, Mare Street, Hackney, E8.

'Yeah, I know where that is,' I told him over my shoulder.

'Thought you would. It's the "knowledge" i'n't? All you

London cabbies have to do the "knowledge" exam so you learn all the street names, don't you?'

'Something like that.'

It was true. Real cabbies did have to do the 'knowledge'. I only knew where Mare Street was because it wasn't a million miles (in fact it was about half a mile) from Stuart Street where I still technically rented a flat at a ridiculously low rent. I hadn't been there for weeks and it was about time I checked up on the sitting tenant.

'You want to go there first?' I asked, just to be sure.

'If it's not too far out of our way.'

'No problem at all.'

I turned left and headed east instead of west.

'The firm will recompense you for the extra mileage,' Oesterlein pronounced confidently.

He was dead right about that.

He was the perfect passenger for the back of a London cab. He sat in the middle of the back seat taking up most of my rear-view mirror, his hands clasped around his carton of tea like he was holding a chalice. He had his iPod earpieces in again and for most of the journey kept his eyes shut, so he would have missed all the sights and attractions of Islington and Stoke Newington had I bothered to point any out.

As we approached Hackney Central station, I knocked on the partition to get his attention. He pulled out his earpieces and leaned forward, looming even larger in my mirror.

'Mare Street coming up,' I said. 'If you just wanted an off-licence, we could have found one sooner, you know.'

'I want to check out this particular one. If you spot it, just slow down and do a drive-by.'

I spotted it easily enough. The big red sign outside saying Ghadji's Wines and News gave it away. I'd always thought Ghadji was something rude to do with donkeys when used as an insult in Urdu, but maybe that was *gadha* and maybe this wasn't

Urdu. There were a lot of languages spoken in Hackney and I couldn't keep up with them all.

'There it is, on the left,' I pointed and slowed Armstrong to a crawl which would have brought in quite a bit of business somewhere like York Way. 'What's so special about this place?'

Oesterlein didn't answer me and I couldn't see anything unusual about the place. It was an off-licence/newsagents, half its window painted out in that opaque paint which meant that children and adults under five-foot ten couldn't get to see all the wonderful alcoholic treats on sale inside.

We cruised by it and only then did Oesterlein speak.

'Can you turn round somewhere and go back up the road?'

'Of course I can, I'm a black cab.'

'And can you pull up on that side of the road, just past the shop? I just need to nip in for something.'

'If you really want to…'

'And keep the engine running,' he added.

For some reason I had already decided that would be a good idea.

As I turned Armstrong around, Oesterlein disappeared from my view in the mirror, bent over his enormous shoulder bag. I heard a zip go and then a thud as something heavy fell out onto the floor panels. Then he was sitting up straight again and reaching for the door handle, waiting for me to do the central locking.

'Don't worry about it, there'll be a nice tip in this for you,' he said, shifting his bulk to get out as Armstrong nosed into the kerb.

I was beginning to doubt his powers as a detective. For a start, he had just assumed I was a cab driver (and that cab drivers always did what the customer ordered) and yet he hadn't noticed that Armstrong's meter wasn't connected to anything. Perhaps he thought I'd just forgotten to set the clock running and he was getting a free ride.

As he got out, he said 'Back in a minute' and started to walk towards the shop. In his suit and with those feet and that giant felt fedora, he would get noticed even in Hackney. And then, watching him in the wing mirror, I spotted something odd about his right hand.

He was wearing what seemed like a purple glove, which he hadn't been wearing when he'd got into the cab. At least, I thought it was a glove, and yet it wasn't.

As he turned into Ghadji's Wines & News, pushing the door with his left hand, I climbed out of Armstrong, leaving my right indicator and the engine on, and opened the door he had just climbed out of. His shoulder bag was on the floor, half unzipped. I lifted it and shook it and immediately found what had made the thudding sound I had heard.

It was a D-shaped three-pound weight, the sort women use in fancy gyms for boxaerobics or jazzercise or whatever they call it this week. The D shape was covered in thick foam rubber, purple foam rubber, and they were designed so you could use them over your feet or in your fists. I hefted the weight in one hand and was impressed. Ossie Oesterlein was wearing its partner like a knuckle-duster. I had been hit in the ribs with a knuckle-duster once not that long ago and the bruise had taken a good month to fade. The memory of that punch had stayed with me much longer.

I stood on the pavement and looked at the shop, wondering if I should go in and rescue him, idly hefting the weight to exercise my right biceps. As I was standing between Armstrong's two open doors, I wasn't causing enough of a scene to attract the attention of any passers-by. You see far stranger things on the street in London than a cabby doing his exercise routine. (I'd once seen one get out of his cab in a traffic jam at Hyde Park Corner and start doing a full 27-move Tai Chi exercise.)

No one gave me a second look. What was worrying, though fortunate, was that no one gave a second look when Ossie Oesterlein came barrelling out of Ghadji's Wines & News with his right arm clutched against his chest, the purple weight still on his hand, but both now covered in blood.

About two seconds behind him was an Asian guy who might or might not have been Ghadji himself.

He was shouting something at Oesterlein, but I didn't take in the words or even note which language they were in.

I was absolutely transfixed by the long shiny sword Mr Ghadji was waving.

Even in Hackney, decapitations in broad daylight whilst out shopping are fairly rare.

Chapter Nine

When sudden violence erupts in public, people say you just act, you don't have time to think. I don't necessarily go along with that. For instance, I remember distinctly thinking that it would be a very bad idea to run *towards* the man coming out of the shop swinging a sword. I also remember thinking, quite clearly, it would be a very good idea to get the hell out of Mare Street as quickly as possible.

I think Ossie Oesterlein had that thought too, and he articulated it quite clearly and concisely by shouting 'Fooking well move it!' at me, just before launching himself head first into the back of Armstrong.

And I even had time for a third idea, though on reflection it probably wasn't one of my best.

I was very conscious that I was still holding the purple D-shaped weight in my right hand. I knew I couldn't drive whilst holding it so, logically, I had to drop it. For some reason it seemed a good idea to use it to discourage the sword-wielding shopkeeper who was getting very close to damaging, at the very least, Armstrong's paintwork.

Now I've never actually putted a shot or thrown a discus, so quite what possessed me I don't know, but I swung my arm like I'd seen them do at the Olympics and let go of the weight, expelling a loud grunt just like athletes are supposed to, in the general direction of the angry Mr Ghadji. He stopped dead in his tracks but the weight, being as aerodynamic as a brick, went nowhere near him, and fortunately nowhere near any other living thing, but when it hit the painted window of Ghadji's Wines & News, it made a dramatic and very satisfying impact.

The owners of Ghadji's Wines & News may have invested in a CCTV camera – just the one – covering the front door (and thankfully pointing down the street, away from me and Armstrong), but they had saved on security glass. The window shattered like ice on a puddle and there was a quieter, stereo-effect smashing sound as the D-weight completed its trajectory. I could only assume it had landed in the Wines section of the shop, rather than the News.

The angry swordsman/proprietor was also thinking on his feet. At first he probably thought: why is this cab driver screaming at me and throwing things? And then he thought: that's my window smashing and that's my burglar alarm going off – and it's making so much noise, people in the street are all looking my way and I'm standing here waving an illegal blade, probably being caught on my own CCTV camera, and there goes that bloody taxi, speeding off towards Hackney Central, jumping a lane of traffic and dangerously cutting up a bus and a white delivery van in the process.

But being a black London cab, Armstrong got away with it, not even attracting an angry blast on a horn.

'That was fooking close,' Ossie Oesterlein gasped from the back seat.

'Relax,' I said cheerfully. 'White vans, black cabs and London buses are the three things all drivers know to give way to and they always respect each other and keep their distance.'

'I didn't mean the traffic I meant that fooking A-rab who pulled a carving knife on me.'

'Did he cut you?'

I could see in the mirror that he was still holding his hand to his chest and there was blood all over his shirt front.

'Not exactly,' he said sheepishly. 'I cut myself on the glass when I smashed in his counter display case thing. I was just trying to emphasise a point.'

'I think you made quite an impression one way or another. We'd better get that hand seen to.'

'I'm not going into any hospital. I don't like hospitals. They ask too many questions and the cops might be on the look-out for us.'

I wondered where the 'us' had come from, but tried to reassure him:

'I seriously doubt that a bit of aggravated vandalism and some broken glass is going to result in an all-points bulletin on you. If that shop-owner has any sense, and I don't think he was an Arab by the way, he'll be more worried about somebody reporting *him* for waving that ceremonial toothpick around in the street. Not to mention the fact that he's got an off-licence with no window and therefore open to the public in more ways than one. Why do you think he didn't chase after us? He knows what the locals are like round here when there's free booze to be looted. He'll be busy for the rest of the day standing guard and filling out insurance claims and going through Yellow Pages looking for a glazier.'

Actually, being a shop-owner in Hackney meant you had the nearest 24-hour glazier's number already in the memory of your phone.

'Anyway, I wasn't thinking of a hospital.'

'You weren't?'

'No. A quiet place just up the road a bit, where I have friends.'

At least I hoped I still had.

'A sort of safe house, is it?' he asked, perking up at the thrill of it all.

'Oh, I wouldn't go that far.'

* * *

There was a parking space outside 9 Stuart Street, but then there usually was since I'd moved in with Amy, as none of my other former house-mates could or would drive.

The Stuart Street flat was the second of three places where I had lived in London. The first, down in Southwark, no longer existed following a bizarre domestic accident with a gas cooker. The third was Amy's place in Hampstead, and now I didn't even live there. Flat 3 had served me well for a number of years, still did and would do in the future just as long as I could keep the rent at a reasonable level. I had once done a couple of favours for our landlord, a Kashmiri wide-boy known as Naseem Naseem. That wasn't his proper name but he always said his family name was too difficult to pronounce and that we should just stick to Naseem, so everybody did and he got to quite like it. He'd shown his appreciation of my help by keeping the rent down to a ridiculous mid-1990s level on the understanding that I never asked for any repairs or redecoration. On his part, he turned a blind eye to the fact that I was mostly absent these days but my sitting tenant was not.

I don't think Naseem was the slightest bit interested in confronting my sitting tenant about the conditions of the lease, or anything else for that matter. Few people were, once they met him, as even though he was getting on in years now, my psychotic and unreasonably violent black cat Springsteen could still inspire terror in the unwary.

But as I had pointed out to Naseem, he was an effective guard cat, as evidenced by the fact that Number Nine was the only house in Stuart Street never to have been burgled. He was also good at pest control. No one had ever seen a mouse or rat on the premises, nor any pigeons on the roof for that matter. Neither did the small, handkerchief-sized garden out back suffer from unsightly weeds as absolutely nothing would grow there, which I think was down to Springsteen's patrolling presence as well, though that may not have been a plus point on an estate agent's particulars.

And why was I thinking about estate agents again?

Because like fluoride and Renault Clios they were everywhere these days and nobody seemed to question them anymore. They didn't even bother to hide, their signs were everywhere. Signs saying 'Flat To Rent' just like the one on the front door of 9 Stuart Street.

'Are you all right, pal?' Oesterlein asked me as we clambered out of Armstrong. 'You look like you've had a right shock. This where you live?'

'No, but a friend does,' I said, fumbling to find the key that would open the front door if alien invaders disguised as estate agents hadn't changed the locks.

It wasn't the time to be paranoid; there was no point. 'They' already knew where I was and what was worrying me.

I felt a surging wave of relief as my key slotted home and the lock turned: I still had my Hackney address.

It wasn't that the flat held particular sentimental value, although some jolly good times had been had by one and all within its rather cramped confines. It certainly wasn't that the flat was the most desirable property in the East End. It wasn't even the most desirable property in the street. I had no equity in it, so its worth to me wasn't measured in cash terms. Why it was so important to have it as an address was because having an address (at least one) was crucial to modern living.

If you needed credit cards, a bank account, a driving licence or even a completely new identity, then you needed an address. Forget the *Day of the Jackal* trick of going round graveyards to find somebody who would have been your age and then applying for a passport for them but with your photograph. Never mind hanging about in one of the three pubs in Woolwich which sell Irish passports for £75 a pop. All you need is patience and an address; you don't actually have to live there, you just have to offer to pay the electricity bill or the gas bill or, best of all, the Council Tax. Once you have one bill or receipt putting your name (or chosen name) together with an address, you're laughing. You can then open a bank account, get credit cards, rent a car, register to vote. I've known people with several sorts of photo ID, including a genuine passport, who were unable to open a bank account so they could make a deposit of fairly legitimate cash because they didn't have a bill to show they'd paid water rates in the last quarter.

Number 9 Stuart Street was my bolt-hole and a rock I could tie an identity to in times of trouble and I didn't want to lose it.

'Up the stairs, first floor,' I said to Oesterlein, ushering him into the hallway. 'Door on the left.'

'Is that your flat?'

'No, it's the neighbours'. Mine's on the second floor, but there may be someone in there who doesn't take kindly to strangers.'

Ossie Oesterlein held up his bleeding right hand with his left until he could tap his nose with the forefinger.

'Say no more, pal. You've got a bit on the side, eh? I understand.'

'Actually, it's a cat,' I said, and there was him already leaving a blood trail.

'A cat? Hey, pal, I just love cats – and they love me.'

He was dead meat.

Fenella answered my knock on the door of Flat 2. I had been banking on her being there in the late morning as she worked from home answering a rank of mobile phones permanently on chargers, responding with scripted replies to text messages and calls on some very dodgy 0800 numbers. It was a business she carried on mostly in total innocence, but only when her partner, Lisabeth, was out at work bullying people into buying useless homeopathic medicines at a local Mind, Body and Spirit emporium.

I was always pleased to see Fenella when I knew Lisabeth was out and Fenella, for some reason, was usually pleased to see me.

'Angel!' she squealed, throwing her arms around my neck. 'Your ears must have been burning!'

From behind me, even though Fenella's arms were acting as
ear-muffs, I heard Oesterlein mutter: 'Angel...?'

I unpeeled her arms and held them against her sides. She was
dressed as she usually was when she was working from home: as
if she'd been standing too close to an explosion in a charity
shop. I doubted that the callers or texters to any of the numbers
she 'managed' had any idea that the 'posh totty' that was talking
to them was slouched on a bean bag wearing an oversized and
threadbare Chicago Red Sox shirt, over-the-knee multi-
coloured striped socks and Ugg boots which looked as if they'd
started moulting.

'So who's been talking about me, Binky?'

'Binky...?' came the echo from behind.

'Oh, it was all very nice, not bitchy at all; not like it usually
is. Mr Naseem is here nearly every day; he's showing people
around the vacant flat. Who's your friend, Angel? Is he
bleeding?'

'*Which* flat?' I asked, shaking her gently.

'Actually it's not so bad now. An Elastoplast would probably
do the business,' said my shadow.

'Mr Goodson's flat of course,' said Fenella, putting her head
on one side and turning the pupils of her eyes on to full beam.
'Downstairs on the ground floor. Mr Goodson; you remember
him, don't you?'

'Yes, of course.' I found I could breathe again. 'But I had no
idea he was moving out.'

'Well he's retiring isn't he?'

'Is he? I didn't think he was that old.' Though it was difficult
to tell with local government officers.

'I know,' Fenella agreed, 'but they can retire at 55 it seems, so
he's packing up and moving to his holiday home by the seaside.'

'I didn't know he had a holiday home. Where is it? Torquay?
Isle of Wight?'

'Oh no, somewhere much more exotic called Burgas. It's
abroad somewhere.'

'In Spain?'

'I don't think so...' she said nervously.

'It's in Bulgaria,' a Yorkshire voice growled in my ear, 'on the Black Sea coast. Property's dead cheap there. Oh, and by the way, I could bleed to death here.'

'Where *are* my manners?' I asked no one in particular and didn't wait for a reply. 'Fenella, this is Mr Oesterlein. He's from Yorkshire and he's had a slight accident. Mr Oesterlein, meet Miss Fenella Binkworthy, an old and distinguished friend of mine.'

Fenella held out a hand in greeting, then pulled it back as if bitten.

'Oh goodness, you *are* bleeding. Come in, come in, let me find you something for that.'

As he stepped into the flat Ossie Oesterlein gave me the cheesiest grin outside Wensleydale and hissed in a very loud whisper:

'So you're Angel hisself, then? And this must be the little pussycat you've got stashed away?'

There was nothing wrong with Fenella's hearing and she did a smart about-turn, squaring up to Ossie who stopped in his tracks as she pointed a finger and its long, tangerine-painted nail first at me and then at herself.

'Please don't get the wrong end of the stick, Mr Oesterlein,' she said in her best Sussex Young Conservatives' accent. '*He's* married, and *I'm* a lesbian.'

Oesterlein's bottom jaw dropped so far, I could see he needed bridge work.

Treating the cut on the back of Ossie's hand took a lot of dabbing with cotton wool balls soaked in TCP and then three sticking plasters because Fenella only had the one size, the ones which fitted around her little toes when she wore the red high heels Lisabeth had bought for her but which pinched terribly (though of course we mustn't tell her). Slightly more embarrassing was the fact that the plasters were designed for kids and each came with a colourful cartoon design, so that Ossie ended up with three smiling green crocodiles in parallel up the back of his hand.

When Fenella retreated to the kitchen, having kindly offered to make us some herbal tea, Oesterlein turned on me and actually raised his fist to my face but the sight of those three happy crocodiles cracked me up.

'Why didn't you tell me you were the Angel I was coming to meet?'

'You never gave me the chance, you just assumed I was the hired help.'

'An easy enough mistake,' he said almost as if expecting sympathy, 'specially when I saw you were driving a taxi.'

'Don't take anything on first impression. First rule of the private detective,' I said rather grandly.

'Fook that for a bunch of soldiers, you conned me.'

'Yes, I conned you into coming down to Hackney instead of driving up west to Shepherd's Bush where you were supposed to go and then I conned you into rushing into an off-licence and throwing your weight around. Throwing your weight around, geddit?'

His expression said he wasn't amused.

'And then of course I conned you out of getting your bleeding head cut off and conned you into escaping from the scene of a crime which might have been down to race hatred for all I know.'

'Now hang on a minute, who said anything about a hate-crime?'

'So you came all the way down from Yorkshire to complain about the price of his Carlsberg Special?'

'Don't be fooking daft. Listen, pal, I admit I might have been a bit out of line...a bit out of my depth in fact; a bit too previous with my actions; but there's a good reason I wanted to come and have a look at this Hackney place whilst I was down in

London. You never said you were a local, did you? For fook's sake, you never said you were Angel, did you?'

So, it was all my fault.

I should have known.

'All right then, I'm Roy Angel, and this is Hackney. My mission was to pick you up from the station, show you your hotel, maybe buy you some lunch and deliver you to the offices of Rudgard & Blugden where, I believe, you had requested a meeting with...er...let's see now, who was it? Oh yes, that would be me.'

Fenella appeared carrying a tray with three steaming mugs.

'Tea up,' she chirped.

Oesterlein beamed at her and said 'Thanks, love' but once he looked into the mug and saw the urine coloured liquid with flecks of green and red leaves floating in it, his expression changed. He looked more frightened than he had when he had been chased out of the shop on Mare Street.

'I think Mr Naseem's just arrived to show some more people around Mr Goodson's flat,' Fenella said cheerfully. 'It'll be nice to have some new faces around the place.'

'I'd better go and check that Springsteen is contained whilst they're in the building,' I said getting to my feet. 'How is he?'

'Temperamentally, same as always; but a bit slower now he's getting older and, to be honest, he does get a bit smelly sometimes. He's eating well, though, which reminds me, you owe me for cat food and kitty litter. I've kept the receipts.'

'Don't worry, I trust you, but I don't trust him so I'll make sure he's out of sight if Naseem's doing a selling job on some unsuspecting punters.'

'In case the new tenants don't like cats, eh?' Oesterlein offered.

'No, in case he doesn't like them.'

I carried my mug with me.

'You stay here and finish your tea, I'm only popping upstairs, shan't be long. And Fenella, don't think Mr Oesterlein is being rude, it's just that in Yorkshire, they don't take their hats off if they're not stopping.'

'Ahm sorry, love,' Ossie gurgled, pulling his fedora off with his bandaged hand. 'Forgetting me manners.'

I had been right in my early assessment, he was as bald as a coot and as he blushed with embarrassment, a pink hue seemed to spread all over his domed scalp. Fenella told me much later that she thought that was rather cute.

On the stairs, I could see the door to Flat 1 was open and I could hear voices coming from inside. I tried to think if I would miss Mr Goodson and decided, on balance, probably not. He'd never done me any harm, always been polite, always paid his share of communal costs and had been invaluable in taking messages for me from the house phone in the days before we all had mobiles. Still, his going was a little piece of the character of the place that would disappear forever, which was sad, and then there was the unknown quantity of new tenants who could undermine the whole delicate balance of the house's social structure.

And then I remembered I didn't live there any more.

But Springsteen did.

Like most domestic cats, he could be in the house but disappear from sight completely for 23 out of 24 hours a day if you ever needed him. Conversely, just now, when I wanted him to stay out of sight, there he was sitting on the landing at the top of the stairs outside the door of my flat, rear offside leg in the fascist salute position, licking clean a troublesome piece of fur so enthusiastically I could hear his tongue rasping.

'Springsteen! It's me!' I hissed, kneeling on the third step down so that we were at eye-level. 'Now I know what you're thinking. You're thinking this is the shit who left you here to go and live in the countryside with a woman who couldn't bear the thought of cat hairs on her designer sofa. Well, you'd be right in thinking that, but trust me, you wouldn't like it out there in the sticks, mate. Oh, sure, there must be lots of wildlife there you could terrorise – it's teeming with bitesize furry things – but hardly any people. You'd hate it, mate, honest you would. It's so quiet out there you'd go out of your mind and you'd miss having Fenella bring you all your meals and all those treats I know she slips you.'

I didn't seem to be making much impression on him. I knew what he was thinking though, he was thinking: Do you feel lucky, punk?

I held the mug of herbal tea I was carrying under his nose.

'See what the nice Fenella made me,' I gushed.

Springsteen wrinkled his nose and slowly unwound, getting on to his feet. The wrinkle in his nose turned into a rippling of his long black fur all the way down his spine. Then he yawned in my face, giving me a grandstand view of his red and black marbled mouth and flashing canines, did a ninety-degree turn and trotted across the landing to head-butt his way through the cat-flap I had built into the door of Flat 3.

Once I was inside, he watched carefully until he was sure I had poured all of Fenella's herbal tea down the sink.

Only then did he feel sufficiently relaxed to ignore me completely.

Chapter Ten

Within a minute, he was back on full alert, the fur up at the back of his neck and his tail fluffed out like a toilet brush: his fairly standard response to a gentle knock at the flat door. It was good to see he wasn't going soft in his old age.

Our visitor was Ossie Oesterlein, who had managed all of three minutes alone in Fenella's company before cutting and running. He stood there holding his mug of herbal tea like a beggar asking for alms.

'I told her there was a phone call for you on my mobile,' he said slightly shamefaced. 'Truth is, I can't drink this cat's pee.'

Then he looked down and saw Springsteen.

'Oh, sorry, pal, no offence.' He reached out his free hand and started to bend his knees. 'Nice pussy…'

'I wouldn't do that,' I said. 'He doesn't take to strangers.'

He didn't much take to people he knew. Fenella had been feeding him and catering for his every whim for two years now and still she wore wicket-keeper's gloves when she fed him.

'All cats like me. I'm a cat person,' said Ossie, but he straightened up when he heard Springsteen's low, rhythmic growl.

'Let me get rid of that for you,' I said, relieving him of his mug and dumping the contents in the kitchen sink. He smiled gratefully.

'I thought we'd better have a private chat, whilst we can.'

'You want to go into the office now?'

'No, here's fine if that's OK with you.'

I gestured for him to make himself at home, not that that would take long. I had left a sofa-bed and two chairs in the living room for Springsteen to lounge on and there was a midi hi-fi system and about a hundred CDs, mostly jazz, in case he got lonely. Apart from that, the flat was bare and the cupboards in the kitchen contained nothing except emergency tins of dolphin-friendly tuna chunks, red salmon and ground beef in chilli sauce (a particular treat), all of which were intended for feline consumption.

Oesterlein settled his bulk at one end of the sofa, pushed his fedora to the back of his shiny dome and placed his broad, blunt hands on his pinstriped knees.

'I suppose you want to know what was going on back there with that Arab,' he said slowly.

'It had crossed my mind. I don't normally raid off-licences before lunch.'

'I wasn't trying to rob him; I was trying to find something out.'

'Questioning with menaces? Is that your usual tactic?'

'Of course not, it was just spur of the moment stuff. I hadn't even thought of coming down here to Hackney until I saw your taxi.'

So it had been my fault.

'Did you just find those weights in your bag?' I asked and he shrugged.

'No. I do use them to exercise, keep in shape. But they also come in handy on occasion. Some of the people I have to deal with, well you have to make a firm impression and quite quickly.'

'You've certainly made an impression on Hackney. You going to tell me why we've been so honoured?'

'Look, pal, I'll come clean. I know what I did was a bit out of order but I thought I'd try and sort it myself before I dumped it in your lap. I didn't know you were you, of course, or that you were a local round here.'

'Whoa, boy! Can you rewind that so we can unpick it?' I realised I was spouting Veronica's management-speak and winced, but it seemed to impress Ossie. 'What exactly were you going to dump in my lap?'

'My reciprocal.'

'Excuse me?'

'My quid pro quo; my reciprocal investigation.' He frowned as if he wasn't sure he was speaking English. 'I do some investigative work for you up north and you help me with a case down here. Didn't they tell you that's how it works? Or do you want me to invoice you for my time?'

'Only if I can charge you for the cab fare, and I would remind you that the meter's still running.'

'It is?' he almost shrieked it. I had found his weak spot: his wallet.

'Relax, I know what you mean. So you've actually dug something up on Margaret Anne Hayes-slash-Pennington for me?'

'Oh yes, on both of them.'

'And the quid pro quo for that is I drive you on a ram-raid?'

'Hey, pal, it wasn't *me* who broke that Arab's window.'

'It was one of your weights,' I pointed out, 'and he wasn't an Arab.'

'I don't give a flying fook what he is, I wasn't after him, I was looking for one of his customers.'

'This is to do with the case you're working on? The case that's now partly mine thanks to our mutual reciprocity agreement?'

'If you want to put it that way.'

'Right, well I'm up for it. How can we soft, southern, Chelsea-supporting hairdressers down here in the big city help you out? Who's the client for a start?'

'The client is me. It's a personal matter. Private.'

'If you want to brief me on the details, we're surely covered by the Private Eye Code of Ethics, aren't we?' I said, banking on the fact that he hadn't read it either. 'Or we could wait until we get to the office, or do it over lunch, or you could fill me in on what you've turned up on my case.'

I thought that all sounded pretty fair but he was hesitating. Perhaps I had given him too many options. The longer he hesitated, though, the more my imagination was working overtime as to what sort of a personal case could bring Yorkshire's finest private detective down to London to ask the help of a rank amateur?

'No, let me go first. It could be a stroke of luck, me running into you this morning and you knowing your way round Hackney.'

'So what's this personal case of yours got to do with Hackney?' I was almost interested now. 'Or should I ask what's it got to do with a grotty off-licence in Hackney?'

'The off-licence is just an address for rented postboxes. I was trying to trace the person who rented one.'

'But the shop owner declined to share those particular confidential details?'

'Something like that – and I might have lost my temper a bit. I just don't like to be ripped off that way.'

'Ripped off as in: lost money, right?'

'Yeah, right. I did my bit, I sent the money Western Union just like it said in the email and...'

'Oh, Christ, Ossie. You tried to buy something off eBay didn't you?'

'How did you know that?'

He looked shocked and impressed at the same time.

'It's the oldest one in the book.'

Under the sofa, right behind his feet, Springsteen settled himself down and I could swear he was grinning.

* * *

Actually, it isn't the oldest one in the book, just a new electronic version of a very old scam. You are offered an absolute bargain which you simply cannot turn down. All you have to do is send the cash in advance. Naturally, you never hear any more.

Such gambits are covered by my Rules of Life Number 14 – When someone offers you the chance of a lifetime, they usually mean theirs, not yours – *and* Number 15 – If it sounds too good to be true, it is.

The Internet has made the cons faster and superficially more sophisticated, but at heart they are still the same basic cons. One of the longest-running is the infamous 'Nigerian Scam' which was a popular crowd pleaser (at least in Nigeria) long before anyone thought of the Internet. Technically, Scotland Yard refer to it as 'Advanced Fee fraud', but, more often than not, it's called a '419 Fraud' after Section 419 of the Criminal Code of Nigeria, where it all started back in the Seventies or maybe even the Sixties. The scammers would send out a thousand (or more) letters to British residents drawn from a borrowed, stolen or bought mailing list, telling them that certain bonds or investments in Nigeria had matured and they were due the dividends. The only problem was that due to 'currency controls' it wasn't possible to just send the hundreds of thousands of pounds owed from Nigeria, you had to supply bank details into which the funds could be paid direct and also send an 'advance fee' or 'transfer tax' of, say, £500, before the dividends could be released.

You would have thought that alarm bells should have rung immediately, but a surprising number of people fell for it, to the extent that it was at one point reckoned to be the fourth largest Nigerian industry. It's not done by post anymore, but by email, and the centre of operations is thought to be Côte d'Ivoire these days rather than Nigeria.

With the boom in eBay, where everyone is looking for a bargain, the scams get more sophisticated but essentially the predators are sniffing for the same old prey: those who are looking for something for nothing, or something for very little. And with a system based so much on trust, there is no shortage of either hunters or those willing to be hunted.

'It was a bargain,' Ossie pleaded in his pathetic defence.

'It always is,' I said patronisingly.

'Do you know anything about ham radio?'

'Of course not. What's that got to do with anything? You're not telling me you're a hamster, are you?'

He snorted in disgust.

'We're called hams or radio amateurs, if you don't mind, and you shouldn't look down your nose at us. It's been a respectable hobby for over a hundred years.'

'So has morris dancing.'

I could see that didn't go down well. He was a big, slightly flustered, very embarrassed Yorkshireman who still had a three-pound knuckleduster in his possession. I judged it was time to back off and feign interest.

'So, this "bargain" you spotted on eBay – it was a ham radio?'

'It was a transceiver, actually,' he said, though it meant nothing to me. 'An Icom and a very tasty bit of kit at a very tasty price. Those things usually retail in America for about $3,000. This one was on auction and the bids were low, only going up in £10 chunks.'

'I've got a very nasty feeling I know where this is going,' I said, but in a supportive way.

Ossie chose to be prickly.

'You know, I just thought you might, pal, what with us dumb northerners being out of our depth when it comes to modern concepts like e-tailing. So what happened then, Mr Smarty Pants?'

'Now this is just a shot in the dark,' I said tentatively, 'but the scam usually goes like this. You are bidding, right?'

He nodded slowly.

'And you get up to a certain figure which you think is a really good bargain, and the clock's ticking away to the deadline. Am I warm?'

'I was the highest bidder at £470 with less than an hour to go – and, yeah, that would have been a bargain. Nobody had placed a bid for two days. I mean two fooking days!'

'But somebody did, right at the last minute, didn't they? Was it a really stupid bid?'

'Yes it was, somebody whacked in a bid for…'

'Let me guess,' I said holding up a hand. '£1,750.'

He looked astonished. Next time I'd try pulling a rabbit from his fedora while he was still wearing it.

'How did you know that?'

'This transmitter thing…'

'Transceiver.'

'Whatever. You said the retail price was $3,000 which is about 1,750 of your English pounds. Somebody bid the spot-on, correct price and all you bargain hunters lost interest immediately, didn't you? You probably went off in a huff, or at least down the pub. Or you kicked the cat, or swore at the wife. Until…'

I paused for dramatic effect and it was working. His eyes were shining and his breathing quickened, which was ridiculous because he *knew* what had happened.

'…you got the email about an hour or so after the auction closed. And it said something to the effect that the winning bid had been disallowed for security reasons or some such excuse, which didn't really register because you were only interested in the bit that said as *you* were the second highest bidder, you could have the item privately if you were still interested, at your last bid price.'

'That's right,' Ossie gushed, 'that's exactly what it said.'

'All you had to do was send an email to the seller at such-and-such an address and he would contact you. It probably said something reassuring as well like "Send no money now" and "On no account send your bank details." So you can't wait to get in touch and the seller – or the guy you think is the seller – comes back wanting to know where you live. Not your actual address, just the nearest town, say. Well, there's no harm in that, is there? So you tell him Huddersfield and he comes back at you saying where the hell's that?'

It got no response.

'OK, sorry about that. Once you say Huddersfield, he says fine, because Huddersfield has several very convenient branches of...'

I waved my fingers like I was conducting an orchestra so we could say it both together:

'Western Union.'

'That's right,' gasped Ossie. 'How did you know?'

'Because if you send money through Western Union and the amount is less than £600, you don't have to produce ID to pick it up at the other end. So next morning, you probably followed instructions to the letter. Took £470 out of your bank account and trotted round to the nearest Western Union franchise, exactly where he's told you it would be, and you sent it off to the address you'd been given and then you hurried home to stake out the postman for the next three days until you were sure your bargain transmitter was never going to arrive.'

'Transceiver. But you're almost spot on. It looked entirely legitimate, I mean, the emails I got were actually from eBay.'

'No they weren't, they were fakes. Somebody had created a template using the Print Screen button – it's on your keyboard, they've all got one – when they've been on the real eBay site and they've rigged up something which looks like an official email.'

'But it was kosher. It had their logo and everything.'

'I bet you didn't check where it came from,' I said smugly.

'How's anyone supposed to do that?'

'Highlight the email in your Inbox, then click on File and go down to where it says Properties. That tells you the address of the sender, whatever it says on the actual thing you're reading.'

'But it *looked exactly* like an official message from eBay!' he protested.

'Who are you going to believe, me or your computer screen?

I bet you've never checked out the eBay on-line tutorial on spoof emails, have you?' He shook his head. 'Or noticed those big warning messages they put all over the site saying whatever you do, do NOT try and buy anything by sending cash via Western Union? For Christ's sake, Ossie, they specifically tell you not to do that, but you just couldn't see beyond the bargain could you?'

I suppose I should have felt sorry for the big oaf, but all I could do was wonder how he'd respond to some nicely worded junk mail from Nigeria or maybe Côte d'Ivoire.

'So what happened next?' I coaxed him gently.

'About four days later, the bloody transceiver was up for auction again on eBay so I contacted eBay and they said they'd had a winning bid but he hadn't coughed up the cash, so the transceiver was up for sale again.'

'And nothing about offering it to the second highest bidder, of course.'

'They said they didn't do that, and I should forward the emails I'd got to them. But I couldn't. They'd disappeared, along with everything else in my Outlook Express. Inbox, Outbox, even my sodding Address Book.'

I sat back in my chair and made like I was sucking on a pipe.

'So, my dear Watson, it seems we have something of a criminal genius on our hands.'

'That right, Sherlock?' he said, playing along.

'Well anyone can find a sucker on eBay and you only have to be relatively clued-up to forge an email, but to send it with a worm or a Trojan horse virus that takes out all the evidence afterwards, that's clever. The profile we're building here, Watson, is of only one possible sort of criminal.'

'And what would that be, oh great detective?'

I sucked on my imaginary pipe as if I meant it.

'Male, undoubtedly. Lives locally, hence the post box in the off-licence. Computer literate, in fact very computer literate and with plenty of time on their hands to surf the Internet.

Moreover, somebody who regards £470 as a decent score, although of course he may be doing the same scam twice a day, with matinees Wednesday and Saturday for all I know.'

'So what *do* you know, Sherlock? And did I ever tell you, Holmes, that you come across as a right pillock when you're like this?'

'What I know, Watson, or at least am pretty sure of, is that we are dealing with a criminal mastermind of the most dangerous sort: one who is about fifteen years old.'

'A kid?' he exploded. 'I've been conned by a fooking schoolboy?'

'I reckon so. I mean, come on, it was less than five hundred quid. No respectable thief would get out of bed for that these days. And he'd know that no normal citizen would bother to try and reclaim such a sum. I mean, the cops wouldn't be interested – "buyer beware" and all that jazz – and the Small Claims Court would just laugh even if you could find somebody to sue.'

And then I realised that I was sitting opposite someone who had travelled a couple of hundred miles just so he could act the bull in the china shop.

'You didn't need to come to London to tell me about Margaret Anne Hayes and the Ellrington case, did you?' I said, losing the pipe-smoking routine. 'You could have told me what you'd found out over the phone. You came looking for the kid who conned you out of £470, even though the train ticket cost you – what – two hundred and fifty?'

'I didn't think it would be a kid,' he said thoughtfully, 'assuming you're right in your deductions, Sherlock, but it don't make any difference. I'm gonna get the little bastard, whoever he is. And don't you get any daft ideas; it's not the principle of the thing, it *is* the money.'

Chapter Eleven

'So you'd settle for your money back? You're not looking for revenge?'

'That's all, I'm a simple man.'

I refrained from commenting on that.

'What name did he give you?'

Oesterlein gave me a look which mixed pity with surprise in equal proportions.

'What good is that?'

'He gave you a name, didn't he? He would have to, for Western Union, so he could get your money.'

'Stephen Danks, but what on earth makes you think that'll help?'

'You never know, it might be his real name.'

Oesterlein snorted so loud, the dozing Springsteen's eye shot open.

'What are the chances of that?'

'Look, I may have been a bit hasty when I said we were dealing with a criminal mastermind,' I said reasonably, hoping that he didn't think I was implying that you didn't need to be a mastermind to con him out of £470. 'We know he knows a lot about eBay and he's computer literate, if that's not a contradiction in terms, a bit like "military intelligence".'

'If you've got a point, get to it.'

'What I'm saying is that the higher the computer skills, the lower the age, usually.'

'So it's a kid; yeah, I got that.'

'A kid who is smart enough to use a postbox to pick up his ill-gotten Western Union drafts, but not clever enough, or old enough, to have set up his own fake address, which would make his life a lot easier. Without a believable address, your legal as well as illegal activities are limited. To open a fake bank account, for instance, is very difficult without a real address. The odds are he probably still lives at home with his parents and he uses his real name because he operates locally where people know him. That's why he keeps his scams relatively modest.'

'Modest? You said he could be doing this every day.'

'He might be, but it doesn't follow that he finds a...victim...every day.' I had almost said 'sucker'. 'And maybe two or three hundred once or twice a month is all he needs to buy himself a new pair of trainers or an iPod or whatever. It's not like he's saving up for a Ferrari is it? I mean, he's not old enough to drive.'

'He could be a druggie, fuelling his habit.'

'I think not. A serious addict would have sold his computer and Internet connection first and thought up this scam later. No, I think we should be looking for this Stephen Danks, who will be a teenager with a computer in his bedroom, proud and loving parents and he's probably doing very well at school. When you got those spoof emails, did you notice what time of day they were sent?'

He shook his head sadly.

'I'll bet they were all sent in the evening, after normal office hours and not during school time. It wouldn't have been proof positive but it's always a good reason to be suspicious. Even the nerd who can fake emails and send a Trojan horse virus to cover his tracks can forget to alter the simple things like his computer clock.'

'I looked up Danks in the London Residential phone book, but there was no listing for the E8 postal area.'

'It was worth doing, I suppose,' I said, trying not to be too harsh, 'but now you get a choice, more people stay out of the telephone directory than go in these days. When I first came to London, it took a professional Strong Man to rip a London phone book in half. These days, I reckon Fenella downstairs could do one.'

I knew that Fenella's partner Lisabeth could; I'd seen her do it.

'So how are you going to find this Stephen Danks?'

'It's not going to be easy. This reciprocal case thing – do we each have to spend the identical number of man hours?'

'I was going to invoice Rudgard & Blugden for five hours' work and about forty quid expenses for finding Margaret Hayes for you.'

'So you found her?'

'Well, I know where she lives.'

And it took him five hours? I'd been working on the case for a week now and hadn't thought of a good question to ask anyone.

I kept a straight face and looked at my watch.

'Five hours should be OK,' I said confidently, 'but let's get some lunch and then I'd better check in with the office and get you to your hotel. But first, I've just got to pop downstairs and have a word with my landlord whilst I'm in the building. I shan't be a minute, just make yourself at home.'

I stood up and started for the door, then stopped.

'Oh, don't take this the wrong way, but try not to touch anything, will you? It upsets the cat.'

'Haven't seen your little pussy since I arrived. I've probably scared him off. Don't worry about it, I told you, cats love me.'

Under the sofa, Springsteen peeked out from behind Oesterlein's size 12 shoes and licked his lips.

By chance, Naseem Naseem was holding the front door open, showing out what I presumed were the potential new tenants of Mr Goodson's flat. From what I could see of them, they were a couple in their mid-twenties, both wearing suits to indicate they were gainfully and professionally employed. It was just the right sort of impression to give Naseem and as they shook hands with him he beamed at them, almost as if giving them his blessing.

As I sauntered down the stairs, I saw the female of the couple add the icing to the cake. With a fluttering of her eyelashes and a girly giggle, she skipped out into Stuart Street and waved a *blip-blip* electronic key at a parked Mini-Cooper, from the back seat of which she produced a bouquet of cellophane-wrapped red roses. Scampering back up the steps she presented them to Naseem and he couldn't have been more impressed if she'd curtsied.

'The new tenants?' I asked, startling him by creeping up behind him as he waved them goodbye.

'Oh! Angel, it's you. I thought I heard somebody padding about in Flat 3.' He juggled the roses and felt embarrassed enough to have to explain them. 'They're for my wife, a present from that nice couple, the Scoulars. Do you know them?'

'Nope.'

He looked relieved. That probably clinched it for them.

'I thought you might. Very nice couple; very respectable. He's in the music business. She's a florist.'

I doubted that. The wrapping round the bunch of roses had a printed bar code just like you would get in a garage forecourt shop.

'I'm sure they'll be ideal tenants and be very happy here.'

'And not cause me any harassment. Unlike some of my tenants.'

I let that go. He couldn't mean me, I was hardly ever here these days.

'Amy sends her love, by the way,' I said, steering him on to safer ground.

His eyes sparkled at the mere mention of Amy's name. That happened quite a lot, I noticed.

'And how is the famous businesswoman Amy May?'

'She is very well, and very pregnant.'

Now the eyes were popping. Naseem had acquired a fair sprinkling of grey in his hair and beard since I had last seen him, but my news made the years fall away.

'You're having a baby. Why that's most excellent. Here.' He thrust the bouquet of roses at me. 'Take these for the young mother. I couldn't explain them to my wife anyway. Do you know if it's a boy or not?'

'We look forward to being surprised.'

'It will change your life, you know,' he said wisely.

'It already has. I now have a regular job.'

'You do?'

He was so surprised it came out as 'You! *Do?*'

'I will have a family to support,' I said, realising that I had quite a strong card to play here, 'and that's why I wanted to ask your advice.'

'Get yourself a good nanny. There are some excellent Polish and Latvian girls looking for work; very qualified, very cheap and also very legal these days. Failing that, you can't go wrong by using the doting grandparents.'

Oh yes you can, if they're like the candidates in my family.

'That's not convenient, they live too far away,' I countered.

'Move them in with you, you won't regret it. I did and now we have a personal babysitter, child-minder, gardener and cook and my father helps out with the accounts.'

Now we were in the realms of fantasy. The idea of my mother cooking anything which didn't go 'ping' when it was ready or growing anything but cannabis in the garden was ridiculous. The thought of trusting my father with a set of accounts was a suicidal one.

'I'll think about it,' I said not to upset him. 'In the meantime, you can help me with my new job.'

'I can?' He seemed genuinely flattered and not at all suspicious.

'I can think of no one better. You see, I need your local knowledge.'

He held up a warning finger.

'This is nothing to do with the flat?'

'Absolutely not.'

'And this will not cost me money?'

'On the head of my unborn child,' I said with one hand on my heart, just hoping I wasn't over-egging it. 'I just need to find someone locally, here in Hackney, so I need a guide, a mentor, a person with local knowledge.'

'A person with contacts and influence? A person of some standing in the community?' he mused, already hooked.

'I couldn't have put it better myself,' I said, which was true. I could have said somebody with an extended family, a natural nosey-parker and somebody who collected a lot of rent in the district, but that probably wouldn't have persuaded him to help me. 'Do you know Ghadji's off-licence down on Mare Street?'

'I know the owner, Roger, very well. He's on the Asian Businessmen's Council.'

'Is that Roger Ghadji?'

'No, no. It's Roger Da Gama. He's from Goa originally. The business was set up by a couple of brothers from Morocco years ago, then they moved into the restaurant business up west, near Leicester Square somewhere and Roger bought the shop but kept the name.'

'There you go, Naseem, that's exactly the sort of local knowledge I couldn't get anywhere else.'

'Well, not unless you went down the town hall and asked to see the licensing applications,' he said modestly, then his face broke into a huge grin. 'Or you hired a private detective.'

I laughed with him.

'Why would I need to do that when I've got you? The thing is, I need to ask this Roger Da Gama about one of the postboxes he holds in his shop. It's being used to con people out of money.'

'How?'

'People send Western Union money orders there for goods they've seen advertised, but the money orders get cashed and no goods are ever sent.'

'So is this job of yours in the fraud business?'

'You might say it's more in the insurance sector.'

You might well say that, if you were lying.

'So what do you want me to do? Ask Roger who collects the mail from that postbox?'

'That would be ever so kind, Naseem, you're a real star.'

'I'm not sure I should, you know. It's probably unethical.'

'I'm not accusing Mr Da Gama of doing anything wrong. He probably has no idea what his postboxes are being used for.'

'If it's cashing Western Union orders, he probably does. His sister runs the Western Union franchise in the travel agent's just round the corner from his shop.'

Oh, brilliant.

'But Roger's an honest man and respectable. He's thinking of standing for the council next year, not that he stands much chance of getting elected, not with his views.'

'Why's that?'

'He's a Conservative. Anyway, I'll ask him about it. Do you know the box number?'

'It's Number 10, so I'm told, and the money orders are made out in the name of Stephen Danks.'

'Not Stephen Danks – The Computer Kid?'

'What? You know him?'

'Everybody does. The *Hackney Gazette* did a big spread on him.'

'I must have missed that issue. What was it you called him?'

'The Computer Kid. He runs his own business setting up computers for people in their homes and connecting them to the Internet. You can call him out for repairs and things, like a plumber. Except cheaper. He's saving up to go to university in a few years' time. He's a child...what's it called? Prodigy, that's it. We're very proud of him in Hackney. He's always winning prizes at his school.'

'So you know him?'

'I know his father, Vikram. He's a solicitor and he's *chairman* of the Asian Businessmen's Council. But you see the calling cards pinned up everywhere, advertising The Computer Kid. In fact, now I think of it, there's one of his cards stuck up in the window of Ghadji's Wines unless I'm very much mistaken.'

Ooops.

I put the bouquet of roses in the back of Armstrong – it was a bouquet rather than a bunch now that Amy was getting them – and waved as Naseem walked off down Stuart Street. He had almost certainly parked his Mercedes round the next corner as he never liked to give advanced warning of a visit to one of his properties.

Re-entering the house, I took the stairs two at a time as soon as I heard the thump and crash of overturned furniture and then the howl of pain coming from my flat. Fenella had heard the commotion too and was opening her door as I rushed by, though I checked my pace when my brain registered that the howl of pain had been human and not feline.

'What's all the noise?' I heard Fenella squeal behind me.

'Just the children misbehaving,' I said over my shoulder.

'You didn't leave your friend alone with Springsteen, did you?'

'I did a risk assessment,' I snapped back, because it was something I'd heard Veronica say.

The door of my flat opened before I reached it and out staggered Ossie Oesterlein, holding his left hand with his bandaged right hand. There seemed to be even more blood on his shirt.

'He just went for me, he just fooking went for me!'

'Did you touch anything?' I asked, trying to keep a straight face.

'No, I was just looking through your CD collection.'

'I did warn you...'

'I don't think I've got any more plasters left,' Fenella said, all concerned.

'Don't worry, I'll pick some up on the way to lunch,' I told her, taking Ossie by the elbow and ushering him down the stairs. 'Be careful when you check up on Springsteen, he may have eaten something that disagreed with him.'

The third corner shop I stopped at sold Elastoplasts without green crocodiles on them and had a postcard in the door advertising the services of The Computer Kid. I turned my mobile on to add the number to the memory and noticed that there were six messages and three missed calls for me. They would have to wait; I thought it far more important to get some protein into Ossie to counter the blood loss.

As I drove into Stoke Newington I concentrated on selecting a lunch venue, partly to distract myself from the swearing in the back seat as Ossie wrestled with the plasters, ripping them open with his teeth. For a brief moment I considered taking him to Kelly's Pie & Mash place down Bethnal Green Road, but decided that might just be *too* much of a culture shock for him. We weren't too far from my current favourite curry hot spot, The Famous Curry Bazaar on Brick Lane, but then they probably had curry houses up north. In the end I told him we were going for fish and chips and shot round to Bill Bentley's on Bishopsgate, where Ossie tucked a napkin into his collar to cover his bloodstained shirt and hid his hands under the table whilst he ordered half a dozen Colchester Natives to be followed by potted shrimps and then a Dover sole. It didn't seem as if his first visit to Hackney had affected his appetite and I treated him to a half bottle of a good Muscadet sur Lie whilst I went for a modest crab salad and a bottle of fizzy Badoit.

'You watching your waistline or summat?' he quizzed me after the waiter had taken our order.

'Got a lot of driving still to do today,' I said in mitigation.

'It's been a funny day so far. Dinner time already and we haven't even got to your office.'

'That wasn't exactly my idea. We had some personal business of yours to take care of, remember?'

'My business which is now your business,' he pointed out. 'And if you're sticking to a reciprocal number of hours, then you should have a result for me by, let's see, about tea time wouldn't you say?'

'I may have been a bit hasty there. I hadn't thought about meal breaks and travelling time. How about if I get you a result before you go to bed in your hotel tonight?'

'By result, you mean you'll have got my money back?'

'Sure,' I said, playing with my cutlery and wishing that Amy and I hadn't given up smoking.

If the worst came to the worst, I'd give him £470 and claim it back from petty cash, having decided I could flannel Veronica more easily than him.

'Well, I can't say fairer than that. Where and when do we beat the lights out of the little toe-rag?'

'*We* don't. I want to do this myself, back at my place in Hackney. I didn't think you'd be that keen on seeing Springsteen again.'

He hugged his wrists to his chest under the crisp white napkin. In profile he looked like a body under a shroud.

'I could do without that, for sure. I've never come across an animal that vicious since the wife left me.'

I didn't rise to the bait and avoided eye contact, as he sounded as if he was not kidding.

'I did warn you about him,' I said, 'and believe me, it was nothing personal. He doesn't really like anything that walks on two legs. Or four. He's not keen on spiders either. Which reminds me, I'd better ring the office. They'll be wondering what I've done with you.'

I turned my mobile back on. Now there were eight messages

and five missed calls, all from the office. Thankfully, it was Laura who answered my call.

'You're *where*?'

'Having fish and chips in the East End. I had to take Mr Oesterlein on a bit of a sight-seeing tour.'

'Sight-seeing?'

'He insisted on it.'

Ossie leaned towards me and said in a very loud whisper:

'Blame me, pal. My shoulders are broad.'

'I intend to,' I told him, covering the mouthpiece, 'now and for the foreseeable future.'

'So are you gracing us with your presence anytime?' Laura was saying.

'Soon as we've finished lunch. Oh, and soon as we've checked into the hotel. Give us a couple of hours. Mr Oesterlein has a positive result to report so I believe.'

Ossie sipped his wine and raised his eyes to the ceiling.

'Good. I know Lorna's been trying to get you. She has some info for you. It seems you're getting good at delegating.'

'It's a knack,' I agreed.

'You're supposed to delegate responsibility, not just work you don't fancy doing.'

'Oh bugger, is that what it means? Listen, do me a favour and ring Amy at home and tell her I'm working tonight and I'll be home late.'

'Well, I'm not sure if I…'

'If you don't want to talk to Amy May, I can text her.'

'No, no, that's fine, I'll do it.'

I just knew she couldn't resist a chance to talk to the great fashion diva Amy May. Few women seem able to.

'And did you get those tickets I asked you to chase?'

'For that Madame Jo-Jo's place? Yes, I got them.'

'Good. You might be working late tonight too. See you soon.'

I ended the call and turned the phone off again. Only then did I notice Ossie Oesterlein staring at me across the table.

'You know Amy May, the fashion designer?'

I hid my amazement and made crossed-fingers with both hands over my place setting.

'Amy and me, we're like that.'

He pulled a face to show he was impressed.

'So what am I supposed to do whilst you're out on a mission tonight?'

'Young Laura from the office is taking you clubbing.'

'Clubbing, eh?' he mused, then he got serious. 'You mean a night club, don't you? I mean, not the rave disco-type clubbing with all that house music?'

'No, not one of them. Nor is it a Working Men's Club with cheap bitter and chicken in a basket.'

'You taking the piss now?'

'No, I'm saying it's a night club, of sorts. It's very popular. It's called Madame Jo-Jo's and it's down in Soho.'

'Soho, eh? With Laura, who has such a nice voice on the phone. Is this a blind date then?'

'Oh, I think you could say that.'

Chapter Twelve

We arrived back at the office in Shepherd's Bush around 3.30 p.m. after calling at Ossie's hotel near the British Library so he could check in and dump his bag.

As I ushered him up the stairs to Veronica's lair, he said:

'With all the women that work here, I only hope one of them knows where the teabags are kept.'

I winced and made sure his body mass covered me from the missiles which would surely rain down on us.

I could tell from Veronica's expression that she'd heard him, and Laura had as well. Lorna just looked like that normally.

They had pushed Veronica's desk back against the wall and arranged five chairs in a rough circle. We could have been set for a focus group discussion, a séance or a meeting of Alcoholics Anonymous.

'It's so good of you to come all this way to deliver your report in person, Mr Oesterlein,' said Veronica after shaking his hand and introducing the Thompson Twins, whilst studiously ignoring me. 'I don't believe you get up to London much, so we're honoured.'

'You should be at the prices they charge,' he said gruffly, though I wasn't sure what he was griping about. He would certainly claim his train fare and hotel bill back from R & B (who would then invoice James Ellrington), and he hadn't had to pay for lunch or a taxi since arriving in town.

'I thought we might all benefit from hearing your report,' Veronica said, ignoring him, 'as we all have an interest in this case. Please, have a seat and let's keep this informal. Any input from our end we'll keep until the end.'

Ossie blinked at that and looked at each chair in turn to see which was the least uncomfortable and which would take his bulk. He sat down carefully, the way a fat man sits down, then took a small black policeman's notebook from the inside pocket of his jacket, snapping the elastic band around it and resting it on his knee. Then there were two minutes of him positioning his huge feet and pulling the creases in his trousers until he was completely comfortable.

It was obvious that Ossie did not like the idea of such a public performance, or maybe he was just disturbed at being outnumbered by females. Strangely enough, none of the women remarked on his hands, covered with six or seven sticking plasters, or the fact that he made no effort to take his hat off.

He started talking in a flat monotone and though we followed Veronica's instruction not to 'input' any questions or observations until he had finished saying his piece, at no time did he seem to relax.

He had started with the newspaper cutting I had faxed him, taken from the *Wakefield Express* on which somebody had written 23rd August 1963. That had turned out to be the Friday publication date of the newspaper and the story actually referred to the wedding of Simon Pennington and Margaret Anne Hayes on the previous Saturday, the 17th.

The local newspaper was still there and Ossie knew his way around their 'morgue' or cuttings library and was able to call up the August 23rd issue on microfiche.

Laura creased her brow at that but I caught her eye and shook my head, sending her a mental memo that I would explain later how people survived before computers.

The report of the wedding followed the standard format of local newspapers (they give the bride a form to fill in), the only difference being that the managing director of a booming local firm merited sending a photographer along. The details were sparse, but Simon Rodney Pennington, aged 32 and the MD of Calder Grove Interiors and originally from Burnley in Lancashire, had married Margaret Anne Hayes, 20, the daughter of Mr and Mrs Colin Hayes, of Sandal, at St Michael and All Angels, Notton. The service had been conducted by the Reverend Ian Davies and the bride had worn a brocade dress trimmed with tulle.

'Tulle' brought confused double-takes from both Laura and Lorna, so I made another note to hold a follow-up seminar on silk exports from Tulle in the Dordogne which were once crucial to wedding-dress making. Sleeping with Amy had taught me a lot.

From the newspaper office in Wakefield, Ossie had driven out to the small village of Notton, about halfway to Barnsley, should anyone be interested.

We weren't.

The current vicar of St Michael and All Angels was, of course, far too young and far too recent to remember anything, but the Rev Davies mentioned in the wedding report had kept a weekly diary of church events, with a view to writing a social history of the parish on his retirement. Every year from 1961 to 1989 was covered in exhaustive and exhausting detail, so exhausting that the Rev Davies had dropped dead within a year of retirement and had never got around to his history project. The Parochial Church Council had inherited the diaries and for a small fee (receipt to follow), Ossie was welcome to consult them, as several thousand people interested in tracing their family histories had done. It was a booming business for country churches.

For 17th August 1963, the Parish Diary recorded the Pennington-Hayes wedding and noted that it had been held in

Notton because it had been the church where Colin and Hazel Hayes, Margaret Anne's parents, had themselves been married twenty-five years before, both coming from the village originally.

The new vicar was able to embellish Ossie's research by volunteering the information that Colin and Hazel Hayes had returned to the village in retirement. In fact, Colin Hayes was still there, buried in the churchyard.

And Hazel Hayes, Margaret Anne's mother, wasn't that far away. Aged 87, she was still alive and living in a posh nursing home for retired gentlefolk at West Bretton, only a couple of miles away, near the Yorkshire Sculpture Park where they had all those big carvings by Henry Moore which were worth millions but you'd have to get a truck in there to nick one.

Pausing only for a quick wash and brush up in the vicarage, Ossie drove over to the High Edge Residential Home and presented himself as a potential customer. Not for himself, of course, but for a fictional mother, aged 75, who was too frail to live alone any more.

Not that his mother was fictional. She was very real, still lived with Ossie's father, and had a season ticket for Leeds United.

Making it clear that money was no object – 'Mother' had substantial savings and a large property to sell as well as private medical insurance – Ossie quickly won the confidence of the duty Matron who supplied him with an armful of colourful leaflets and a promotional DVD, as well as giving him a tour of the facilities and grounds.

He then did what all private detectives did, which was not lying but creating an alternative truth.

We all nodded wisely in agreement.

Casually, he dropped into the conversation with Matron that he had been recommended High Edge by a very nice lady, a Mrs Pennington, whose mother was a resident there. Matron had said that was odd, as there was no one called Pennington in residence.

That *was* odd, because he was sure that Margaret Anne had said High Edge. There wasn't another residential home nearby, was there? Oh, Margaret Anne *Hayes*; of course, now Matron twigged it. Hazel Hayes' daughter, that was who he meant, and of course the daughter's married name was Pennington, how silly of Matron.

It was always wise to remember one of Ossie's personal rules of life: if you ask somebody the right way, they'll tell you anything.

Of course, he didn't know Mrs Hayes' daughter that well, but she'd seemed really nice. Oh she was, she was, Matron had agreed. Did she visit her mother often as she lived quite a way away, didn't she?

This was what was known as extrapolating on an alternative truth, we noted. Otherwise known as fishing or guessing.

Well, it was difficult, now that her husband had retired and they'd gone to live in Dorset. Oh yes, she'd said, and Lyme Regis was such a lovely place, wasn't it?

Matron was sure it was, but she didn't know it personally. Mrs Hayes had shown her photographs of her daughter's house though, a really lovely house in a village called Upwalters. Looked like the picture off a tin of Christmas biscuits. It was probably near to Lyme Regis.

Ossie had refused the offer to meet Mrs Hayes that day, but said it could be useful if his mother seemed interested in High Edge.

Back in his office, above the pub in Huddersfield, he had made a few phone calls until he had located the personnel department of the company that had taken over the running of Calder Grove Interiors, Simon Pennington's old firm. Pretending to be from the Tax Credit Office in Preston he demanded verification that they were still paying a pension to one Simon Pennington, who had retired in 1996.

We were impressed that he knew the date, but he said it was an educated guess based on the fact that Pennington had been

32 in 1963 and that most people in Yorkshire still retired at 65.
And why did we all look shocked and scared at that?

He reminded the personnel department that they must on no
account divulge Mr Pennington's National Insurance number,
nor any bank details, even to the Tax Credit Office over the
phone, as that would be an offence, and so the poor little
jobsworth on the end of the line was only too happy to answer
the easy question and, yes, they were still paying Mr
Pennington's company pension every month.

And could they just confirm that the address the Tax Credit
Office had, in Upwalters, Dorset, was still the current one for
him?

Oh yes, that was right: Stone Cottage, Frome Street,
Upwalters, Dorset.

'Where the hell is Upwalters?' Lorna asked sulkily as Ossie
relaxed at the end of his presentation.

'How the fook should I know?' he snarled. 'Get yourself an
RAC road atlas. Bloody hell, am I the only detective in the
room?'

'I've got a map in Armstrong, I'll just nip and get it,' I said to
avoid answering his question.

As I started down the stairs, I heard him say 'All this
nattering, I'm parched. Don't you have kettles down 'ere?' in
the broadest Yorkshire accent he had tried all day.

Whilst I was getting the road map and on my own, I jumped
into Armstrong and sneaked in a couple of phone calls. They
were not particularly private, I just didn't want to give any trade
secrets away and when I got Oesterlein's money back that
evening, I wanted it to be a nice surprise as I was sure he had
absolutely no confidence in my ability to deliver.

As an insurance policy I rang Amy to make sure she had got a
message about me being late home. She said she had and I said not
to worry, it wouldn't be late late; it would be before-the-pubs-shut
late. And yes, I agreed, she had heard that before but this was

work, not pleasure and I really wanted to prove I could do this job. I wasn't sure she believed that until I casually asked if she could make sure she had £500 in cash in the house just in case I needed to borrow it tomorrow morning. And no, I wasn't being pursued by loan sharks or bookmakers, and I certainly hadn't bought anything stupid cash-on-delivery over the Internet. (Though I didn't tell her how close she'd come with that one.)

Amy had grizzled and griped and said she would have to make a special trip into Cambridge, but she would have the cash. In our time together we had not once argued about money, working on the principle that I never had any and she had more than she knew what to do with. It had seemed a good arrangement.

Back in the office, Ossie still hadn't got the cup of tea he had been dropping such subtle hints about all afternoon; and he was continuing to drop them so that the whole tea issue was rapidly turning into a diplomatic stand-off of Cold War proportions, with Ossie on one side and the female employees of R & B Investigations on the other.

'Right, got the map. What are we looking for?' I said jovially trying to lighten the mood.

'Upwalters,' said Ossie, croaking a bit as a really thirsty man would, 'in Dorset.'

I opened the AA road map to the Dorset/Devon pages and placed it on Veronica's desk.

'Near Lyme Regis, you said, didn't you?'

'Yeah, but I was just saying that to the nice Matron in the maximum security twilight home; making conversation, like, whilst we were chatting over a cup of tea… I've no idea where it is really. Lyme Regis was the only place I could think of. Well, be honest, who's heard of anything else from Dorset?'

'The Tolpuddle Martyrs,' said Lorna.

'The Thomas Hardy books,' Veronica chipped in, though from the look on Ossie's face she would have got more of a reaction if she'd said Thomas the Tank Engine.

'The Cerne Abbas Giant,' said Laura, then caught my eye and started smirking at the thought of the giant phallus on the famous warrior figure carved into the chalk hills north of Dorchester; a phallus which the Victorians reputedly tried to grow grass over.

'I always liked the cut of his jib,' I whispered to her, turning to the index to find a map reference for Upwalters. 'Remind you of anyone?'

She choked back a giggle and whilst apparently fascinated by the road map, she kicked me gently on the ankle.

'Found it,' I said, pointing proudly. 'It's down on the Isle of Purbeck near a place called Wareham.'

Then, as if I'd just had a flash of inspiration: 'Cream teas! They do them in Dorset.'

'That's Devon,' moaned Lorna.

'No, he's right, they do lovely cream teas in Dorset as well,' said Veronica, playing along for once.

'Nice one,' whispered Laura, biting down on her bottom lip.

'So, do you feel better now you've found it on a map? Happy now that I wasn't making it up?' said Ossie through cracked lips, forcing out every dehydrated syllable.

'We have never doubted the quality of the information you have provided in the past, Mr Oesterlein,' Veronica soothed, 'and we don't now.'

'Naturally we will check the address for Mrs Pennington, to see if it's still current,' drawled Lorna.

'It is.' Ossie tore a sheet from his policeman's notebook and offered it to them. 'That's the phone number, according to 118 118 or whatever the fook Directory Enquiries is called these days. And 192.com People Finder says that she and Mr Simon Pennington were both registered on the electoral roll as being at that address for at least the last four years, so I've saved you a job looking that up.'

'You've been very thorough, as usual. We are in your debt.'

Veronica was polite, businesslike and genuine with it, but she wasn't going to be the one to make the tea.

'Mebbe not for long, eh?' Ossie grinned and winked in my direction, even came up behind me and clapped one of his huge hairy paws on my shoulder. 'If our friend here is as good as he thinks he is.'

'I'm sorry, I don't understand,' said Veronica.

'Reciprocal cases,' I volunteered. 'Ossie worked my case in Yorkshire and he's got a case of his own which needs someone to work the London end.'

'What *sort* of case?'

'A confidential one.' I looked at Ossie and he nodded. That had been the right thing to say.

'And if my pal Angel gets me the result he's promised tonight, we'll call it quits and start a new slate. Nobody owes anybody anything.' He beamed at his own largesse.

'What do you mean get a result tonight? I thought Laura was taking him to Madame Jo-Jo's tonight.' This, unbidden, from Lorna.

'Well, that could be a result of sorts,' I mused softly.

Laura almost ruptured something trying to prevent the laughter. She slapped one hand over her mouth and waved the other in the air as she scurried from the office in the general direction of the kitchen. I could only assume she had found out what sort of cabaret went on in Madame Jo-Jo's.

'What's up with her?' asked Ossie.

'She's gone to put the kettle on,' I said.

"Bout fooking time,' he said magnanimously.

'I managed to get a few answers for you,' Lorna said and then had to remind me: 'From the tasks you set me yesterday.'

'Oh yeah, right. Good work; well done.'

'So do you want me to tell you now or shall I send you an email some time next week?'

Ossie pursed his lips and I could tell he was thinking 'Sarky cow'. I know I was.

'Perhaps Angel would prefer a private briefing,' Veronica said, playing the peacemaker.

Perhaps that was what management was all about: stopping the staff from killing each other. How boring a career choice was that?

'I've no objection to you listening in, Veronica,' I said with my second-best smile.

'I was thinking of Mr Oesterlein,' she said grimly.

'I doubt anything Lorna said would worry him. Would it Ossie?'

'Hey, I'm off the clock on this one.' He held up a bandaged hand. 'It's JD, Job Done, as far as I'm concerned, I've done all that was asked of me, and if Angel here does the same tonight, then that's JD all round and I can go back to God's own country tomorrow. You carry on, love; pretend I'm not here.'

The expression on Lorna's face said that would be like trying to ignore finding a tarantula in her low-fat yoghurt.

'I shouldn't think any of this is sensitive information,' she said pointedly, 'as it wasn't a very onerous task I was given.'

Ossie made a face and said, 'Onerous...' quietly, under his breath.

'James Ellrington belongs to a thing called the Thames Motor Yacht Club and has been a member since about 1980. He bought a forty-foot motor cruiser from another club member about eight years ago and renamed it or relaunched it, or whatever it is they do with boats, the *Margaret Anne*. It's moored at Sunbury and he's down there at least once a week tinkering about, though he doesn't seem to go out much on it.

'The man I talked to – who said he was a volunteer duty officer and claimed to know Ellrington – mentioned the fact that Ellrington and his wife used to go across to France quite often when she was alive. I asked if the boat had been named after her and he said no, her name had been Sandra, but she'd died of cancer two years ago. He couldn't think why Ellrington had called the boat the *Margaret Anne*. Other than that, a fine upstanding member of the messing-about-in-boats fraternity as far as I could tell.

'I did check the electoral roll for his address in Wimbledon and there was a Sandra Ellrington listed for 2002, but not since, and no listing for the son, Peter Ellrington.'

'Nothing from Criminal Records Bureau?'

'Not yet, but give them a chance. They're not the fastest.'

'You can say that again,' muttered Ossie.

'Well, thank you Lorna, an excellent JD there,' I said and then had to explain. 'Job Done, JD. Or maybe that should be JWD: Job Well Done. And here's Laura with the tea, so it's JD there as well.'

'Erm...Angel?'

'Yes, Veronica?'

'If Mr Oesterlein's been tracing people in Yorkshire for you, and Lorna's been checking out a yacht club for some reason for you, and Laura seems to be acting as your social secretary, not to mention making cups of tea when it's clearly your turn on the roster...'

There was a roster?

'...then I'm curious to know exactly what *you* are doing on this case.'

'I like to think of it as directing the overall strategy of the investigation,' I said.

It sounded good and meant absolutely nothing.

I was beginning to get the hang of this.

Chapter Thirteen

I didn't have much of a plan to get Ossie Oesterlein's money back. In fact, as plans went, it was pretty thin. If it failed, my Plan B was positively anorexic.

I had rung the number on The Computer Kid card and got a dedicated answering machine which told me to leave a message. I gave my name as Fitzroy and the Stuart Street address and said it was an emergency and my PC seemed to have jammed, just frozen up and I needed to get something out if it by tomorrow and I would really, really appreciate a call as The Computer Kid came highly recommended. The machine told me someone would get back to me and sure enough, at about five o'clock, I received a text saying that The Computer Kid could do a house call at about eight that evening. I sent a text back saying that would be fine by me, and by eight he should have finished his homework.

Basically I intended to get him alone and appeal to his better nature, stressing the fact that I was much easier to deal with than the mad Yorkshireman he'd actually conned. If he didn't see reason, then Plan B was to lock him in my flat with Springsteen.

Plan C would be to lock him in my flat with Fenella. Plan D would be to let Lisabeth find them there. Hopefully it wouldn't come to that; I really didn't like unnecessary violence.

Which was why I was very diplomatic when Veronica

marched me into the office kitchen for a 'one-on-one ongoing caseload assessment and client review'.

All that turned out to be was her pinning me to the sink unit with a steely glare and saying:

'So what are you going to tell our client?'

I should have guessed it would be a trick question.

'I was thinking of giving him a ring and saying: "You wanted us to find your girlfriend, we have. Please put cheque in post." And that would be it. JD, job done.'

'And you think that's wise?'

'Why wouldn't it be, Veronica?'

'Do we know what James Ellrington will do with this information? Have we any idea what his intentions are?'

'Only that they are honourable.'

'And how do we know that?'

'He told me they were. He let the love of his life slip through his fingers in the Sixties and now, when he's got time on his hands, he's thinking of what his life might have been, he's trying to reclaim a bit of that "Angel's share" of love that's evaporated over the years. The expression comes from the French: *la part des Anges*. It's what they say when cognac evaporates whilst it's maturing.'

'I thought you said it was something to do with making whisky in Japan?' she said, to prove she had been paying attention.

'Same principle. Anyhow, the point is James Ellrington is our client, our customer, and the customer is always right. Right? Why should we be investigating his motives?'

'But you obviously have some misgivings yourself. You went down to Wimbledon and you had Lorna check out his motor boat or whatever it was, I know you did, I've seen the work logs.'

'What work logs?'

'Lorna's. I've got a feeling it'll be a cold day in hell before I see yours.'

I decided to ignore that particular barb.

'I admit I had my reservations about Mr Ellrington, I mean you have to, don't you? Someone who still holds a torch for a girlfriend he hasn't seen for 42 years? That's not normal behaviour is it?'

'Obviously not for you. How long did you remember your first girlfriend? Forty-two days? Or forty-two minutes perhaps?'

'I could answer that at least five different ways, all of which would get me into trouble,' I said, immediately thinking of a sixth which was even funnier, but twice as dangerous. 'But we're not talking about *me*. We're talking about a man who, whilst to all appearances is respectably and happily married, buys a boat and christens it – or whatever they call it – the *Margaret Anne* after his first true love, then gets his wife to go out sailing on it and they even have their photograph taken on the deck and the picture is put on the mantelpiece in their front room on open display. Doesn't that strike you as a bit odd?'

'What makes you think Mrs Ellrington didn't know, and didn't mind, about his old girlfriend? It was all a long time ago.'

'I just try to imagine what my mother would have done if my father had named a boat – or a dog, or a pet tortoise – after one of his old flames when they were married. Defenestration is probably not the word for it, but it would have been a start.'

'So the late Mrs Ellrington didn't know that her husband carried a torch for someone else?'

'I certainly hope not. If she did, that would make it even weirder. In my experience, relationships work better and last longer if there's a healthy proportion of ignorance about what went on before.'

'Your vast experience, eh? Is ignorance the basis for your relationship with Amy May?'

'You're damn right it is.'

'So you don't tell her about your past?'

'I certainly don't flaunt it, like Ellrington did with his boat,'

I said, adopting a highly moral tone. 'He had his chance with Margaret Anne and he blew it. Now he wants to spend his retirement worrying about what might have been. He should have moved on. He should have grown up.'

'Everyone has to grow up,' said Veronica with an edge in her voice.

'No they don't *have* to. Growing old is inevitable; growing fat is very probable; but growing *up*, that's optional.'

She couldn't think of anything to say to that, so I decided to end the sermon there. Anyway, I had a schoolboy to intimidate.

I dropped Ossie Oesterlein off at his hotel on my way back to Hackney, so that he could put his feet up for half an hour and gather his strength for a night on the town with 'young Laura' who really was a 'tasty bit of crumpet'. I told him that Laura, like most females in London, secretly adored being called 'crumpet' in public, though it wasn't cool for them to show it, and that I thought it a good idea that he rested up before he visited Madame Jo-Jo's, as it could be a long night.

He laughed at that and while he was in a good mood, I asked if I could borrow his policeman's notebook.

'There's nothing much in it,' he said.

'That's fine, I just might need to take notes and I've nothing to write on.'

He poked it through the sliding screen from the back seat and dropped it into my lap.

'You sure we shouldn't do this together?' he asked. 'I mean, if there's a thumping to be dished out, I'm your man.'

'Thumpings are not on the menu tonight,' I said, though I couldn't speak for what might happen at Madame Jo-Jo's.

'So what you going to use to get my money back, then? Harsh language?'

I took a deep breath and held my head up high.

'If it comes to that.'

* * *

I got to Stuart Street with nearly an hour to spare. Realising that I was almost certainly going to miss out on dinner, I thought about ordering a take-away, but only for about two seconds until I remembered that my options locally were limited to a kebab the size of an elephant or a pizza of such uncertain origin that it was the equivalent of a game of Russian roulette delivered to your door. I compromised on sharing a tin of dolphin-friendly tuna chunks with Springsteen, though neither of us could really understand what the dolphins saw in them.

I had made my presence known to Lisabeth and Fenella and told them not to be disturbed by any strange noises coming from my flat later that evening.

Fenella had brightened up immediately and said: 'So, it'll be like the old days, will it?' with that stunning smile of hers and a hundred watts of pure, shining innocence. Then Lisabeth had growled, 'It'd better not be', and the lights had dimmed in Fenella's face and perhaps, just a little bit, in the world.

I had made myself concentrate on the business at hand and asked if there was anyone else home that evening, which meant in effect Miranda and Doogie, the couple in Flat 4 at the top of the house. Luckily they were at the local multiplex, seeing a new film which Fenella quite fancied but Lisabeth had vetoed on the grounds of dubious morals. (The film's, not hers.)

In some ways that was a pity, as Doogie was a good man to have in your corner. Oddly enough, Doogie was also the only thing on two legs Springsteen hadn't taken an instant and homicidal dislike to, possibly because Doogie was an up-and-coming chef in a leading West End hotel and often brought little meaty treats home as bribes. Or perhaps it was because Doogie was Scottish. Who could tell how a cat's brain worked?

The doorbell rang, dead on eight o'clock.

I slipped a Hayseed Dixie CD into the player, but kept the volume at a modest level. The sound of music, any music (even with Hayseed's dubious lyrics), coming from a strange flat would put strangers off their guard, because somebody obviously lived there. It would also help to put Springsteen on edge.

Even though I had told the girls in the flat below that I was expecting a visitor, Lisabeth was on guard on the stairs as I jogged down to get the front door.

'It'll be for me,' I said over my shoulder and she grunted something but I knew she would hang about to get a good look at my visitor.

As I was opening the door it occurred to me that Lisabeth almost certainly had assumed it would be a woman.

'Mr Fitzroy? You called about a computer problem.'

'And you're the answer to my prayers. Do come in, it's upstairs, first on the right.'

I wondered if I should offer to give The Computer Kid a hand with the big gunmetal case he was lugging, but he seemed fit enough to manage the stairs with it, though he did break stride and hesitate when he came to Lisabeth still standing in the doorway of Flat 2.

I thought she was going to say something, but instead she just shook her head and walked backwards silently and very slowly into her flat. For once I couldn't tell what she was thinking, and I was rather glad of that. I was sure she had been expecting me to meet and greet a woman, and the fact that it wasn't a woman, but a slim, bespectacled Asian youth, probably surprised her.

The fact that he was still wearing his school uniform really threw her.

'That's not a computer, that's a CD player.'

'Really, is that where I've been going wrong?'

I closed the flat door and leaned my back against it.

'This is a wind-up, isn't it?' said The Computer Kid. He pushed his glasses further up his nose with his left forefinger. They were gangsta glasses, with oval lenses and a big frame curving round his face like ski goggles. They could have been a fashion statement or they could have had a practical use, like they wouldn't fall off when he was bending over the intestines of a computer. They were certainly expensive and the school uniform was too, but then it was from a posh school.

'I wouldn't wind you up, Stephen, I need your expert advice.'

'So where's your PC then, and I don't mean that mangy pussy cat.' Springsteen automatically moved closer to him. 'How do you know my name anyway?'

'Wasn't it on your calling cards? The ones in the shop windows?'

'No it isn't. Now tell me what's going on here, or...' He hefted his metal suitcase, still in his right hand, and looked down at Springsteen mooching towards his legs. '...the cat gets flattened and I start screaming "Pervert" at the top of my voice.'

'I can't stop you screaming,' I said, pulling Ossie's notebook out of my pocket and rooting around for a pen. 'But I wouldn't try and touch the cat. That wouldn't sound good in court.'

It wouldn't sound good down at Casualty when they tried to staunch the bleeding either.

'So who's going to court?'

He didn't sound worried and his expression, as vacant as any teenager's when dealing with someone outside their peer group, didn't change.

I found the biro I had stolen from Veronica's desk, pulled the top off with my teeth and wrote 'Cat' in the notebook. The Computer Kid didn't seem particularly worried by this.

'Maybe both of us,' I said, 'but I'll be in the witness box.'

'Seeing as how you enticed me here under false pretences, I think you're the one who should be considering your legal position very carefully, as I am a minor.'

'Of course you are.' I made another note. 'I was forgetting that your father is a solicitor, isn't he? Will he be defending you do you think?'

Still no reaction. Cool kid. I flipped a page in the notebook and began to read the notes I had made about five minutes before his arrival, from my talk with the Features Editor of the *Hackney Gazette* that afternoon.

'Just let me refresh my memory,' I said because I thought that sounded official. 'Yes, here we are. Vikram Danks, solicitor, pillar of the Asian community, assistant treasurer of the Hackney and Stoke Newington Conservative Club, member of the Council of Governors of Homerton University Hospital Foundation Trust and said to be a potential candidate in the next local elections.'

'So?'

The Computer Kid put down his metal case, folded his arms across his chest and stared at me. He wasn't exactly shaking in his trainers yet. Springsteen ambled across the floor until he was within sniffing range of the case.

'So I didn't get a chance to find out if he listed ham radio among his hobbies.'

'You're a bleedin' cherryhead, mate,' said The Computer Kid. It was probably an expression he'd picked up in the playground. 'I don't have to listen to this.'

He dropped on to one knee and snapped the catches on the metal case, opening back the lid to reveal an interior of foam rubber with cut out slots for bits of equipment, just like a professional photographer would use to protect his lenses. I recognised two different sorts of flash drives, a stack of re-writeable CDs, a pair of thin pliers and a small canister with an aerosol nozzle that could have contained WD 40 for all I knew. There was even a cushioned pocket for a mobile phone, which he reached for and flipped open, pointing it at me like a stun gun from *Star Trek*.

'I can have a picture of you sent back to my computer at home before you can touch me,' he said defiantly, though still keeping cool.

'I have no intention of touching you, Stephen, I just wanted a chat about ham radio equipment. We can go chat in front of your father if you prefer. Is he at home tonight? Let's see,' I

consulted my notebook again, 'you live on Charnock Crescent, over by London Fields, don't you?'

'You know a lot,' he said, keeping the phone pointed up at me. Springsteen strolled over to take a suspicious sniff of it and for the first time that evening, probably that year, The Computer Kid looked slightly worried.

'Call your moggy off, mister. I don't want cat hairs in my equipment case.'

'It's his flat, I'm afraid, and I wouldn't make any sudden moves.'

Which of course he did. The youth of today, they just don't listen do they?

He transferred the mobile phone to his left hand and reached into the case with his right, grabbing for the small aerosol canister which had a long thin plastic tube for a nozzle.

'I really wouldn't do that,' I said.

Springsteen was still intrigued by the phone/camera, probably trying to judge if he was in focus or not, when The Computer Kid took leave of his senses and squirted the aerosol into his face and whiskers.

I suppose it could have been mace or pepper spray or even the WD 40 oil I had originally thought it was. It might even have been deodorant. All would have been nasty and, in such a case, much against all my principles, I would have had to beat the little shit to a pulp.

Fortunately, the aerosol contained only compressed air, used for blowing bits of broken biscuit and cigarette ash out of all those nooks and crannies in a computer keyboard. So it proved relatively harmless, at least to Springsteen if not to The Computer Kid.

It did take him by surprise and then he sneezed, which sent a wave rippling down his fur, all the way to his tail. Then he was moving too fast even for the digital camera in the phone to pick him up, though if it did sound it probably caught the menacing growl just before he slashed at the hand holding the phone with his claws and in the same fluid move sank his teeth into the hand holding the aerosol.

Before young Master Danks has started to howl in pain, Springsteen had cleared the open metal suitcase and was heading for the kitchen.

JD.

Job done.

'How long is it since you had a tetanus booster?' I asked helpfully. It was something I was used to asking in Stuart Street.

The Computer Kid sat on the floor cross-legged, dabbing at the punctures in his skin with a tissue.

'I did try and warn you,' I said, 'he doesn't like sudden movements.'

'Bloody animal.'

'Now, don't sulk. You started it.'

'You conned me into coming here and you set that untrained beast on me.'

'"Untrained beast"? That'll sound good in court, until they hear it's a cute little pussy cat.'

I didn't bother to tell him that Springsteen was certainly older than he was. And hadn't really ever been 'cute'.

'What do you keep talking about court for? Just what is going on in that head of yours? What's this all about?'

'I keep telling you, but you just don't want to listen. It's about ham radio.'

'I don't know nuffin' about no ham radio,' he said and though he spoke quietly, I could tell that his voice was regressing back to his primary school.

'I'll tell you something, Stephen, neither do I. In fact I think it's a bit of a geeky hobby where all you get to do is talk to other geeks. Still, a lot of hobbies are like that but people do get obsessed with them. They begin to see things that aren't there: like bargains on eBay.'

'Oh.'

'Yes "Oh". You've been a naughty boy, haven't you?'

'Don't know what you mean.'

'I think you do. I'm not sure what the proper charge would be, but I'm sure they'll find something under the Theft Act, the Sale of Goods Act, the Computer Misuse Act, the Data Protection Act, the Cruelty to Animals Act, and, of course, those nice people at eBay will want a word, not to mention the nice people at Western Union.'

'You sound like my PD teacher,' he whispered with a hint of defiance, 'and you can't prove anything in court.'

'I don't intend going anywhere near a court.' Now I had his attention. 'I'm going to tell your Mum and Dad on you. Now don't look at me like that, I'm sure your father will understand. He must be very proud of his son the computer prodigy.'

I made a show of consulting the notebook.

'*I think, even at this tender age, Stephen is a sure-fire candidate for Cambridge, such is his grasp of Computer Science.* That was your headmaster, speaking to the *Hackney Gazette*, so it must be true. You don't want to spoil press coverage like that, do you?

'Well, your Dad certainly won't. I hear Vikram Danks is the coming man in local politics. It can't be good for him if the story gets out that his son's little eBay scam has deprived a disabled ham radio operator of a vital piece of equipment, not to mention nearly £500.'

'Disabled?'

'Yes, since he was confined to a wheelchair, Rabbi Oesterlein finds that his radio is his only link with the world outside his room.'

'Rabbi?'

I wondered if I'd overdone it, but hell, he was an impressionable kid so I should impress him.

'He's quite well known, I'm told. Some of his London relatives were incensed when they heard how he'd been robbed – yes, robbed, Stephen, it's an ugly word isn't it?'

'You sure you're not my PD teacher?'

I ignored him, not wanting to have to ask what a PD teacher was.

'You're not listening again. What I'm telling you is that there are people in Hackney looking for you, Stephen. If you don't believe me, ask Roger Da Gama at the convenience store where you rent your postbox.'

That hooked him.

'Have you been round there today? Yes, I think you have. Notice the shop window? Anything unusual about it? You ought to consider your position very carefully, young Stephen.'

'What are my options?' he sighed. A bright lad.

'You've got just the one,' I said, working on the principle that the youth of today has far too much choice. 'Give me the £470 you scammed out of Rabbi Oesterlein for the radio transceiver he never got, and I lose all interest in having a chat with your father. Face it, Stevie boy, there are some things parents are better off not knowing.'

'And that's it?'

'That's all I want, a straight refund. If eBay or Western Union send the heavies round, you're on your own. Maybe you should cool it with the Internet scams for a while, say until you've got a student loan to pay off. Just out of interest, how many times have you pulled that stunt?'

He didn't answer that. He said:

'I don't even know what a transceiver is and I certainly didn't know this Oesterlein guy was a Rabbi.'

How could he?

Neither did the Oesterlein guy.

I gave The Computer Kid a lift to his house on Charnock Crescent. He said that his mother would be relieved to see him getting safely home by taxi. I even supplied him with an Elastoplast to put over his scratched hand.

The house was big and impressive, with steps up to the front door and lights on in all the windows.

'You'd better come inside if you want your money,' he said as I pulled up to the kerb.

'Will the family be in?'

'Looks like it, but hey, no sweat. You're a cab driver waiting for your fare and I left my wallet at home. What could be more normal? They won't bat an eyelid.'

I was impressed with the lad's logic and also the fact that he had a wallet with £470 in it.

'They won't think it odd, inviting a taxi driver into your bedroom?'

'If you think you're going anywhere near my bedroom, then you are a perv. Front room downstairs, that's my office. No one goes in there except our cleaning lady.'

He may have had his own office and a 'flying doctor' computer repair business whilst still only thirteen, but he wasn't allowed a key to the door. I half expected a butler to answer his ring on the doorbell, but it was a tall, clean-shaven Indian wearing a white shirt, blue tie and pinstripe-suit trousers held up with blue braces. He had a mobile phone clamped to his ear and was talking in a language I didn't understand and couldn't properly identify, but might have been Gujarati or Urdu. There was a time, when I lived in Hackney, I could swear in eight recognised Indian languages and one sub-dialect. Nine, if you counted English.

The man I presumed to be Vikram Danks waved his son into the house without pausing in his phone call. His son said something to him in yet another language, pointed at me and then pointed at Armstrong parked out on the road.

His father nodded vigorously, smiled politely at me and indicated I should come in and make myself at home. He seemed a nice guy for a solicitor.

The Computer Kid's office was a fairly typical den for a modern thirteen-year-old boy: one desk, one chair, three computers and two shelves full of computer manuals but no real

books. There were posters Blu-Tacked to the wall of course –
there always are – but these were not the usual suspects. No
footballers, pop stars or supermodels here. Instead, they all
featured cars: lots of them and all were Ferraris. I recognised the
Testarossa, the Berlinetta and a couple of Dinos but then I lost
track.

Stephen took down a large manual with the title *Java Script
Made Easier* from the shelf. My instinct was to ask 'easier than
what?' but I resisted the urge. The manual wouldn't have told
me, however, as Stephen had carefully hollowed out a secure
hidey-hole in the central couple of hundred pages, from which
he produced a roll of notes the size of a hamster straining inside
a thick rubber band.

'You have done this before, haven't you?' I said, trying to
keep the admiration out of my voice.

'It's a perfect victimless crime,' he said, starting to count out
notes on to the desk.

'No it bloody isn't.' I thought about Ossie Oesterlein who
would by now be on his way to dinner with Laura and then on
to Madame Jo-Jo's. 'Just because you never get to meet or even
see your victims, it doesn't mean they don't suffer terribly.'

'Suppose not,' he grunted. 'But they really are gullible, as well
as greedy. How did you find me anyway?'

'Not allowed to say, young sir, trade secrets and all that. Just
bear in mind I did it without a computer.'

Even as I said that, the main computer on his desk emitted a
bleeping noise. He stopped counting out notes and picked up a
wireless mouse, clicking until the desktop view on the monitor
cleared and another image came up.

'What the hell is that?' he said to himself.

I knew immediately. It was a photograph he had taken on his
mobile phone back at Stuart Street. A photograph he must have
taken and sent accidentally. It wasn't easy to make out if you
didn't know what it was, but through the black and grey blur I
could recognise Springsteen's right paw slicing through the air

just before the moment of impact. And was that just a flash of canine tooth in the background?

'Turn it into a screen-saver; show everybody that you're a cat lover.'

'Yeah, right,' he said but I think I saw a flicker of a smile.

'There's four hundred and eighty,' he said as he offered me a wedge of notes. The roll he had counted from didn't seem to miss them.

'I said four seventy.'

'Ten for the taxi.'

'Fair enough.'

'Useful set of wheels, those. I mean, having a black cab in London must come in handy.'

'It does,' I agreed but I didn't want to give this kid any more ideas. 'You really should find a new hiding place for that bank roll, you know.'

'Just as soon as you've gone,' he eyeballed me.

I glanced at his poster display.

'You saving up for a Ferrari, then?'

He pointed to one of the posters showing a classic (i.e. more than ten years old) red sports car.

'That's the one I fancy. The 246 GTS. That one's a 1973 model. I reckon I'll have saved up enough by the time I'm old enough to get a licence.'

I didn't know about that but I was pretty sure he would be driving a Ferrari before I was.

Chapter Fourteen

The next morning I drove a bald head with a hangover inside it to the station and made sure it was pointed north.

There was absolutely no reason why I had to chauffeur Ossie Oesterlein to King's Cross. The hotel could have called him a genuine cab or he could have walked it in ten minutes flat.

But I wanted to make sure that he had picked up the envelope containing £470 which I had left at reception the previous evening whilst he was out on the town, and of course I wanted to stress that I had been absolutely true to my word in recovering his cash. There was also the bonus, despite Veronica's sour face, that it got me out of the office for the morning, as I had things to do.

After my negotiations with The Computer Kid and a quick detour to Ossie's hotel, I had gone home to darkest Cambridgeshire to find Amy, wearing a white boiler suit, squatting in front of the television doing stretching and breathing exercises. She had a DVD playing but it wasn't an exercise video, it was *Casablanca* which just happens to be the favourite film of both of us: she likes it for the sparkling on-screen chemistry and cruelly restricted love scenes between the Humphrey Bogart and Ingrid Bergman characters; I like it for exactly the same reasons but between Bogart and Claude Rains.

'You're early,' she said without taking her eyes from the screen.

'I told you I wouldn't be late,' I said, trying to think if we had any beer in the fridge.

'But I didn't *believe* you. Not when young Miss Sheridan let on you were going to Madame Jo-Jo's.'

'Who's Miss Sheridan?'

'Laura Sheridan, the doe-eyed brunette who works with you,' breathed Amy between pelvic thrusts.

'How did you know her surname?' I asked automatically, kicking myself for admitting that I did not.

'She's listed as an operative on the R & B Investigations website.'

There was a website?

'I never intended to go to Jo-Jo's. Laura took a client, well, not a client as such, more a colleague.'

'Did this colleague know it was a transvestite cabaret bar? Did young Laura?'

I looked at my watch.

'They do now. Is there anything to eat?'

'I picked up some Cajun chicken and salad when I was in Cambridge getting your £500 float this afternoon. And I got you some beer. You can't say I don't love you.'

'As if.'

'And by the way, your father rang.'

'Now what?'

'Nothing, he sounded fine, quite chipper in fact. He checked out of the hospital this morning and he's back in his flat. Kim collected him in a cab, though he says she wore a hoodie the whole time in case there were any press photographers around. He seemed a bit disappointed that there weren't.'

'He always was a bit of a media tart.'

'He mentioned something about you running an errand for him.'

'It's on my To Do list. I just don't get a minute to myself these days; it's work, work, work.'

To be sociable I ate from a plate balanced on my knee sitting on the sofa and watched the television screen over her shoulder as she continued her exercise routine.

'What's young Laura like?' she said suddenly, out of the blue, in the middle of one of her squat thrusts. I cursed myself for bringing her the roses; I might have known it would make her suspicious.

'She's one of our graduate trainees,' I said through a mouthful of lettuce, 'young, and she is doe-eyed and brunette, though I don't know how you knew. Bright, keen to learn, young, independent, fairly reliable. Did I mention young?'

'I think she's got the hots for you.'

'Me? How do you work that one out, you never actually having met her.'

'It was all in her voice. I bet she gives you *that* look when you're not watching.'

'*What* look?'

'One like that,' she said pointing to the screen.

Casablanca had reached the point where Ingrid Bergman was pleading with Sam to 'play it for me'.

'She doesn't look at all like Dooley Wilson,' I said.

'Wrong!'

'What do you mean wrong?'

'The *right* thing to say to your wife who is stuck out here on the prairies, miles from a decent shopping experience, who is pregnant, who can't smoke or drink and is rapidly going spare with boredom, is that she *does* look like Dooley Wilson.'

I realised I had finished the bottle of Dos Equis I had been drinking, but decided this was perhaps not the time to go and get another.

'What's up, babe?' I got down on the carpet with her and put an arm around her shoulders. 'You're not having second thoughts are you?

'About what? The baby, the house or you?'

'Any or all of the above.'

She shook her head in my face and I tasted her hair.

'Oh, don't worry about me, I'm just depressed. All the books say I should expect to be. I think I'll have a T-shirt made up saying "Next Mood Swing: Five Minutes". It's just that everything is suddenly so different. I mean, me staying at home tending the Aga and you going out to work every day. I'm positively jealous. How bizarre is that?'

'It's pretty strange,' I agreed, 'but I'm getting used to the commuting and I think I could make quite a success of this job and get to enjoy it if I stick at it and put my heart and soul into it.'

'Do you mean that?'

She looked up at me from under her fringe. It was probably a *'that'* sort of look.

'No, not really.'

Then she smiled.

'Thank God for that, I thought you were going soft on me. Let's go to bed and you can tell me all about your day at the office.'

'You want to hear about my day at the office?'

'No, not really.'

For once, no one said anything when I rolled into the office just after 10 a.m.; in fact they were all so polite and smiley-smiley that I was instantly suspicious. I said in a loud voice that it would be a good idea if Laura helped me make coffee for everyone and once I had her in the kitchen I asked what was going on.

'Nothing's going on,' she said. 'What makes you think there is?'

'I'm an hour late and no one has so much as raised a plucked eyebrow.'

'We knew you'd be late in.'

'You did? How?'

'Amy rang in, talked to Veronica. She said you'd been working late and she had a load of tasks lined up for you in the new house, so basically it was her fault you had overslept.'

'I always knew that sleeping with the owners would pay dividends.'

'Yeah, it's all right for some isn't it? Nobody cares that I only got three hours' kip last night, or makes allowances for my hangover and I bet no one is going to help me do my outrageous expenses claim for last night.'

'I can help you there,' I said cheerfully. 'How did it go?'

'It was an education,' she said, thinking about it.

'I bet they don't have places like that in Huddersfield,' I said.

'I meant for me; I've no idea what Ossie thought of it all. He seemed to be enjoying himself well enough when I left to catch the night bus home.'

'Taxi,' I corrected her.

'Excuse me?'

'You took a taxi home, according to your expenses. Right?'

'But then I would have got a receipt,' she said, wide-eyed and innocent.

'I can help you there,' I repeated.

I gave Laura a five minute tutorial on creative expense accounting and then stuck my head around Veronica's office door to tell her I was going to check up on Ossie. She scowled at that and muttered that he was a big boy now and could surely find his own way home. I agreed, but said I had to make sure he was happy with the outcome of his 'reciprocal' case which I just happened to have cleared up for him in record time and therefore he wouldn't be billing us for his time on the Ellrington case.

Veronica supposed that would be all right then and asked if I had decided whether or not to tell James Ellrington that we had found Margaret Anne Pennington, née Hayes. I had said I didn't think we had an option if we were a professional business. Wasn't the customer always right?

'Not as often as you'd think,' she had said enigmatically.

* * *

I rang Ossie's hotel to learn that, although he had officially checked out, he had not, unlike Elvis, left the building. A cautious receptionist said she thought she could find him in either the coffee shop or the bar and I asked her to get a message to him that a taxi was on its way.

'Thought it would be you,' he said as he slung his bag into the back seat of Armstrong then climbed in after it.

He seemed to be dressed exactly as the day before apart from having no cravat and no hat, but I wasn't going to ask.

'Did you get the money I left?'

'Aye, I did, though it was bloody careless leaving it at reception like that.'

'It was in an envelope,' I protested. And I had made sure that the night porter I had left it with had seen me arrive in Armstrong. If something was delivered by a London cab driver, few people questioned it. It was almost as good as being a policeman sometimes.

'You have any trouble with the little toe-rag?'

'Not at all. Very quick to see reason he was, no thumping required.'

'Did he say why he was cheating innocent buyers on eBay?'

'Partly because he can and partly because he's saving up for…er…for driving lessons.'

'Bloody Nora,' sighed Ossie. They were his last words on the subject.

'How was your night out with Laura?'

He cleared his throat and seemed to have difficulty doing so.

'She's a nice lass, sure enough, but no stamina. She wimped off about two o'clock.'

'What did you think to the club?' I asked, checking in the mirror to catch his reaction.

'Different,' he said, rubbing a hand across his chin as if to check if he had remembered to shave. 'Don't think it would catch on up north, mind you. Not in Huddersfield anyway, it would be more of a Manchester thing.'

And I thought those would be his last words on that subject as well.

Before we made the station, I pulled in near a pharmacy and asked Ossie to do me a favour and pick up a prescription for me. He grunted his displeasure but I told him it was against the Hackney Carriage By-Laws of 1888 to leave a passenger in an unattended cab on double yellow lines in a bus lane and he reluctantly agreed, taking my father's prescription and the three £10 notes I handed him.

He was back within two minutes, thrusting a paper bag at me and obviously anxious to make a quick getaway.

'There was no change,' he said grumpily. 'And I got some bloody funny looks in there. Those are fookin' expensive tablets if you ask me.'

'You're absolutely right; in so many ways,' I agreed.

On the concourse at King's Cross, we shook hands and he hefted his bag and checked the big departure board to get the right platform.

'If you're ever up north, look me up and we'll go out for a night on the pop.'

'If I'm up north and at a loose end, you'll be the first I'll call,' I said, thinking: only if The Samaritans are engaged.

'And if you're ever in that fancy club of yours down Soho,' Ossie spoke without making eye contact, 'you can ask if they've found my hat. One of the waitresses might know where it is. Little blonde thing with big boobies, called Carl.'

Instead of going back to the office, I drove down into Westminster to my father's flat in Morpeth Terrace and as it was by now approaching lunchtime, I toyed with the idea of picking up a pizza to take with me but in the end was rather glad I didn't as Kim McIntosh was in the flat, slaving away over a hot stove.

The house porter (it was that sort of a block of flats) had recognised me and buzzed me in and Kim had left the flat door ajar. From the kitchen there came the sound of a radio playing the Kaiser Chiefs, although it may have been Arctic Monkeys, it was difficult to keep up these days. Wafting on the music came a variety of savoury smells: onions, garlic, meat and possibly nutmeg.

Kim was stirring with a wooden spoon in a deep frying pan on the electric range; another saucepan held a bubbling white sauce. She was wearing a blue and white hooped top and stonewashed 501s, both protected by a long green cook's apron bearing the logo *Hoskin's Brewery*, which was one of my father's treasured possessions.

'What's all this, then?' I announced myself. 'I thought you were a student. Why are you not doing pot noodles?'

'I lost the recipe for boiling water, so I'm making a lasagne from memory. You do use nutmeg, don't you?'

'It's the secret ingredient, so if I told you to use it, I would have to kill you.'

She laughed and whooshed a can of tomatoes into the pan. I don't know if her cooking was improving my father's recovery, but her laughter certainly would.

'Are you going to risk joining us? There's plenty and I'm not using any salt, so it'll be healthy even if it tastes crappy. Kit...your father...doesn't have much of an appetite at the moment. It's probably the drugs he's on.'

'Which reminds me, I've some more for him. Where is he?'

'He's in the study, trying to read up on hypertension. Knowledge is power, he says, so he's reading everything he can find about stroke and blood pressure. He seems determined to become the perfect patient. I've never seen Ki...your father... concentrate on anything so hard before.'

'It's all right, you know.'

'What is?'

'To call him Kit. I know he's my father, you don't have to keep reminding me. And you should hear some of the names I call him.'

She smiled and went back to some furious stirring.

'It's not his name that's a problem, it's you.'

'Me?'

'It's just that I find talking about your father and me, in front of you, is a bit weird. Has he talked to you about us?'

I instinctively felt for the pills in the pharmacy bag in my jacket pocket.

'No!' I said, rather too quickly.

'He hasn't mentioned that we were planning on getting married?'

'Oh, that. Of course he's mentioned *that*.'

'And how do you feel about that?'

She concentrated fiercely on her cheese sauce.

'What on earth has it got to do with me? You're both grown ups, over 21 and know your own minds.' Even as I said it, I was thinking that my father only qualified under one of those three criteria. 'In the words of the Greek goddess of victory: just go for it.'

She smiled at that and looked at me, still stirring.

'So you're cool with things?'

'Will I have to call you Mother?'

She whipped the wooden spoon up like a rapier and pointed it at me, a blob of white sauce dripping down her front on to where her chest strained at the green apron.

'Don't you frigging dare!'

That was a relief. I couldn't handle another Mother.

Instead of a 'Hello' or even a 'What are you doing here?' the first thing my father said was: 'Did you get my prescription filled?'

I was mildly curious to know if he would have greeted me like that if Kim had been there and not laying tectonic plates of pasta in an ovenproof dish.

'Yes I did. And good morning and my, you're looking well. You've obviously not telephoned dear Mama have you?'

'How do you know I haven't?'

'Because you look guilty.'

'I meant to, it's just the stroke…it makes you…slower. I get tired so easily now.'

I held up the bag from the pharmacy and shook it so he could hear the box inside rattling.

'Probably not a good idea to use these then,' I suggested.

He held up his hands in surrender. It was good to see he could use his left side again, even if the hand was shaking.

'You'd hit an invalid, wouldn't you?' he snarled. 'Get me a phone, I'll ring her now.'

'My God, I didn't realise what a bargaining chip four little blue tablets could be,' I taunted him and his expression turned to pure outrage.

'Four? That fucking consultant only gave me four?'

'Remember your blood pressure, Dad, calm down. You don't have to phone Mother. I knew you wouldn't, so I've arranged for you to have a nice day out at the seaside where you can tell her all the news face-to-face. I've even laid on suitable transport, door-to-door, which I think you'll approve of,' I said, thinking of Jane Bond's Aston Martin.

'I don't know why you're trying to kill me, Fitzroy, you know there's nothing in the will.'

'Come on, Dad, grow up and face the music. You've got to tell her about Kim, anyway. You haven't done that yet, have you? You've probably not even told her about the stroke, she might have wanted to come down and nurse you through your rehab.' He winced violently at that. 'And we had a deal that you would tell her she was going to become a grandmother. Do it all at once: one-stop shopping. Get it all off your chest. It won't kill you, it will make you strong.'

'This is your mother we're talking about, isn't it? I'm going to need a bodyguard.'

'I've thought of that as well.'

* * *

That afternoon, as I hacked it back to Shepherd's Bush, I had a sense of things finally coming together. My father was visibly improving and, under Jane Bond's strict supervision, he would soon have the Mother situation sorted. Between us, Ossie Oesterlein and I had discovered the whereabouts of James Ellrington's long-lost girlfriend (though I hadn't actually checked that she was still alive) and Ossie's 'reciprocal' case was done and dusted. A few loose ends to tie up, a report to write, some expenses to fiddle and the odd invoice to send out and that would be that. Surely I was due a few weeks' holiday by now.

Judging by the black looks I got when I returned to the office, the influence of Amy's sick note that morning was obviously waning.

Laura had a pack of Paracetamol tablets on her desk and was nursing a bottle of mineral water. She looked the most approachable.

'Why is everybody giving me the evils?'

'Everyone wants to know if you're going to play Cupid and put the star-crossed lovers in touch with each other,' she said.

'Is there any reason why I shouldn't?'

She shrugged her shoulders and then winced as if it had inflamed her hangover.

'No reason. It's your case, your judgement call.'

'Hang on a minute,' I said loudly so that Lorna and Veronica in her office could hear. 'James Ellrington hired us in good faith and paid good money, to find someone for him. We found them, we tell him. That's what we're supposed to do, isn't it?'

'If you're sure,' Lorna said.

'Sure about what?'

'Sure it's safe.'

'What do you mean "safe"? Why shouldn't it be?'

'Perhaps Margaret Anne Pennington doesn't want to see her old boyfriend after all these years,' Lorna said, rather smugly.

'Then she can tell him to piss off,' I said. 'We are talking about adults here, no, they're more than adults now, they're pensioners for Christ's sake. They're grown-ups, not teenagers in love.'

'She might still be uncomfortable, having an ancient boyfriend crawl out of the woodwork. It's almost like we've been helping him to stalk her.'

'Oh, get real, Lorna. Would we be having this conversation if Margaret Anne Pennington had asked us to trace James Ellrington?'

I didn't get an answer to that, just silence, so I stomped off to my desk and phoned James Ellrington.

'Mr Ellrington? This is Rudgard and Blugden, Confidential Investigations.'

'Is that Mr Angel? Do you have some news for me?'

'We think we may have. Would it be possible for you to call in to the office here, so we could discuss things?'

'Have you found her?' I heard him sucking in air with excitement as he spoke.

'We have a very strong lead and I need to discuss how we progress things,' I said diplomatically.

'I fail to see what could be up for discussion. I mean, you've either found her or you haven't.'

'Let's talk about it, shall we? When could you...?'

'I can be at your office for eight-thirty tomorrow morning.'

'I can't,' I said. I wasn't *that* keen. 'Can we make it eleven?'

'I'll be there,' he said and hung up abruptly.

I put the phone down and looked at it for a minute, then I recalled the name of the estate agents on the For Sale sign I'd seen outside Ellrington's house and called out to Laura, telling her to give them a ring.

'About what?'

'About a house on Manor Road in Merton Park. It's on their books, or it was. I wanted to know if they've had any offers yet. And do try and be charming.'

I didn't quite catch what she said in reply but the word 'swivel' was involved.

Half an hour later she stood in front of my desk, reading from a sheet of paper:

'The estate agents offered to fax over the details of Manor Road, but they said there may not be too much point. They've had four offers this week alone, all at or above the asking price. Seems like it's quite a desirable area.'

'What was the asking price?'

'£385,000, for a quick sale and it sounds as if it was. Why did you want to know?'

'No particular reason,' I said. 'Just making sure James Ellrington could pay the bill for my outstanding services.'

And it looked as if he might have enough change to buy his old girlfriend a really large bunch of flowers.

Chapter Fifteen

'Upwalters? Where exactly is that?' asked James Ellrington calmly and politely.

'It's in Dorset on what's called the Isle of Purbeck, which is on the coast near Poole and Bournemouth,' I told him.

'I know where Poole Harbour is.'

As someone who messed about in boats he would do, but I probably wasn't supposed to know he had a boat as he had never volunteered the fact.

'It's a beautiful part of the country. I used to go on holiday around there when I was a kid,' said Laura who was supposed to be taking notes of the meeting, not contributing tourist information. 'Corfe Castle is wonderful, and you could go across to Brownsea Island, which I think is where the Boy Scout movement first went camping.'

Laura was also present, so I had a witness to what I was telling James Ellrington in the certainty that Veronica was bound to blame me for anything which went wrong.

'Yes, it's a lovely coastline,' Ellrington said dismissively, looking at me across the desk, not her. 'And you're sure she lives there, at this Stone Cottage address?'

'As sure as we can be.'

'What do you mean by that?'

He was leaning forward in his chair, his arms hovering over my desk. He was freshly scrubbed and recently shaved, dressed

smart/casual in shirt and tie and green blazer, but I noticed that
the forefingers and thumbs on both hands had faded oil stains,
the sort of stain which washing with soap only fades to grey and
to get rid of completely you need a nailbrush or some chemical
solvent. It was the trademark of men who mess about with
engines.

'I meant that our latest evidence puts her at that address and
we've every reason to believe she lives there, but we haven't
physically *seen* her there or made personal contact.'

I noticed another thing about him. On his forehead where he
was rapidly receding, though not yet enough to be classed as
'follicley challenged', he was definitely sweating.

'So you're sure this is her address?'

'As I said,' I struggled, 'as far as we can tell. Short of actually
going there and knocking on the door, we are virtually certain
that Margaret Anne Pennington lives in Frome Street,
Upwalters.'

'Hayes,' he said quietly, staring distractedly at his hands.

'Excuse me?'

'Margaret Anne Hayes. She was Margaret Anne Hayes when
I last saw her,' he said, almost in a whisper.

'And you last saw her in...what? The 1970s?' asked Laura
slyly.

'No, 1963.' Ellrington was emphatic. Then he focused back
on me: 'Can you do that?'

'Do what?'

'Find out if she's really there, at that address.'

I reached for the phone and looked at my notes.

'We have a phone number for that address. 01929 55...'

'No!'

His hand shot out and grabbed mine before I could punch the
first number.

'I don't want you to call her like that, out of the blue, I want
you to go down there. Personally.'

'And do what?' I asked, genuinely at a loss.

'Simply confirm the situation; that it is her and that she lives there.'

I flicked a glance at Laura. She was chewing on the end of her pen and staring at Ellrington as if hypnotised. I would get no help there.

'And what do you want me to say to her, Mr Ellrington?'

He stared at me as if I was an idiot. His whole face became sharp and foxy and mean.

'I don't want you to *say* anything to her, just establish her whereabouts, perhaps see if she has a particular routine.'

'You mean sort of spy on her?'

Now I really did feel stupid.

'Isn't that what people like you get paid for?'

He had a point, but I felt on safer ground here.

'There will indeed be additional costs involved. Overnight accommodation in Dorset, car hire and my time of course.'

'None of that is a problem. When can you go?'

He was already getting up out of his chair. I looked at Laura again for help but she just pulled an I-don't-know face.

'I'm afraid I'm tied up this weekend,' I lied automatically, 'so I suppose sometime next week.'

'How about Tuesday? Tuesday would be good, wouldn't it?'

Good for what?

'Well, yes, I could go down to Dorset Tuesday and Wednesday if I can reschedule all my other meetings.'

Now Laura was giving me a 'what meetings?' look. She really wasn't being supportive at all.

'Excellent, that's settled then. You will ring me, won't you, as soon as you've identified her? Let me give you my mobile number as I may not be at home.'

He reeled off some numbers and Laura, earning her keep at last, wrote them down.

'Now I don't care how much this exercise costs, but I insist you call me on that number whilst you are in Dorset. I may have further instructions for you. Is that clear?'

'You're the client, Mr Ellrington.'

He nodded as if to say yes he was, and I'd better not forget it.

We shook hands as he was leaving and his palm was hot and damp.

'That bloke is well strange,' said Laura when he was gone. 'He didn't ask any of the obvious questions.'

'No, I noticed that,' I said, wondering what the hell she was talking about. I wasn't going to ask her to enlighten me. I didn't have to.

'I mean, after all these years and he doesn't ask if she's still married, if she's got kids or even grandchildren. He doesn't ask if she's got her health – I mean, we are talking about a woman who must be 62 by now – but does he ask after her? Does he hell, he just wants you to go in as the advance guard and "identify her" like a ranging shot, to clear the decks before he makes his move.'

'It's his money and if he wants to play it that way, we'll take it.'

'Oh come on, Angel, even you must have felt a bit creeped-out, or maybe it's not a man thing. But you'd think, after 42 years apart, the first thing he would ask, if he really is the sort of guy who's been carrying a torch for his first true love, would be *is she happy*?'

'Maybe he doesn't care whether she is or not.'

'What the fuck's that supposed to mean?'

'I don't know, yet,' I said.

On the plus side, Amy didn't mind that I would be taking a little break by the seaside, figuring that even I couldn't get up to much mischief with a 62-year-old woman in rural Dorset. And there was the added bonus that I would be there when Jane Bond chauffeured my father up to the Essex (but let's call it Suffolk) coast to Romanhoe for a show-down with my mother. Dorset was far enough away for me to be out of range of the fall-out from that one.

The surprise bonus was that Veronica actually approved of the idea; even though I wasn't one hundred per cent sure I knew what the idea was.

'You do have a plan, don't you?' she had asked.

'Of course I do,' I had told her.

My plan was to play it entirely by ear.

'There again, it might be simpler just to introduce yourself to Mrs Pennington and tell her what this is all about.'

'It certainly would,' I'd agreed, 'but it's not what the client wants.'

'Pfui!' was what she'd thought of that. 'This is a small village we're talking about isn't it?'

'I suppose so,' I had said, wondering where she was going with this.

'Well, even the best surveillance operatives get spotted by their subjects occasionally, so just how well are you going to blend in with the locals down in Thomas Hardy country? What if she challenges you to explain yourself? You're duty-bound to tell the truth.'

I was? Where was that written?

'I get the message, Veronica,' I had assured her. 'You're really quite devious when you want to be, aren't you? I'm impressed.'

There was a downside of course.

After all the lectures I had endured from Veronica about how Laura wasn't my personal assistant and how I shouldn't treat her like a secretary or an office junior, Veronica, a non-driver, had instructed her, a non-driver, to hire me a car for my out-of-town expedition. She had accepted all my arguments, like the fact that Armstrong would stand out like a sore thumb on the rolling Purbeck Hills, and that Ellrington had already agreed to foot the bill. Yet she was unwilling to let me do the hiring, suspecting, quite rightly, that I would use my old and distinguished friend Duncan the Drunken over in Barking.

As it happened, Duncan had a barely-used Mercedes S-class

available that week, but Veronica was able to announce that I was too late and Laura had already hired me a car from a local firm in Shepherd's Bush.

Which is why Tuesday morning saw me, teeth gritted, heading for the M3 in a cherry red Vauxhall Astra.

At least, by travelling mid-week, I wasn't going to be mobbed by flying columns of motorbikers heading for the south coast, or jeered at by grinning children in the backseats of people carriers as they overtook me with ease. I might even avoid the traditional weekend tailback of caravans as soon as the A31 leaves the New Forest.

Somewhere near Basingstoke I stopped at a big service station for a double espresso and a doughnut and then explored the mini shopping mall. I bought a Landranger Map covering Bournemouth and Purbeck, a bottle of mineral water, some nicotine chewing gum and, because the Astra came with a CD player but no CDs, a couple of bargain-bin compilation discs: *I Love Salsa* and *Punjabi Lounge*. I carefully folded all my receipts and tucked them into my wallet.

Once clear of Bournemouth, I followed signs for Wareham. Laura had booked me a room at The Priory Hotel there because 'it looked really posh' on the Internet and she was feeling guilty about hiring the Vauxhall for me. She had even programmed Ellrington's mobile phone number into my phone and made sure it was fully charged before I left Shepherd's Bush. I didn't care what Veronica said, it was nice to have staff.

Wareham turned out to be a town of two halves. A modern sprawl on the north bank of that schoolboy's favourite, the River Piddle, and the older half, an earth-walled Saxon town squarely occupying the land between the Piddle and another river, the Frome.

The site of an ancient priory was actually marked on my map, at the very southern edge of the old town, on the banks of the Frome itself, and so I headed for it, assuming, correctly as it turned out, that The Priory Hotel would be nearby.

As I nosed my way through narrow streets, I was half expecting to be dazzled by signs for Copper Kettle tea-rooms and badly lit antique shops, but instead I noted a plethora of Chinese and Indian take-aways, at least one kebab shop and what seemed to be dozens of pubs. There was also a shop with a pavement display of plastic spades and buckets, fishing nets on bamboo sticks and beach mats.

The Priory was certainly posh enough to justify its prices and my room had a view over the real ruined priory and a green and pleasant river meadow. The River Frome itself twisted away into the distance and, although not a wide river, seemed to have more small boats plying up and down it than cars on a stretch of the M25. The boats were making a better average speed as well.

When I had checked in, the pretty receptionist had asked if I had 'overnight moorings' and when I asked if that was what they called the car park round here, and that if it was then I'd found it, she had giggled an apology and said that she was so used to guests arriving by boat that she forgot people still drove cars.

I took the opportunity to ask her for directions to Upwalters, resisting the urge to say what quaint names these Dorset villages seemed to have, a platitude she would have heard a million times before. She directed me to cross the bridge leading out of Wareham and take the road for Corfe Castle and Swanage, which she said with a hint of reverence as if it was the thriving metropolis where all the action happened. But I wasn't to go to Corfe Castle (though it was well worth a visit); I had to take a side road to the right, possibly signposted to Creech, East Creech or perhaps Creech Bottom. Down the hill and through the woods and then the road forked at Cocknowle. Turning left would take me into Church Knowle, but right would lead me to West Bucknowle and the next village after that was Upwalters. The road signs probably wouldn't say Upwalters, but rather Kimmeridge or maybe even the Dorset

Coast Path. I would have gone too far if I found myself on the famous fossil beach at Kimmeridge or in the middle of a tank training exercise on the Ministry of Defence's extensive ranges around Lulworth Camp.

I thanked her and went to find the Astra, making a mental note to write to the Dorset Tourist Board to tell them they weren't paying her enough.

Leaving Wareham via the bridge over the River Frome, I was impressed with the view of the river meandering in great curves eastwards across the flat, marshy landscape, though for most of the vista I could only tell where the river was by the hundreds of yacht masts poking out above the reeds. Somewhere over to my left the Frome emptied into the enormous Poole Harbour where I knew I could catch a high speed ferry and be in the Channel Islands in time for tea, or St Malo or Cherbourg for dinner. It was a tempting thought; just the sort of thought I wasn't allowed to have any more.

Once I found the turning off the Swanage road, I left the afternoon tourist traffic behind me apart from a pack of suicidal cyclists determined to fill every inch of the narrow lanes which twisted through the dark woods and sunny fields filled with cows or sheep or sometimes both. When the signs began to point towards East Creech, the road started to rise quite steeply and run along an obvious ridgeway, the far end of which would, I guessed, be guarded by Corfe Castle. I lost all the cyclists on the incline and didn't see another vehicle until I cruised into Upwalters itself.

Frome Street turned out to be the main, and as far as I could tell, only street in Upwalters. It was lined with solid, low, stone cottages, each one having window boxes as if it was a local by-law. The doors of the cottages fronted the road, but the inhabitants were protected by a built-up pavement with a kerb two or three feet high, requiring steps to be cut into it at regular intervals. Such an arrangement certainly discouraged on-street parking as you'd need a tank to mount a kerb like that, but then again, the girl back at my hotel had said there was a tank training ground round here somewhere.

I scoped the village for some communal point where I might put my detective skills to work tapping into local gossip.

There was no village church that I could see, but there was a tiny Post Office (also offering newspapers, confectionery, toiletries, coal, kindling wood and video rentals according to the sign on the pavement) and, I discovered with relief, a local pub, though only an eagle-eyed and very thirsty tourist would have spotted it.

The Ilchester Arms didn't have a proper pub sign, rather a coat-of-arms chiselled into the stonework above the front door. A small painted sign said 'Entrance and Car Park and Beer Garden At Rear through Archway' but gave no warning of how narrow the entrance was. It was probably fine for the days when the visiting darts team from East Creech (or wherever) arrived in a horse and buggy, but it didn't make any allowances for motorised transport with a wider wheelbase than a Model T Ford.

I reckoned that the Vauxhall Astra could just about do it without scraping the paint off one or both sides, then thought why was I hesitating? It wasn't my car.

It was Sod's Law of course that the first vehicle I had seen in half an hour was coming straight at me, heading out of the archway as I was heading in.

It was a big green Land Rover complete with bull bars and a row of spotlights across the roof. It looked military and big and I didn't have room to argue with it, but if the driver could get that thing through the archway, what sort of a wimp was I worrying about an Astra?

Discretion being the better part of most things, I slammed the Astra into reverse and backed out into the road. The Land Rover, which had never actually stopped its progress, merely slowed down, nosed out and turned left to head down the road away from me. The uniformed driver held up a hand half in salute, half in a grateful wave and I noticed that it was a woman with her hair tied back in a thick pony tail. I also caught a glimpse of a logo of wavy lines painted on the driver's door and the stencilled words LULWORTH RANGERS, though I noticed as it pulled away in a splutter of exhaust fumes, that it had civilian rather than army number plates and, rather incongruously, stickers in the back window supporting the RSPB and the National Trust. Either the army was going soft or some of our better known charities were getting more militant.

I swung the Astra back into the archway with absolute confidence and, once through, discovered quite an extensive, but empty, car park. The original stone-built pub had been extended at the rear with a totally out-of-character single-storey conservatory romantically labelled the Function Room and there was a fenced-off area like a corral containing some battered plastic garden chairs and tables, all tinged with green mould. That I presumed was the Beer Garden, but all seemed deserted.

The pub itself was stone-floored and *olde worlde* in an authentic, rather than theme pub, way in that the dust on the tables and the smell of damp soot from the fireplace were quite genuine. There was a dart board on the wall in one corner, a bar billiards table in another and traditional black hand pumps on the bar. To encourage the passing trade, one wall had a large wire grille with pockets for leaflets for local attractions, including, curiously, coach trips to London's West End to see *Billy Elliot*. There was a blackboard near the bar which said 'Guest Beers' but the rest of it was blank, but on the plus side the bar top had several new, orange house bricks with real red-topped matches piled in their indents or 'frogs' which showed that smoking was still allowed and positively encouraged in Dorset pubs.

It seemed, though, that customers were not. For one dreadful minute I thought that the news of all-day licensing had not filtered down this far and that the pubs still closed in the afternoons, as they had since 1915.

Then there was rumbling from somewhere behind the bar and suddenly there was a short, ferret-faced man wearing a tweed waistcoat and a bright yellow bow-tie, glaring at me from between the beer pumps.

'The kitchen closed at two o'clock. We'll be doing food again at seven,' he snapped before I had even opened my mouth.

'That doesn't matter, I'd just like a drink please.'

What I should have said, of course, was 'Gimme four fingers of bourbon and some information', but I just didn't have the nerve.

'So what'll it be?' he asked, feigning interest.

I pointed to the nearest pump.

'I'll try a pint of Palmer's, please,' I said.

'It's off,' he announced, almost with glee.

'Then I'll have the Badger Bitter, please.' I pointed to the next pump.

'Barrel needs changing and the new one only came this morning. Won't have settled yet.'

I kept smiling and remained polite.

'Do you have any draught beer?'

'We've got Foster's and Guinness,' he said and I gave him his victory.

It was almost like being back in London.

'I'll have a pint of Guinness, please.'

He slammed a pint glass on the dispenser and snapped open the tap.

'That'll be £3.80 please.'

It was exactly like being back in London.

'Nice village,' I said, biting my lower lip whilst I waited for the stout to settle.

'It's quiet enough,' he grunted.

I glanced around and located the Gents toilet. I didn't want to go but I thought I might do a random bit of vandalism on my way out.

'Have you had the pub long?' I asked.

'Why? You looking to buy one?'

I wondered if he kept his Mr Congeniality Award next to his framed certificate from the Good Pub Guide.

'No, I couldn't stand the pace. I was just wondering if you knew the people round here.'

'I've been in this neck of the woods for thirty years and in this place for about five,' he said, finally handing over my pint, 'and not a day off for good behaviour.'

'Pub not trading well?' I asked though it was a question of who was I going to believe? Him or my own eyes?

'Not as well as I was led to believe when I bought into it. We're off the main tourist routes here and the food side of things has gone downhill since the wife left. I've tried to do theme nights but the reception's so bad round here, you need a satellite dish to get decent football on the box and they won't let me put one up in a conservation area, just like I couldn't get a music licence because the pub's part of the local estate leased to the National Trust. Same reason I can't put up a decent sign and they complained about the Christmas decorations last year.'

It was true: ask people the right way and they will tell you anything; sometimes when you haven't actually asked them.

'You ex-army?' I asked, guessing already that he was.

'Yes I am. Armoured Corps before it became bloody Logistics or whatever it's called these days. This place was to be my pension.'

'All your mates said they'd come and drink here, didn't they?'

'They did too, for a while. It was just like being back in the Sergeant's Mess in Lulworth Camp,' he said proudly.

'I bet it was,' I said, putting on my best fake smile. 'But the locals haven't supported you?'

'No they have not!' he blustered as if he had just realised the fact. 'And it's not as if there's another pub in the village. There isn't.'

'That's why I'd never go into the pub business; there's just no pleasing people.'

'You can say that again. What line of work are you in, then?'

'I'm a National Insurance Inspector.'

His reaction was, predictably, silence.

I have found, over time, that if you tell people you're a musician, they want you to play something for them. If you say you're in IT they want you to fix their computer or upgrade their Office package for free; a doctor, and they want you to take a look at an abscess on their leg; a lawyer and they want free advice; a bestselling author – they simply don't believe you. But if you want to be left alone, say you're a National Insurance Inspector, though with publicans, pretending to be a VAT Officer or, even better, an Environmental Health Inspector, tends to produce the most dramatic results.

'Do you know where Stone Cottage would be by any chance?' I asked casually, sipping my pint, which tasted distinctly musty. How on earth had he managed to ruin draught Guinness? That takes skill.

''Course I do. Out of here, turn left, last cottage before you leave the village.'

That's the other part of the trick, of course, tell them you're a National Insurance Inspector but immediately suggest you are looking for someone else, not them.

And, naturally, the sour little git behind the bar, who was already down in my book as a total misfit and sleaze monkey, couldn't be more helpful.

'That would be the Penningtons you would be after,' he said cheerfully.

I hid my face behind my pint and shrugged as if to say that I couldn't possibly comment.

'Pity you didn't come two minutes sooner, you just missed her.'

I put down my glass and reached into my pocket for a piece of nicotine gum.

'Missed who?'

'Maggie Pennington. She was here delivering me some new

leaflets.' He pointed to the rack of tourist information on the wall. 'Wouldn't stop for a drink, of course, that would be beneath her and her sort, but she expects me to give her leaflets out at no extra charge doesn't she? Just slaps a pile on the bar and pisses off. Throws that bloody Land Rover of hers around like she owns the place.'

'Would that be a green job with Lulworth Rangers on the side?'

'That's the one!' he said enthusiastically as if I'd made some great discovery.

'So what's a Lulworth Ranger, then?' I asked Ferret Face. 'Is that like a Texas Ranger?'

'No, but she acts like it is.'

Chapter Sixteen

The leaflets which 'Maggie Pennington' had left for free distribution to the hordes of customers visiting the Ilchester Arms were for something called the Tyneham Trail.

'It's a deserted village, only four or five miles over towards Lulworth. It's very popular with the tourists,' the publican had said, pushing one at me.

Glancing round the bar, I could see how a deserted village would be more popular with tourists than his pub. A night in a graveyard with flesh-eating zombies would probably attract more visitors.

I nosed the Astra out of the car park and turned left, following the direction the green Land Rover had taken. I made a point of slowing down as Upwalters began to peter out and there, on the left, was a thatched cottage with a small front garden protected by a stone wall about three feet high. On the garden gate was the legend Stone Cottage. It didn't look as if there was anyone at home, and I wasn't ready to pay a house call yet. I doubted that James Ellrington would count a fleeting glimpse of the driver of a disappearing Land Rover as a positive identification.

Once out of Upwalters the road rose quite steeply until it was running on what seemed, from the map, to be the curved backbone of the Purbeck Hills. Suddenly the landscape changed. The soft, dark woods and the meadows, where the wild flowers grew as high as a sheep's eye, were gone behind me. In front of me, as far as I could see, was gorse and heathland and green undulating hills where the sheep had to hang on for dear life, and then there was a white edging of chalk cliffs to the landscape and, beyond that, the sea.

There was even a parking space offering a free panoramic view as long as I promised not to camp overnight or start cooking on a barbecue; so I pulled the Astra off the road, took in the view and got my maps out.

The contour lines told me I was less than 600 feet above sea-level, but it seemed much higher as the view was spectacular and I had it all to myself. Due south of me, as near as I could guess without a compass or GPS, was Kimmeridge Bay and the famous Kimmeridge Ledges, which even I had heard of. That was where the white cliffs turned black with natural oil deposits and there was even an oil well marked on the map. Over to the west was a large bay shaped like a huge bite out of the coastline, albeit with slightly overlapping front teeth. This, it appeared, was known as Worbarrow Bay which contained something called Arish Mell, which may have been a cliff feature, or a smaller bay, or even a misprint from an Ordnance Survey map of one of the Outer Hebrides. Beyond Worbarrow, and out of my sight line, was Lulworth Cove, an ideally picturesque and almost perfect horseshoe-shaped harbour, and beyond that, over the hills, would be Durdle Door, the natural arch of limestone jutting out into the sea which had become the perfect icon for Dorset's Jurassic Coast. It was called that because of the richness of its fossil finds and not, as once maliciously rumoured, because of the average age of the population of Bournemouth.

My maps were also, worryingly, dotted with red letter warnings of Danger Areas to the left of me, to the right of me, and especially – in capital letters – in the exact direction I was heading. The warnings must refer to the army training ranges around here, I reasoned. They couldn't possibly be anything to do with me.

I located 'Tyneham Village' on my map and, judging by the contour lines, it was nestled in a hollow between the hills, near the sea but not visible from my scenic picnic spot because of the folds of the land, even though it could not have been more than three or four miles away as the seagull flew.

The leaflet I had picked up in the pub told me why I should take the Tyneham Trail. When the landlord of the pub in Upwalters had said it was a deserted village, I had assumed that meant a fairly ancient site: a fourteenth-century plague village or an eighteenth-century victim of the enclosure craze, when small farms were blitzed to make large ones.

In fact Tyneham had been a going concern as a village as recently as 1943, when it became a quite spectacular casualty of World War II in which it was totally destroyed by the enemy. The enemy in question, though, was not the Luftwaffe this time, but the British government, who decided that the parish of Tyneham was the ideal place to extend the army's tank driving schools and gunnery ranges.

Taking the church bells with them, the population of 252 souls were evacuated leaving over a hundred properties in the care of teenage conscripts driving Sherman Tanks with 'L' plates on them and trigger-happy artillerymen trying to get their eye in before the Normandy landings on the other side of the Channel.

Their deal with the War Office had been that they would be allowed back after the war and presumably compensated for any damage or unexploded shells left lying around. Of course that never happened, the army's Gunnery School seemed fond of the place and in 1948 issued a compulsory purchase order.

The village was left to rot, fall down and suffer vandalism and even arson, proving that even in beautiful Dorset, teenage yobs have to have something to do. Eventually the church and the tiny village school were repaired and restored as museums and access to the public was allowed again, for those curious to see a frozen segment of rural life from the 1940s.

Ironically because of the army's presence and the constant banging of big guns, the people might have been frightened away, but the wildlife had not. Since farming had not been allowed for sixty years, the local environment was also blissfully free of fertilisers, pesticides and all the other crap that humans bring with them to the party. It was now held up as a natural wildlife park in microcosm. The army had done an outstanding job protecting every known species of vole, tree, fern and herb, not only from Nazi invaders but from farmers, property developers and probably Dorset County Council.

There was no mention of the Lulworth Rangers on the leaflet though I had seen plenty of military signs about firing ranges at the side of the road, along with instructions about how the roads would be closed if a red flag was flying. Or perhaps that was open when the flag was flying. I began to wish I had paid more attention.

In truth, I was distracted by the scenic emptiness of it all. It really was quite stunning and, above all, calm. I decided never to moan about Toft End in Cambridgeshire being out in the sticks again. This really was the end of things and if you went too far, you could fall off the edge.

A nice place to retire to, for people who liked fresh air and scenery and weren't worried about not having a decent pub to call their own. People like Mr and Mrs Pennington, for instance.

Which brought me back to the matter in hand. It was four-thirty on a fine, sunny summer's afternoon. I was over a hundred miles from the office and my mobile was switched off. There was a warm breeze coming off the sea, the sort that makes your skin itch. I had a rented car with half a tank of petrol and I was wearing sunglasses. I was perfectly fixed to go chasing a ghost from the past.

And where better to start looking for a ghost than in a ghost village?

* * *

The road down to Tyneham, or 'Tigeham' as it had been recorded in the Domesday Book (it was a pretty thorough leaflet I'd been reading), was single track, steep and punctuated with sharp, blind bends. I met three cars coming up as I was going down, more than I'd seen all afternoon. This must be where all the tourists were, I thought, and when Tyneham finally came into sight I realised I was right.

The village was deep within a fold of the hills almost as if it had been deliberately hidden away from prying eyes for centuries. Even when the signs told me I was there, it seemed as if the place was just one big car park containing about two hundred cars, with dogs playing, kids running around and parents sitting on tartan rugs by their own exhaust pipes, drinking tea from Thermos flasks and realising that they looked just like their parents did twenty years ago.

But the village proper, or rather the shell of it, was off to the right, along the Tyneham Trail, bearing left after the village pond, where no cars were allowed. No cars except big green Land Rovers marked 'Lulworth Rangers'. I was on the right trail.

The Land Rover was parked next to a stone wall behind which was the husk of what had been Post Office Row. There was even an ancient telephone box, painted white, with filigree iron work on the top and the word TELEPHONE just in case the villagers hadn't known what it was. Curious, I went up to the box and peered in through the glass.

It was a genuine old phone box or at least it was good enough to fool someone who had only seen one in old black-and-white movies. There was the huge bakelite receiver with its thick brown wire, curled on its cradle, the dial with finger holes where you actually had to dial the numbers rather than pressing them, the metal money box with slots for coins far bigger than anything in circulation today and, of course, the legendary Button A which you pressed when you made a connection and Button B which you pressed to get your money back.

'It was hardly ever used,' a voice said behind me. 'Possibly never.'

'I'm sorry?'

I turned to face an elderly man wearing a green uniform with a badge on the breast pocket bearing the same Lulworth Rangers logo as on the side of the Land Rover. He was taller than me and fit, with the freshly-scrubbed pink complexion of someone who gets plenty of fresh air and a full head of wavy white hair, and he could have been old enough to have used the phone box in anger.

'The telephone,' he said, 'was only installed in November 1943, though the village had been petitioning for one for years. In December 1943, the entire village was evacuated as part of the war effort. Mebbe nobody ever got to press that Button A.'

It was the way the old man said 'mebbe' instead of 'maybe', betraying a faint trace of a Yorkshire accent that should have set the alarm bells ringing.

'I'm not sure British Telecom have actually improved their customer service record since then,' I said and he smiled at that.

'It was the Post Office in those days, not BT,' he said, 'but you've probably got a point.'

'And this was Post Office Row, was it?' I asked, not wanting him to wander off.

'Yes, that was the post office.' He pointed to the second shell of a building in a row of four cottages, or what was left of four cottages after their roofs, doors and windows had been removed. 'The end cottage was known as Shepherd's Cottage.'

'Let me guess,' I said. 'Because a shepherd lived there?'

'I can see nothing much gets by you.' There was the faint Yorkshire lilt again, buried but not dead. 'Shepherd Lucas he was called and it was said that what he didn't know about sheep wasn't worth knowing.'

'I'll assume that was meant as a compliment to him. Are you one of the official guides? You seem to know all the history of the place.'

'No, nothing so grand. All I do is clean up after the visitors.'

He jerked a thumb towards the car park which was slowly starting to empty.

'It's a bit like pulling a plug in a bath. Gets near tea time and they realise there's no refreshments provided here, so one or two start sneaking out and the rest follow on. Herd instinct I think it's called. They're all frightened that the fish and chip shops and the pubs will fill up before they get there.'

'So what time do you officially close?'

'We don't really. Dusk, I suppose. I mean, it's not as if there are many doors to lock, is it? And there's nothing much left to pinch. Our biggest problems are litter and lost dogs. You'd be surprised what people leave behind; we picked up 81 mobile phones last summer and not one person came back to look for one. We ended up giving them to charity.'

'Do you take out the SIM cards first?'

'The what?'

'Never mind; just a thought. Was there a pub in the village?'

'No, I don't think there ever was, but over there' – he pointed to the wood beyond the car park – 'is a track down to Worbarrow, which was a tiny settlement where they fished for mackerel and crabs. My guess is that a fair amount of smuggled booze found its way into Worbarrow Bay in the good old days.'

'The old days don't seem to have been so good to Tyneham,' I said.

'Nor to Worbarrow, which went the same way. There's very little left of it now. At least some of the Tyneham cottages are being restored slowly.'

He moved to the back of the Land Rover and opened the rear door. Inside was a variety of brushes, shovels and bin bags, with which he began to arm himself.

'Well, I'm on my early evening litter patrol. Are you on your own?'

'Yes, I was just passing and thought I'd have a look at the famous deserted village.'

'No one is *just passing* this place,' he said.

'No, you're right. I had some time to kill and I was in a pub in Upwalters and the landlord gave me a leaflet.'

I took the Tyneham Trail leaflet out to show him and he nodded and smiled.

'You were in the Ilchester Arms were you?'

'It could have been; it seemed to be the only pub around.'

'It's our local,' said the Ranger. 'Tom the landlord gave you that, did he?'

'Yes.'

'He's a miserable git isn't he?'

'Oh yes.'

The elderly Ranger was now snapping on a pair of latex surgical gloves and he saw me looking at them.

'Have to wear these nowadays, some of the things we have to pick up.'

'They should pay you danger money – or do you do it for the love of it?'

'No, they pay us. Not a lot and the taxman takes most of it, but it keeps us fit, gets us out of the house. If you're interested in the village, you should have a word with Maggie.'

'Maggie?' My voice was croaking for some reason.

'My wife. She's another OAP – Over Active Pensioner, that's what they call us round here. She'll be tidying up in either the church or the schoolhouse. Just follow the road along here and bear left, you can't miss it. Anyway, you've got the Tyneham Trail map there, haven't you?'

'What? Oh, yes. Maggie, you said?'

'You won't miss her. She's dressed in the same Jolly Green Giant uniform I am, except hers fits better. Mind you, I have to say that, I've been married to her for forty years.'

Forty-two, actually, I thought, but I didn't mention it.

* * *

I found Margaret Anne Pennington, née Hayes, alone in the churchyard. She was picking up day-old cigarette butts which had been stubbed out on a two-hundred-year-old gravestone and placing them in a plastic bucket, cursing under her breath. I heard 'Sodding smokers, how bloody *dare* they?' as I approached and was torn between startling her and allowing the further flow of invective.

Then suddenly she wasn't muttering, she was speaking out loud.

'Please treat the church and houses with care; we have given up our homes where many of us lived for generations to help win the war to keep men free. We shall return one day and thank you for treating the village kindly. Especially if your refrain from putting your bloody cigarettes out on someone's grave, you ill-mannered, uneducated, in-bred bunch of shits!'

'Maggie?' I said, from far enough away to be unthreatening.

She straightened up and said: 'Yes?'

'Your husband said I'd find you here.'

'Simon? Is there anything the matter with Simon?'

'Not at all. I was just chatting to him down by the old post office and he said you'd be here and that you were the fount of all knowledge on the village.'

She waved her plastic bucket at me.

'Well, I'm an expert on its rubbish,' she said, then she put a hand to her mouth. 'Oh dear, did you hear my little rant? It was actually something the villagers wrote in 1943, a notice they pinned to the church door as they were leaving. Well, the bit about treating the church and houses with care was, I sort of added the tirade against smokers who don't take their butts home with them.'

'I didn't know you allowed the ill-mannered, uneducated and in-bred into Dorset,' I said with a grin.

'Normally they are stopped at the Hampshire border,' she grinned back, 'but one or two get through occasionally. They let me in, for instance, though that was a few years ago now.'

'I went undetected for a whole day, but the Lulworth Rangers finally caught up with me.'

She looked down at her green uniform as if noticing it for the first time, then at me with a big smile.

'We always get our man.'

When she smiled I could see why one man had stayed 'got' for forty-two years and another wished he had been.

I knew she was sixty-two, or thereabouts, but she had taken such good care of her skin that she could probably lose eight or nine years in a police line-up. She filled the fairly shapeless green uniform in all the right places without any unsightly bulges. She looked slim and trim and healthy. Perhaps it was down to clean living and country air, in which case, I reckoned that my father was doomed.

'Is there anything I can do for you?' she was asking and I made an effort to concentrate.

'Not if you're busy, it's just that your husband said you knew all there was to know about the village.'

She looked at her small, square, gold wristwatch.

'Well there's a family of Dutch people looking round the church and they haven't seen the schoolhouse yet, which means they'll be here for ages yet. So if you want a quick guided tour, I'm sure I can manage one, though it's not part of the job description.'

'Exactly what is a Lulworth Ranger?'

'Basically we're part-time guardians of the countryside around Lulworth and this bit of the coast. We're a "partnership" organisation, whatever that means, but we get some funding from the army, the Environment Agency and the National Trust and, God bless it, the National Lottery. We pick up litter, report fallen trees or abandoned cars and stop the grockles' dogs from eating the local wildlife.'

'Grockles?'

'Sorry, tourists, visitors. It's what they call them down here. My husband's retired now, and it gives us something to do that's actually worthwhile and a damn sight more interesting than basket-weaving or playing bingo.'

'Are you from around here originally?' I asked innocently.

'Goodness me, no. Simon and I are both from God's own country.'

'Texas?'

She frowned at that.

'No, Yorkshire. Oh, I see what you mean – Texas Rangers.'

'Sorry. Have I just blown the free tour?'

'Not at all; come on, we'll start in the schoolhouse.'

The church and the tiny school, because they were in effect museums, were the only buildings in the village to have roofs, all the others were open to the elements and most reduced to a single storey. Some of the cottages, peeping through the trees in the dappled afternoon sunlight, looked like genuine casualties of war. Where doorways and windows had been removed, it looked as if a giant hand had pulled teeth from a stone mouth. My first impression was that the cottages of Tyneham had been individually and carefully bombed, for nothing remained of the interiors except, in one bizarre case, cast iron fireplaces on both the ground and first floors, even though the intervening ceiling/floor had disappeared and so one fireplace appeared half way up a wall, above another fireplace.

One particular ruin, called Rectory Cottages, was reduced to a single storey wall which had been buttressed to keep it upright at some point. The removal of the upper floor and windows had left a crenellated battlement effect. If it hadn't been surrounded by trees in full green leaf and backdropped by the rolling Purbeck Hills, it could have been the Alamo just before the final assault. There were other stretches of chest-high stone wall, some recently repaired, marking out long-forgotten boundaries in among the trees and long grass. They reminded me of some of the earliest battlefield photographs taken during the American Civil War, where one side would hunker down behind a stone wall and blast the hell out of the attacking side. It all added to the ghostly air of wartime devastation, but then the village *was* a scene of wartime devastation even if the battle of Tyneham had been fought without a shot being fired.

A complete circuit of the village with Maggie, even at a leisurely pace, didn't take much more than fifteen minutes and she assured me she had shown me everything there was to see. In fact, if she hadn't pointed out some of the ruins hidden among the trees I would have missed them completely.

The green Land Rover had moved from the fish pond at the end of Post Office Row but I could see it in the distance down the track near the woods at the far end of the car park. There were still dozens of cars parked up and a steady stream of tourists walking back up a path which seemed to run down the side of the woods.

'What's down there?' I asked Maggie, wanting to prolong contact for as long as possible.

'That's the path down to Worbarrow Tout,' she said, holding a hand up to shield her eyes from the sun.

'Worbarrow *what*?'

'Tout. Don't ask me, I just work here. It's the promantery... peromentry...prom...oh, bugger it, it's the headland which sticks out into the sea here in Worbarrow Bay. There used to be a little cluster of cottages and a coastguard station but it's almost all gone.'

'Oh yes, Mr Pennington mentioned it,' I said, sneakily inserting the surname which neither of them had mentioned. She didn't respond to it, but then again she didn't deny it. I would take that as cast-iron confirmation of her identity when I wrote my report for James Ellrington, or rather dictated it while Laura typed.

'The army have got giant targets down there on the landward side,' she continued. 'You can walk the path right down to the sea or there's another one through the wood. There's nothing much to see down there, except the sea, but it's a nice walk and

I take the girls down there every morning for their nine o'clock constitutional.'

'The girls?'

'My dogs: substitute daughters, I suppose, or grand-daughters. We've always had dogs and they've all been bitches. If we'd ever had real daughters they would probably have been bitches too. Have you got children?'

I was slightly startled by that. It wasn't something I got asked regularly.

'No, not yet,' I said honestly.

'I've always thought them over-rated,' she said and I couldn't tell how serious she was being.

'That's what my mother says,' I said in agreement.

Chapter Seventeen

Margaret Anne Pennington wandered across the grassy field towards the Worbarrow path and the Lulworth Rangers Land Rover, where her husband was using the bonnet to set out the contents of a traditional wicker picnic basket.

'I must leave you now,' she had said, 'because it's our official tea-break and Simon gets very grumpy if he doesn't have his tea on time.'

I had thanked her for the tour and headed for the Astra, watching her walk away. Despite the over-generous cut of her green uniform and the thick-soled, eminently sensible work boots, her walk was a feminine sway, not a military march. Although it was impossible to tell with that uniform on, I suspected she would have taken as much care of her figure as she had of her skin.

As I climbed into the Astra, I dug out my mobile and thought to myself that James Ellrington was going to get a very upbeat report – just what he wanted in fact. There across this field in a quiet, sunlit little Dorset valley with just the faintest salty tang of sea spray in the air, was the object of his desire, his lost dreams, his evaporated 'Angel's Share'. The only trouble was that Margaret Anne, or Maggie as she seemed to be called now, was chatting and laughing and sharing a flask of tea with the man she had been married to for the best part of a Golden Wedding stretch. She didn't seem to be missing an angel's share of anything.

There were three messages on my phone, all from the office, and at least one of them would be Lorna telling me to turn my phone on. They would have to wait, I had a far more important call to make and I was pleasantly surprised to find that my phone had a decent signal here in Tyneham.

'Amy, it's me.'

'Hello you, where are you?'

'I'm in darkest Dorset and it's a beautiful day.'

'Can I assume from your buoyant mood that you've found the missing girlfriend?'

'It was a lot easier than I thought it would be, but I'm not telling Veronica that. In fact, I'm looking at her right now.'

'Who? Veronica?'

'Good God, no. The missing teenage sweetheart. Except she's not a teenager anymore.'

'Is she a woman worth waiting for?'

'I'd say so.'

'So she's not old and wrinkly and living in a maximum security residential home?'

'Far from it, but speaking of old and wrinkly, have you heard anything from my dear father?'

If everything had gone to plan, Jane Bond would have collected my father from his flat in Morpeth Terrace in her classic Aston Martin that morning and whisked him off up to the Essex coast in a surprise attack on my mother. I was sure that my father would be so impressed with the Aston Martin, not to mention his attractive and well-groomed driver, that he would put his fear to one side and finally grow up and face his responsibilities.

'Not from your father,' said Amy, 'but Jane Bond rang me from a call box in a pub somewhere called Wickham Bishop's or somewhere like that, where your father had insisted she take him for lunch.'

'So why was Mrs Bond grassing him up?'

'I don't think she was complaining, she was just checking it was OK for your father to drink so much. He seemed to be stocking up on Dutch courage.'

'I can see why he needed it. Have they actually got to Romanhoe? I haven't heard the radio all day, have there been any reports of violent deaths in East Anglia?'

'Not so far. I'll continue to monitor the police frequencies,' she said dryly. 'So are you coming home tonight?'

'They've booked me in to a really nice hotel and I've got a few things to do for my client, so I'll probably get an early start in the morning, back about lunchtime.'

'So you won't be going into the office?'

'Why?'

'It's called working for a living. I know it's unreasonable, but they sort of expect you to turn up every day.'

'I knew that. It's just that this case is virtually wrapped up. JD – Job Done, as we say in the private eye business – and I reckoned I was due a few days off before they gave me another case to crack.'

'Oh, grow up and get real,' she said, which I thought was a bit harsh.

No sooner had I jabbed the phone to end the call than the damn thing rang. I knew it was a mistake to keep it switched on; it ran the batteries down unnecessarily and if the set wasn't on, the CIA's low orbit satellites couldn't pinpoint your location. The added bonus was you didn't have to talk to Lorna.

'Don't you ever check your fricking messages?'

'Why, good afternoon, Lorna,' I said patiently, 'and it is a fine one, so is there any reason to spoil it with that sort of potty mouth language?'

'Who's got a potty mouth?' she blurted.

'You have. You were swearing.'

'No I wasn't.'

'Yes, you fucking were, but let's not dwell on that. You must be psychic; I was just about to ring you. What's the problem?'

'Where are you?' she ploughed on grimly.

'Where I'm supposed to be. Isn't it on the office Intranet diary?'

She took a couple of deep breaths to calm down.

'What exactly is your situation, Angel?'

'I'm sitting in my snug little hire-car. It's parked of course. I'd be breaking the law if I was driving and talking to you at the same time, wouldn't I?'

I gave it a beat and then said: 'That's not the sound of teeth grinding I can hear is it?'

'Have...you...located...Margaret...Anne...Hayes?' she said slowly and deliberately.

'Of course I have. She can run, but she can't hide, not when I'm on her trail.'

'Oh, perleese spare me the bullshit.'

'Really, Lorna, your language is dis-fucking-graceful some-times.'

'Oh stop being so childish. When are you going to grow up?'

That was twice in two phone calls within two minutes; whatever could it mean?

'I blame lack of role models,' I said. 'Anyway, enough of this chit-chat, what did you want to know about Maggie?'

'Maggie?'

'She goes by the name Maggie Pennington now.'

'So you have located her?'

'I'm looking at her right now.'

'*She's in the car with you?*' she hissed in an anxious and urgent whisper.

'Don't be ridiculous, I've got her under surveillance, as we field operatives like to call it,' I said smugly.

'Has she seen you?'

With the phone still clamped to my ear, I got out of the Astra and parked my buttocks against the offside wing. Across the field, the Penningtons, enjoying their picnic high tea, saw me looking at them and both raised what looked like paper cups in my direction. With my left hand, I waved back enthusiastically.

'No, my cover's not blown. It's a knack I've developed, just blending in with the scenery. They never see me coming.'

'So you haven't talked to her about Ellrington? Veronica wanted to know.'

'No, I haven't. I thought the client came first.'

'Yeah, well, that's the other thing. Your client has been phoning us every half hour since about three o'clock wanting to know why you haven't called him like you were supposed to.'

'Because I'm on the phone to you is why I haven't called him yet. Give me a break! I've got a load of messages to get through first.'

'They'll be from me,' she said rather smugly. 'I thought you might like to know that the Criminal Records Bureau came back on their enhanced check on Ellrington; he's got a record.'

'This is the son, Peter, right?'

'We asked for both father and son to be checked,' she said quietly.

'Who authorised that? I don't remember anything being said about checking up on James – our client, the guy who's paying the bills.'

'Veronica thought it would be a good idea, just to be sure.'

'Oh, did she? So what turned up?'

'The son, Peter, has got a record. Cautions, fines and Community Service Orders in the early 1990s.'

'How old was he?'

'Nineteen, he was a student.'

'So the offences were drug-related?'

'Yes, they were. How did you know?'

'Shot in the dark. Anything else?'

'After 1994, it gets more serious. Three short prison sentences: three months and four months, both for Class A possession and dealing, and then six months for robbery and assault in a place called Middleton, wherever that is.'

'It's up in Manchester.'

'Is that important?'

'Probably not. Anything else?'

'Doesn't look like it. His last offence seems to have been two years ago, nothing since.'

'And did Veronica's suspicious mind find anything on the father?'

'Not a thing. James Ellrington does not have any sort of record; there seems to be absolutely nothing against him.'

'Oh yes there is,' I said. 'He's in love.'

Lorna snorted in my ear.

'How bad can that be?'

'Can be fatal.'

I treated myself to a piece of nicotine gum before calling the mobile number Ellrington had left with us. It was almost six o'clock and the Tyneham car park was virtually empty now, leaving just me and the Astra at one end and the Penningtons finishing their tea at the other.

My call was picked up immediately, so quickly in fact it made me jump.

'Yes?'

'Mr Ellrington? This is Roy Angel of Rud...'

'Where are you?'

And good afternoon to you, sir.

'I'm in Dorset, as we agreed I would be.'

'Where precisely?'

Sitting on the bonnet of a car parked in a field on top of a cliff, possibly slap-bang in the middle of a Ministry of Defence artillery range, but he probably didn't mean that.

'I'm near Upwalters.'

'What do you mean "near"? Where exactly are you?'

If I'd had the map in front of me, I would have given him a grid reference.

'I'm in a place called Tyneham, just a few miles from Upwalters.'

'Wait.'

I wasn't expecting that, but he was the client and he hadn't paid the bill yet, so I waited and listened to dead air and then a variety of thumps and bangs and finally he was back on.

'Where did you say? Tyneham?'

'It's between Upwalters and Lulworth, towards the coast.'

'I've got it now.'

He was tracking me on a map! Perhaps he was pre-empting my mileage claim.

'What are you doing there?' he nagged.

'It's where Maggie Pennington works,' I said, thinking that might shut him up for a second.

'Margaret Anne Hayes,' he said immediately. Then, and I could picture him doing a double-take: 'What do you mean she *works*?'

I hadn't been expecting that either.

'Hey, don't shoot the messenger. All I'm saying is that the woman now known as Maggie Pennington works as a sort of park ranger down here, protecting the countryside, clearing up after the tourists, that sort of thing.'

'Are you sure it's her?'

'As sure as I can be without a contemporary photograph or a DNA match.'

'So you've actually seen her?'

'I'm looking at her now,' I said and the phone went dead, almost as if the signal had gone. 'Hello?'

'You can see her?'

'I told you, I'm looking at her right now.'

I swear I heard him suck in his breath.

'Can she see you?'

'No, I'm under cover,' I said, waving across the field to the Penningtons.

Margaret Anne waved back.

'How does she look?'

What sort of question was that? It might as well have been a woman asking it, there was no right answer. I couldn't possibly win; it was a no-brainer.

'She looks fit,' I said.

'*Fit?* What do you mean by that?'

'I mean fit and well and active, not sitting in a bath chair blowing bubbles and drooling.'

'Don't take that tone with me,' he snapped.

I had been such a nice, faithful, well-behaved gun dog all day long and this was the thanks I was getting.

'I'm sorry about that, Mr Ellrington, I'm just confused as to what you want me to do. I've made a physical identification of Maggie Pennington like you asked me to. What do you want me to do now?'

'Her name is Margaret Anne Hayes,' he said firmly. 'You're staying at The Priory in Wareham, aren't you?'

'Yes.'

How did he know that? Lorna probably.

'Then go back there now and I'll contact you in an hour or so.'

He ended the call before I could say anything, leaving me looking at the dead phone in my hand.

I wondered if there was a manual of Best Practice for the new Private Eye and if there was, did it have a chapter on what to do when the client started to lose it?

I climbed back inside the Astra and sat there for a good five minutes looking across the grassy meadow, watching the Penningtons pack up their picnic things, being extra careful not to leave a crumb of litter. I was sorely tempted to walk over there and tell them what was going on.

But what was going on? What could I actually say?

Hello, Mrs Pennington, can you remember when you were called Margaret Anne Hayes and you were still at school and it was back in Yorkshire? Television was in black and white and The Beatles hadn't really got going? You lost your heart and your virginity, so I'm led to believe, to an immature schoolboy from a mining village, who got a little taste of the life of the great and good, not to mention privileged, and then *he* decided that *you* weren't good enough for him. Remember him? Well he grew older, but he probably didn't grow up, because he's decided that an important piece of his life has been missing – you, Mrs Pennington. You're his 'Angel's share', that portion of his life which evaporated, slipped through his hands. And now he wants to reclaim that lost share. He wants to...

What the bloody hell did James Ellrington want?

I drove slowly up the hill out of Tyneham. Even though I knew it was there, the remains of the village disappeared rapidly from sight, the summer foliage of the trees adding to the natural camouflage provided by the fold in the hills in which it nestled. The village had probably remained hidden and safe from enemy action for a thousand years until the very army that was supposed to be defending it booted it out of existence.

Driving through Upwalters, I slowed as I passed the Ilchester Arms. Through the archway entrance the car park looked just as empty as earlier that afternoon. There was a light on in the bar fronting the street, though. It must have been Happy Hour in there.

I saw virtually no other traffic until I was approaching Wareham. In fact I had been generally surprised by how under-populated the immediate area seemed to be given that this was the height of the tourist season. Still, Wareham was busy enough, with a horde of early evening drinkers crowding the square outside The Granary restaurant. It wasn't right to call it the town square because only two sides of the square were town buildings. The third was the road and bridge across the Frome and the fourth side was the river itself, still busy with small rowing boats and flotillas of ducks on the look-out for spare crisps or chips thrown by the 'grockles'.

I parked the Astra and walked round by the church to The Priory. I had fully intended to have a shower, check out the restaurant, have a good dinner and the finest wines known to humanity (on expenses of course) and then get an early night with a good book. I had even brought a good book with me from my window sill bookshelf in the office.

I did manage the shower and I was on my way to the restaurant when the pretty receptionist who had been on the desk when I had checked in waved to me from the snug little bar where she was now on duty.

Naturally, it was only good manners to give her my custom, as none of the other residents seemed to be doing so, and we had the bar to ourselves. I didn't have the nerve to use 'I'm a private dick down here on a case' as a chat-up line, so I relied on the equally corny:

'So what do you do for amusement in the evenings round here?'

'Well, if the boat carrying this week's supply of crack cocaine hasn't docked yet, we normally stay in and read a good book.'

Trust me to get the wise guy and although she had a lot more obvious advantages than the landlord of the pub in Upwalters, I was beginning to worry for the future of the licensed trade in Dorset.

'Is that a good book?' she asked, leaning over the bar to look at the paperback I had put down under my room key.

'It's a very good book indeed.'

'*Farewell My Lovely,*' she read upside-down. 'Never heard of it. What's that about then?'

'It's about unrequited love,' I said.

And that was precisely when I should have bitten my tongue until it bled.

In fact I almost did, as James Ellrington walked into the bar and sat down on the bar stool next to mine.

Chapter Eighteen

'I need you to do something for me, Mr Angel,' said James Ellrington.

'Where the hell did you come from?'

'I told you I would contact you here this evening.'

'I was expecting a phone call, not a personal visit. How...?'

'I believe you are still working for me, that you are still "on the clock" as you would put it. In fact, I'm probably paying for your hotel room, so I see no reason why I shouldn't call on you here. Your billable hours are continuous are they not? Or do you have a sliding scale for overtime? Neither matters, I am quite happy to pay for your time.'

'You came on your boat, didn't you?' I said, not listening to him.

It turned out to be a dangerous thing to say.

He wanted to borrow my car, or rather have me drive him somewhere. I couldn't see the immediate harm in that and I was not going to get any instructions from the office. They would all have gone home by now, so I was on my own, reliant on my own initiative to make the correct executive decision. I knew then that it would all end in tears.

It wasn't as if he wanted to go out and rob a convenience store, if they had such things in Dorset, or had a drive-by shooting in mind. It was fairly obvious where he wanted to go,

I just hadn't a clue what he had in mind to do when he got there.

'I want you to drive me to Upwalters,' he said firmly.

'Is that a good idea?'

'I just want to see where she lives.'

'We can't just turn up there in the middle of the night, they'll set the dogs on us.'

'Don't be ridiculous, it's barely dark yet and anyway, I repeat, I only want to see her house, I've no intention of announcing myself just yet.'

It was a curious way of putting it, but he was the client and he was paying for car hire and the petrol and me. I smiled at the nice barmaid, told her that duty called and that I'd be back. She looked upset to be losing one definite and one potential customer; but I suspected that she would get over it.

James Ellrington couldn't get over the fact that Margaret Anne had a job and began to ask questions about Tyneham and the Lulworth Rangers as soon as we were in the Astra and heading out of Wareham across the bridge.

I described the place as best I could and what the Penningtons did, even using Simon Pennington's description of them being 'Over Active Pensioners'. In fact, I tried to mention Simon or 'her husband' as often as I could yet I failed to get any obvious reaction from him. The nearest he came to being emotional was when he murmured to himself 'So she can drive a Land Rover' and I could sense him smiling as if it was something he could be proud of.

The drive through the darkening evening didn't take long. I don't think we saw another car on the road once we had left Wareham, although I did see headlights arcing spookily over the crests of the hills around us.

Upwalters was dark and deserted as we drove along Frome Street, with only a feeble orange glow from one window to show where the Ilchester Arms was. Given what I had already seen of the pub, though, that one lighted window was tantamount to putting up a flashing neon sign advertising free beer and pole dancing.

With no street lighting, Ellrington wasn't going to see much but at the far end of the village I slowed down to kerb-crawling speed to point out Stone Cottage. It was just possible to detect a faint glimmer of lights, or maybe a television set, around the edges of the curtains masking the front windows.

'Pull over,' Ellrington said excitedly. 'Stop somewhere where we can see.'

'See what?' I complained, but as soon as I could I negotiated a U-turn and headed back into the village, parking on just sidelights with Stone Cottage about twenty yards away on our right.

'Can't we get any closer?' hissed my passenger, straining forward against his seat belt, almost pressing his nose up against the windscreen.

'What we could do is walk over there and knock on the door and then run away,' I snapped. 'Isn't this all a bit childish? Look, I've got a mobile phone. Why don't you ring the house and say hello there, remember me? You could ask if they fancied popping out for a drink. There's a very quaint village pub just up the street.'

'No, no, no,' he said quietly, 'not like that. Not like that at all. I want to see her alone; get her on her own, that's most important.'

'Well, you're not going to do that like this,' I said firmly.

'Perhaps if I walked by the house a couple of times…'

'Oh, grow up,' I said, trying to snap him out of his mood, 'we look suspicious enough as it is just sitting here without lurking about the street on foot, peering in at windows. How far do you think we'd get before someone called the local plod or came after us with a shotgun or set the dogs on to us? I don't think they take too kindly to snooping strangers around these parts.'

He sat back in his seat with a jerk, as if I'd hit him with a cattle prod.

'You said she had dogs.'

'What?'

'Earlier, you said that she might set the dogs on us. So she has dogs, right?'

'That's what she said this afternoon.'

'What sort of dogs?'

'*I* don't know! They might be Yorkshire Terriers, they might be Rotweillers. They might be Yorkshire Rotweillers – God, there's a thought. She just said she had dogs – bitches, female dogs, called them her "girls" and said they were substitute children.'

'I bet they're poodles,' said Ellrington, but I got the impression he was speaking more to himself than to me. 'Her family always had poodles when she was young. And they were never able to have children, so she would have got poodles, black ones; I'll bet you anything. And I bet she takes them for a walk every morning, she always did when she was young.'

'Yes she does,' I said without thinking, 'down at Tyneham.'

'How do you know that?'

'Because she mentioned it. Something about taking the girls "for their nine o'clock constitutional" down the path to the sea.'

'That's it then!' He slapped his knees with the palms of both hands. 'I'll meet her down at Worbarrow tomorrow morning. I'll need you to give me a lift, first thing, though, I haven't got a car here.'

'Does that mean I can go back to the hotel now and have a drink and some dinner?'

'By all means. I'll call for you at seven.'

He could call at seven. Whether I would answer was another matter.

As I turned on the ignition he reached out a hand and grabbed my left arm.

'Wait. Just one more minute. Please.'

And so we sat there in the dark looking across a dark street at a dark cottage and when I thought he'd had his minute's worth, I put the Astra into gear and moved off. All I could think of was how much more relaxed I would be about driving around my definitely unstable client in the light of day, and wondering – just casually – if that barmaid would still be on duty at the hotel.

What, of course, I should have been worrying about was how James Ellrington knew that Margaret Anne walked her dogs down to Worbarrow, when I'd never mentioned the place by name.

He had also said 'they were never able to have children' meaning the Penningtons as a couple. He hadn't said 'she couldn't have children' which was something he might possibly have been aware of. He had said they couldn't.

How the hell did he know that?

James Ellrington asked me to drop him off just as we reached the bridge taking us back into Wareham, saying that he would walk along the tow-path on the south bank of the river to get back to his 'moorings'. He didn't offer any more information and it was the only thing he said to me on the journey back from Upwalters. He got out of the Astra and walked around the rear end to cross the road and disappear through a small gate in the roadside fence. I had the distinct feeling I had been dismissed.

Back at the hotel, my barmaid was off duty and the sea bass was off the menu. I had to settle for a crab salad followed by strawberries and clotted cream. I took my coffee into the bar and ordered a large brandy from a balding, middle-aged man wearing a uniform which said he was the Night Porter. He was nowhere near as attractive as the barmaid he had replaced and I suspected, from his accent, that he was either Polish or Latvian, and from his skill with the bottles behind the bar, that his natural calling was not as a barman.

As there were no other customers to irritate, I settled myself in an armchair in a corner of the bar, pulled out my phone and called Amy. She sounded remarkably cheerful and I could hear music in the background, possibly The Killers' new album.

'How are things on the home front?' I said.

'Oh, hello, you. Home front still intact. How are you getting on down by the seaside?'

'Still haven't made it for a paddle, but I have seen the sea, if only from a distance.'

'Given your track record with ships, I'd keep it that way.'

After my recent experience being winched off a freighter full of would-be Russian gangsters by the Essex Coastguard, I had every intention of keeping both feet firmly on dry land.

'I will; no more messing about in boats for me. Talking of messing about, have you heard from Father Dear?'

'Not him, but your friend Mrs Bond rang about twenty minutes ago to say they were just about to leave Romanhoe.'

I looked at my watch.

'Christ, they made a day of it, didn't they?'

'Sounds like everybody had a good time, that's for sure, and Mrs Bond sounded to be still sober.'

'Thank God one of them was. So it all went well, then? My mother was perfectly happy to learn that she was about to become a grandmother and that her ex-husband is still planning to marry a page three model despite having a stroke?'

'Amazingly, given that scenario,' she said dryly, 'nobody died. But did you have to arrange it so that your mother got all this news at the same time as seeing your father arrive with a very glamorous personal chauffeur in a flash Aston Martin? If you've ever got serious news for me, promise me you'll just send a text, OK?'

'So you think Mrs Bond is glam, do you?' I asked, knowing that Amy threw other women compliments like lions threw scraps to hyenas. I had once caught her watching a TV make-over show and when I'd asked what it was she'd said: 'It's called *Munters Into Babes*.' Once I had worked out that she'd made that up, I seriously thought of pitching the title to Channel 5.

'You know she is. God, I wish I had skin tone like that now, let alone when I'm a senior citizen.'

'I don't think Mrs Bond actually qualifies for a bus pass just yet, but I think she's quite looking forward to becoming an Over Active Pensioner and growing old disgracefully.'

'How is your pair of ancient lovebirds getting on?'

'I wouldn't call them ancient,' I said.

'All right then, chronologically challenged. How's that?'

'Not much better, and to answer your question, my client is beginning to act really strangely.'

'Keeps calling for regular updates, does he?'

'Worse than that: he's actually here in Dorset, came down on his boat on the spur of the moment and now he's hoping for the big reunion tomorrow morning.'

'What does the ex-girlfriend think of this?'

'She's blissfully unaware of it all. So's her husband, who seems quite a nice old boy.'

'And what's your role in all this?'

'I don't really know. Chaperone? Referee? Getaway-car driver? I'm just playing it by ear.'

'You always do,' she said, 'but just don't expect everybody else to do the same.'

'What do you mean by that?'

'This client of yours – James whatsisname – he has a boat?'

'Yes.'

'Where does he park it?'

'Sunbury on Thames. What the hell has that to do with anything?'

'So he's taken his boat down the Thames, turned right at Kent, gone into the Channel and ended up in Dorset?'

'I suppose so, why are you going all nautical on me?'

'I was just thinking that that's hardly spur-of-the-moment stuff, is it? That requires organisation and planning. Pre-meditation, wouldn't you say? It's just something you should keep in mind – and be careful. You're dealing with pretty strong emotions here.'

I digested what she had said.

'You know, you're much better at this detective business than I am,' I conceded.

'How long has it taken you to work that one out, Sherlock?'

The phone in my hotel room rang at 7 a.m. and a husky accented voice, unfortunately that of the Polish/Latvian Night Porter, told me that my visitor was in Reception waiting for me. It rang twice more whilst I was in the shower, once while I was packing my overnight bag and once more while I was brewing the complimentary packet of instant coffee, but I didn't answer any of them. I wondered if James Ellrington was taking the same pills my father had been prescribed. If he was, it probably wasn't a good idea to keep him waiting. Well, not too long; but then I hadn't asked to be woken up at seven.

Down at Reception I made a long slow pantomime out of paying my bill, though that's usually the hotel staff's job, not the customer's, while James Ellrington hopped anxiously from one foot to the other, checking his watch every thirty seconds, muttering to himself and slowly going pink in the cheeks and the ears.

Eventually, I tucked my credit cards away and turned from the desk to face him.

'We do have time for breakfast, don't we?' I asked hopefully.

It wasn't a comfortable drive back to Upwalters, the two of us in the Astra, him all revved-up and anxious and me trying to eat the two slices of toast and marmalade sandwiched together I had raided from the hotel breakfast spread. I had, after all, paid for bed and breakfast, or rather the client had. I thought he might have been reassured to see I wasn't wasting his money, but he had other things on his mind.

Uppermost seemed to be keeping his appearance in pristine

condition, checking himself every few minutes in the vanity mirror in the passenger's sun-visor, and jerking away nervously every time I changed gear whilst holding my toast, in case he suffered collateral damage from the crumbs.

He had dressed in full Regatta-strength Yacht Club chic: blue blazer, fawn slacks, white shirt and a tie which looked regimental but probably wasn't. He had shaved carefully and used far too much aftershave and I was sure I detected hair gel which had been, in his case, applied more in hope than expectation.

'Slow down,' he ordered as we once again drove into Upwalters, though once again there was little to see.

The curtains were open in Stone Cottage and there was no milk on the doorstep, but whether either fact meant anything was beyond me at this time of the morning. Maybe it just meant that somebody had opened the curtains and they didn't do doorstep deliveries in Dorset. Who knew? Who cared? James Ellrington did.

'Does she have a car?' he asked.

'I don't know.'

'You don't know?'

'When I saw the Penningtons yesterday, they were in a Land Rover, but that was a work vehicle. I don't know if they have a car as well.'

'Margaret Anne will have a car. She always liked driving and she always was a careful driver. She was very strict about drinking and driving, absolutely terrified of having to blow into a breathalyser, not that she ever had to. If she had a car, where would she keep it?'

'I've no idea, somewhere behind the house I should think. Look, why don't we just go on down to Tyneham, see if she's there?'

'Yes. Yes, do that,' he said, still looking back at Stone Cottage as if willing her to materialise through the walls.

I accelerated out of the village, genuinely hoping that

Ellrington's long-lost girlfriend would be down the road
walking her dogs, as that might just make James Ellrington chill
out a bit. He was becoming more distracted by the minute and
genuine memories were obviously becoming twisted in his
private fantasies. For instance, he'd said Margaret Anne was
terrified of breathalysers, yet the blow-in-the-bag breathalyser
hadn't been around in 1963, it was only introduced in 1967. The
guy must be cracking up.

There was a low-lying ground mist in Tyneham which had not
yet been burned off by the early morning sun, but then it was
only about 8 a.m. and the sun was hardly awake. If it was
possible, it gave the place an even more haunted look than
normal, like an over-lit Hammer horror film set.

As we drove slowly down the hill to the village, I tried to get
some instructions out of my client who had remained tight-
lipped since we had left Upwalters.

'Just how do we play this?'

'Play?' he said vaguely. 'We make sure she's alone and then
you tell her I'm here and want to see her. Then you leave us
alone.'

'I tell her? I tell her that her former childhood sweetheart,
whom she hasn't seen for forty years, is here in the wilds of
Dorset, hiding in the back of a rented Vauxhall Astra just
waiting to jump out and yell "Surprise!" What if the poor
woman has a heart attack?'

'Don't be ridiculous, she won't have a heart attack. It will be
a surprise, but not a shock. She's always known I would come
for her one day.'

He'd been worrying me for some time; now he was beginning
to scare me. He twisted his head round to look over his
shoulder into the back seat as if measuring it up as a place of
concealment.

In the end, he settled for skulking down in his seat, his eyes
level with the Astra's dashboard, as we entered the precincts of

Tyneham and I turned left and parked in the car park. He didn't need to be so cautious because the only living creatures looking at us had either fur or feathers and wings, and none of them seemed interested in us.

I turned the engine off and we waited for the ground mist to clear which it did rapidly, leaving a sheen of dew on the grass.

'So, if she turns up, you want me to what?'

'Approach her without frightening her,' he said as if he had rehearsed the scene he was describing many times in his head. 'Tell her that you have a message from me, that I would like to see her and that I have only her best interests at heart. If she agrees to see me, you come and get me.'

'And if she runs away screaming at the very idea?'

He shook his head seriously.

'Oh, she won't do that, but if she shows any hesitation at all, then tell her she will not hear from me again.'

'Well, that seems fair enough,' I said and I did think it all sounded harmless enough, though I didn't like the way Ellrington's right leg was shaking as if the nerves in it were twanging out of control.

'Listen!' he hissed suddenly, reaching out and grabbing my left arm.

Then he shrank even lower in his seat, almost sliding on to the floor, as a BMW Series 3 Touring, one of the small Beamer estate cars, came round the corner and entered the car park. It drove by the Astra slow enough for me to see that the driver was a woman and that the boot area behind the back seat was caged off with a grille to contain two substantial dark doggy shapes. The BMW carried on towards the far end of the car park where the woods and the path to Worbarrow started.

'That was her!' Ellrington squealed, so excited he almost stuck his nose above the dashboard. I really didn't know how he could be so sure from that fleeting glance. I wasn't and I'd been chatting to her the day before.

'Are you sure? It's been a long time since you saw her,' I said.

'It's her. Look! Poodles! What did I tell you?'

In the distance, the BMW had parked and the driver had opened the tailgate, releasing two bouncing dark brown shapes which began to circle her legs with such speed, it looked as if she was standing in a miniature dust-devil. I had to concede that it was Margaret Anne Pennington, wearing green Hunter Wellingtons and a Barbour raincoat open over jeans and a bright red jumper.

She reached into the pocket of her coat and produced a bright yellow ball, throwing it roughly in the direction of the Astra. The two dogs took off after it and we had a good view of them coming towards us at about fifteen miles an hour, then skidding into a U-turn as one of them caught the ball. They were indeed poodles, standard poodles, not the small ratty highly-manicured useless ones that rich useless women carried in old Hollywood movies.

The dogs bounded back towards their owner, who had turned and was walking off to the right of the wood, heading for the Worbarrow path.

James Ellrington began to strike my arm with the back of his hand.

'Go on, go on. Get after her,' he was saying, his right leg jerking up and down like a jack-hammer. 'Catch her up.'

I thought that was pretty rich advice for a man who'd given her a 43-year head start, but I followed my client's instructions, got out of the car and strode purposefully across the wet grass.

'Maggie!'

I hadn't meant to shout in any sort of aggressive way, but I wanted her to know I was on the path far enough behind her not to be an immediate source of danger. It also helped to alert the dogs, who turned, barked and started lolloping towards me to investigate. When Margaret Anne turned – and there was Ellrington's voice in the back of my head insisting that was her name, not 'Maggie' – and saw me, I stopped in my tracks, put my hand up and waved cheerfully, adding:

'Hello there!'

She put her head on one side and gave me a good look, then whistled for the dogs to come to her. They skidded around and bounded back if not to heel, then roughly into the vicinity of her legs. As I started walking towards her, she produced the yellow ball and threw it for them in the other direction and they went haring off down the path which led to the sea, while she waited for me.

When I was ten feet away from her she said:

'Hello, there. I didn't expect to see you again and certainly not so soon and so early.'

She was relaxed and looked fresh and healthy. She was wearing a minimum of make-up, but she had taken the trouble to put make-up on even at this time in the morning when out walking the dogs and not really expecting to be seen by anything other than a satellite with a really good camera.

'I wasn't really planning on coming back so soon,' I said, pushing my hands into my pockets and aiming as I walked for a point at least two yards to the side of her. I wanted to be totally non-threatening and not at all in her face. 'But I've got a message for you, Mrs Pennington.'

Her brow creased and her stare hardened.

'Simon…?' she said in a whisper.

'No, it's nothing to do with your husband. I've got a message for you from someone else.'

It took her a nano-second to digest that and then she put two fingers into her mouth and blew a two-note whistle (something I had never been able to do) and the two poodles came bounding down the path.

'Sheba! Jezebel! Sit!' she commanded, pointing at the ground and the dogs put the brakes on and skidded to a halt near her feet and between us.

'And just who the bloody hell are you?' she asked in a voice which could have been inquiring if I took sugar in my tea.

'My name is Angel and I'm a private detective from London. I came down to Dorset to find you, Mrs Pennington, and now I have a message for you.'

'I've never had any dealings with private detectives,' she said quite coolly. 'I don't know anything about them.'

'That makes two of us then,' I said, giving her my best smile.

Chapter Nineteen

I showed her a business card, which she read and handed back to me as if keeping it was agreeing to some sort of contract, and then she suggested we walked as we talked.

'My dogs don't mind us talking, but they do expect their walk,' she said and I saw no reason to get on the wrong side of Sheba and Jezebel. 'So what exactly do you want with me, Mr Angel?'

'I'm just the messenger, Mrs Pennington,' I pleaded.

'So what? So I shouldn't shoot you? I knew you were up to something yesterday but it didn't sink in until last night.'

'What made you suspicious?'

'You knew our surname was Pennington, but I'd never mentioned that and I was sure Simon hadn't been so formal with a visiting tourist.'

'That's very clever,' I said.

'Please don't patronise me. Just because there's snow on the roof it doesn't mean the lights have gone out.'

'I wouldn't dream of patronising you, Mrs Pennington. What I meant was that was very observant and perhaps you should be the detective.'

'You sound as if you don't really want the job, Mr Angel.'

'Sometimes I wonder,' I admitted.

'That makes it sound as if you're a bringer of bad news.'

'I may well be.'

'Are you trying to scare me, Mr Angel?'

'If I am, I'm certainly getting nowhere fast.'

'Don't be so sure. Why not just get it off your chest?'

'I had no idea I was ever going to be talking to you like this. My job was to find you and that's all I was doing, up until yesterday.'

'When you found me.'

'Yes.'

'And then things changed?'

'My client's instructions changed.'

'What sort of a client would want to find me in the first place?'

'James Ellrington,' I said.

'Oh,' she answered.

We walked on and she said nothing for nearly five minutes, keeping her eyes on the ground and even ignoring the two poodles when they romped around her feet. They got so fed up with their mistress's indifference that they even came and sniffed my legs but they soon got bored with that and galloped off down the path. To our right was the wood, fenced off with three strands of barbed wire and the occasional Ministry of Defence sign telling people to Keep Out. To our left, the hills were marked out as a gunnery range with targets indicated by huge painted numbers, the furthest and highest a giant number 3. We had walked about a quarter of a mile and I could definitely smell the sea now.

'I knew he would,' she said suddenly.

'I'm sorry?'

'He always said he would come for me when he was free. It was the last thing he said as we parted.'

'He said that back in 1963?'

'What?' That seemed to confuse her. 'Well, yes, it was certainly a long time ago, more years than a lady should be asked to admit to.'

'Mr Ellrington has certainly not forgotten you and has gone to considerable lengths to find you. And I have to say he is ecstatic that we have found you.'

She still had her head down as we walked so I couldn't read her expression. All I knew was that she wasn't running away screaming at the news I'd brought, which I suppose was something.

'How is he?'

I judged that it wasn't the time to be brutally honest and tell her I thought he was a regressive, anally-retentive obsessive and, anyway, I wasn't a psychiatrist.

'He looks very well,' I said, but not convincingly.

'For his age, you mean? You must find this very amusing, this lover's quest among the senior citizens.'

'Not at all, I'm jealous if anything.'

'That's awfully polite of you. You lie very convincingly. But James really is well?'

'Yes he is. From what I've seen of him he's very active and fighting fit.'

'So I can assume he is now free?'

'I don't quite understand, I'm afraid.'

'He said he would come looking for me when he was free. I take it he is free?'

'He's recently retired I believe...' I stumbled, knowing it was not what she wanted.

'His wife. How is Cheryl?'

'I'm sorry, I don't know anything about his wife. I understand that Mr Ellrington has been a widower for about two years.'

'Two years?' she said to herself, then aloud: 'But yes, of course, he would be sixty-five now and retired.'

'Yes he is,' I said.

'So he would be free from *all* ties now...'

'Yes, I suppose so.'

We continued in silence. The dogs had disappeared ahead of

us and the path was rougher now, with the exposed foundations of demolished buildings off to either side. I presumed this was what was left of the Worbarrow settlement. And then the path narrowed and became difficult to negotiate even for walkers due to seemingly random outcrops of bare rock. As we got closer, they turned from natural rock to man-made concrete lumps, many with rusty iron reinforcing rods jutting from them like spines on a fish.

Mrs Pennington saw me looking.

'World War II tank traps,' she said, reverting to tourist guide mode.

'They were expecting an invasion here?' I asked, looking round just to make sure I hadn't missed anything of vital strategic importance, like an oil refinery or a coal mine or even a road. To anywhere.

'At the start of the war, yes they were. Look, that was the first line of defence.'

She pointed off the path to a tangle of concrete blocks and rusty metal sheets.

'What the devil's that supposed to be?'

In fact, there was a small, weather-beaten information board which would have told me, but Mrs Pennington knew the script.

'It's called an Allan Farrell turret, I'm guessing after the man who invented it. Basically it's a hole in the ground big enough to take one man standing up, with a metal turret to cover his head. There would have been a slit in the turret where the soldier would stick his tommy-gun through.'

'So it was like a buried tank, which couldn't move and was badly armed and there doesn't seem to have been any way of getting out of it.'

'I don't think they caught on,' she admitted.

'Just as well the invasion didn't come here, then, though it's a beautiful spot to do sentry duty.'

We were standing on the edge of the shingle beach which sloped gently down into the clear blue/green water of

Worbarrow Bay, the promontory point of Worbarrow Tout rising to our left with its incongruous army designation of a giant numeral 3.

'Yes it is beautiful, isn't it?' she said. 'The water's so clean too, though it is bloody cold. You don't get too many grockles because of the shingle. Holidaymakers with kids prefer sand.'

'Your girls seem to like it.'

The two poodles were sliding and skittering across the pebbles, barking at the gentle waves hissing up the shore.

'Go on then,' she shouted to them and raised her arm, almost in a fascist salute. The poodles understood perfectly and splashed out into the surf with yelps of doggy glee.

'There they go,' she said somewhat distracted, 'just like naughty children. Simon and I never had any children, so I spoil the dogs instead. Do you have any children, Mr Angel?'

'No,' I said, keeping it short and honest, though she had already asked me that the day before.

'Does he?'

'Mr Ellrington? I think he has a son.'

'Who would be 34 or 35 now?'

'I suppose so, I don't really know.'

'He said Cheryl always wanted a boy.'

'If you mean the late Mrs Ellrington, I'm afraid I can't really comment. I have no brief for that; all I was told to do was find you.'

'And that you've done,' she said, turning to me with a smile. 'Here I am, you found me.'

'You're taking this very well,' I said. 'In fact you don't seem particularly surprised that your childhood sweetheart has come looking for you after forty years.'

'Why should I?' she smiled coyly. 'It's happened before.'

'When did you last see James Ellrington?'

Even as I said it I knew it sounded like 'When did you stop beating your wife?' and I couldn't actually think of a good reason why I was asking it, except that I felt it was somehow important.

'1970, the year The Beatles broke up.'

Let It Be. Laura, the pub quiz queen, had been right all along. James Ellrington had been economical with the truth from the start.

'Shall we head back?' Margaret Anne was saying. 'It'll give the dogs a chance to dry off.'

'Of course,' I said, falling into step at her side. 'Look, Mrs Pennington, I don't know how to put this and I'm not sure that it's at all important to anything, or that it means anything, but I feel I have to ask.'

'Please ask away, Mr Angel. Actually, I was beginning to think you were a poor sort of detective as you seem afraid of asking questions.'

'It's usually the answers that scare me,' I said.

'I'll try not to frighten you. What was the question?'

'You say you last saw James Ellrington, my client, in 1970. He told me he last saw you in 1963.'

'So what's your question?'

'Who's lying?'

'Neither of us, if it's any of your business, which I doubt it is. What has he said about us?'

'He's said you were childhood sweethearts; well, not exactly in those words. That sounds a bit twee, but the sentiment was there. You were his first love and he only realised later that you were his one true love. I'm sorry if this is embarrassing for you.'

'It's not at all. I think you're more embarrassed than I am.'

She had a point there.

'Anyway, he said that, basically, he had let you go and now he regretted it because a certain proportion of his life had evaporated...with you not being there.'

'That's really quite romantic,' she said and she was smiling now; smiling big time, her hands deep in the pockets of her Barbour, hugging it to her thighs.

'Yes, I suppose it is,' I said weakly.

'But you don't believe it, do you, Mr Angel?'

'Something's not right.'

'The sentiment is true, only the timescale confuses you,' she said in the sort of voice which reminded me of schoolteachers I had known, sometimes too well. 'But because you have, essentially, acted the gentleman up to now, I think you are owed an explanation.'

I resisted the temptation to ask for the bit about acting as a gentleman to be put in writing.

'James and I were...well, put it this way, James took my virginity – not that it was fiercely contested! It was enthusiastically and, I'd like to think, energetically given.'

I was getting the feeling that this was altogether far more information than I either needed, or wanted.

'Anyway, we were young and we thought love was all you needed. And then the real world came crashing in. James wanted a career; I wanted a husband, so we parted.'

'He always regretted that,' I said, feeling I had to stick up for my client at some point.

'Yes I know, he told me so, but by the time he did it was too late.'

'In 1970?' I said, still not sure what I was missing.

'Yes, in 1970. Simon and I and James and Cheryl, we'd all been married for seven years. Seven years! The Seven Year Itch they called it back then. Do you know what I mean by that?'

'It was an old movie with Marilyn Monroe, wasn't it?'

'That's right. It was all about the urge to have an affair after seven years of marriage. Seven years! These days they don't seem to wait seven minutes.'

'I don't think it's compulsory,' I said and she smiled at that.

'No, of course it isn't, but it happened. James had been posted to Leeds and he contacted my mother. She told him where Simon and I lived.'

That was mothers for you.

'Didn't it worry you, your mother setting an old boyfriend on to you?'

'Oh no, I understood perfectly that mother only did it out of spite. She never liked James, thought he was a jumped-up "scholarship boy" who didn't know his place. She thought Simon was a much better catch. After all, he had a proper job with prospects; James was just a student. A bright one, but then my mother never understood things like universities. She actually sent James the report of our wedding from the local newspaper and, in her mind, letting James see how happily married and successful Simon and I were would serve him right for breaking her daughter's heart.'

'And had he?'

'Oh yes, he had, but mother's plan misfired. As soon as James and I saw each other again, we were all over each other. "At it like knives" I believe the expression was, back then. I was 27 and James was 28 – or perhaps 29 by then – both respectable, married people, and we were doing it in the backs of cars, in hotel rooms, out in the countryside, in the cinema; we just didn't care and it was a wonder we weren't arrested. Once we even did it in a churchyard! Oh dear, now I *am* embarrassing you.'

'No, I'm not embarrassed,' I lied. 'Exhausted perhaps, but not embarrassed.'

'There you've put your finger on the problem.'

'I have?'

'The problem was I didn't exhaust James. Perhaps I inspired him. Anyway, about three months into our little affair, James's wife Cheryl announced she was pregnant. There was nothing else for it. James got himself posted out of Yorkshire and I said goodbye to him for the second time, but I always knew I'd see him again, sometime, somewhere.'

'How do you feel about that?'

She reached down and patted one of the poodles on the head in an absent-minded way.

'Scared, thrilled, confused, excited, all those things. Would it shock you to hear that the very idea makes me rather horny?'

It was a worry in that Ellrington was waiting in my car and I didn't fancy the idea of them replaying their passion in the back seat. Still, it was a rented car, so what the hell?

'Would it shock you to know he was here in Dorset?'

Her hands flew to her hair.

'Here? See him? Today?' she asked, breathlessly.

'If you want to; if you're absolutely sure.'

'Oh yes,' she said and she smiled a smile which lit up her face as if she'd stepped into a searchlight.

'Then let's head back to my car,' I said, taking the yellow ball from the poodle who was offering it.

Trying to ignore the doggy drool it was coated with, I hurled it down the path towards Tyneham and the dogs set off at the charge, with us following at a brisk but more dignified pace.

'This was the message you had for me? That James wanted to see me?'

'Yes, but I wasn't sure how you would take it, so I thought if I could get you...'

'Oh my God!' she screamed.

James Ellrington hadn't been able to wait in the car. He was on the Worbarrow path striding purposefully towards us, his arms outstretched.

The two poodles had spotted him and were racing towards him, barking wildly. And then, with a loud sob, Margaret Anne was running towards him too.

'So what did you do?' asked Amy.

'The decent thing, of course, I left them to it.'

'You did?'

'Yes, of course, not that I could really stop them. She was over him like a rash and I would have needed a crowbar to prise them apart.'

'Oh perleeese,' said Amy in my ear. 'They're not actually *at it* are they?'

'No, they're sitting in her car talking. They have been for over an hour now.'

'Are the windows steamed up?'

'No, but mine are, mainly because I've got two wet dogs asleep on the back seat. I thought I'd better take them in rather than have them panting over the shoulders of the two young lovers.'

'Very noble of you, but they're hardly young lovers, are they?'

'Oh, I don't know, call them Grey Panthers or Over Active Pensioners, whatever, if the flesh is willing and the mind isn't weak, where's the harm? What's the big deal about not accepting growing old?'

'Don't you mean growing up? I think you've found some fellow travellers down there.'

'You could be right,' I admitted. 'Speaking of sixty-year-old teenage hooligans, how's my father?'

'On fine form, really chipper, full of the joys of life.'

'This was after seeing my mother?' I queried to make sure we were talking about the same person.

'Yes, it all went very well, or so Mrs Bond said.'

'And he told her about Kim McIntosh?'

'Yes.'

'And he told her you were pregnant and she was going to be a granny?'

'Yes.'

'And he's still able to walk?'

'With a positive spring in his step.'

'You sure you got the right man? Did you run his DNA? Check his fingerprints? Do a retina scan?'

'On the drive up there, he borrowed forty quid off Mrs Bond to buy your mother a bottle of champagne and some chocolates.'

'That sounds like my father, but I can't really believe my mother took the news without violence. We don't like surprises in my family.'

'Maybe you should give her more credit.'

'Why? Bank managers never did. Oh-oh, gotta go, they're on the move.'

'What are they doing? Adjusting their clothing?'

'Just getting out of the car.'

'So what happens now?

'I've no idea. I'll ring you again when I'm heading back.'

'Give my love to the young lovers,' she chirped.

'I will but I don't think they need it. They seem to have more than enough.'

They got out of her BMW and began to walk towards me, holding hands and gazing dreamily into each other's eyes. I decided to bring them down to earth with a touch of reality and climbed out of the Astra, releasing the two poodles who tore across the grass towards them. As they neared their prey, Margaret Anne held out a hand like an old-fashioned policeman's Stop sign to prevent them jumping up and planting muddy paws on the two lovers. They barked and yapped and zipped off to sniff the BMW to make sure it was still theirs.

James Ellrington looked the happiest I had ever seen him and the moonstruck expression on his face only slipped when we all heard the sound of a car coming down the hill into Tyneham. All three of us turned to look and I think all three of us let out a little guilty sigh of relief to see a Ford Galaxy packed to the gunnels with a family of obvious holidaymakers claiming their place in the car park as the first visitors of the day. We all seemed to take it as a sign that we should get going. But where, exactly?

Mrs Pennington carried on walking towards me and when she was close enough for me to smell her perfume, she held out her right hand for me to shake.

'You were a bringer of good news for me, Mr Angel. Would "angel of mercy" be too cheesy a thing to say?' she beamed, determined not to be embarrassed.

'It probably is, but by all means say it in front of the client,' I said nodding towards Ellrington.

She allowed herself a small laugh at that, but Ellrington didn't. Suddenly he was all business.

'You must go, my darling,' he said to her, 'and Mr Angel can get me back to Wareham.'

'Sure,' I said. It was on my way home and he was still my client, though a thank you for a job well done would not have gone amiss. Perhaps he was planning to add a big tip on to the bottom line of the invoice Rudgard & Blugden were going to send him.

He walked Mrs Pennington back to her car, at one point slipping his arm around her waist, something she reciprocated. When they got to the Beamer, she opened the tailgate to load the dogs and then the couple embraced and treated themselves to a long, lingering kiss. When they eventually unstuck themselves, Ellrington opened the driver's door for her and she climbed in and started the engine. As she pulled away, she waved frantically at him and as the BMW went by me, she smiled and waved at me and I think she mouthed the words 'Thank You', then she was out of the car park gate and accelerating up the hill, the two dogs staring stupidly out of the rear window with *what-the-hell-was-that-all-about?* expressions on their faces.

Ellrington himself trotted towards me like a big puppy. His shoes and the turn-ups of his slacks were wet with the dew and spattered with mud, but he didn't seem to mind. If there had been any more bounce in his step, he would have been skipping.

As he got nearer, he clapped his hands together and rubbed them. 'JD,' I thought and felt sure he was going to offer me a bonus or name me in his will or at least say thank you. Instead, he completely blindsided me by walking straight past me, staring directly ahead, towards the Astra where he climbed into the passenger seat, slammed the door after him and began to strap on his safety belt.

Not a word; not a bloody word.

Perhaps he was overdosing on love after all those years going cold turkey, but meeting up with his long-lost lover had not improved his attitude to the hired help.

The drive back to Wareham didn't make him any more grateful or talkative. For most of the journey he sat there with his hands clasped in his lap and his eyes glazed. He could have just had an orgasm or gone into catatonic shock; it was often difficult to tell the difference.

He became mildly animated as we drove through Upwalters again, but he didn't ask me to stop or even slow down. He did turn his head though and stare at the Penningtons' cottage as we cruised by, watching it through the rear window until long after we had left the village and he couldn't possibly see it.

As we came to the bridge into Wareham, he spoke for the first time.

'Can you park the car and come with me to my boat, Mr Angel? There's something I want to show you. It's not far.'

I made a point of looking at my watch before I agreed, but I didn't see how I could refuse. In theory he was still paying a daily rate for the services of Rudgard & Blugden, so he was still the client and I was his hired man. There was always the possibility that he had a bottle of champagne on ice or a pile of cash he wanted to tip me with for a job well done.

I left the Astra in the square which fronted the river, outside an Italian restaurant, and Ellrington and I walked back over the bridge to the south bank and down on to the tow-path.

The path was flanked by a ditch and water meadow where reeds and bulrushes grew taller than me and made an impenetrable screen from behind which came the constant rustling and twitching of invisible wildlife. To our left was the river, where rowing boats were already being hired by the hour from the landing near the bridge and families of inexpert rowers were terrorising the duck population. On the other bank was The Priory and its immaculate lawns running down to the water's edge, and the river and the path were curving away from

Wareham and suddenly the town had disappeared from sight and we were in boat land.

Yachts and motor cruisers and things I could only classify as floating gin palaces were moored two or three deep as far as the eye could see. Occasionally there would be home-made, rickety wooden jetties the width of a single plank extending out on stilts to the furthest moorings but it seemed as if the majority of boat owners simply hopped from one deck to another to get ashore. I had no idea how much any of the craft were worth but there were hundreds, if not a thousand of them tied up there, giving off a constant tinny, tinkling sound every time a passing rowing boat sent ripples across the surface of the water. If they had been cars and double-parked like that on a street in Hackney, the traffic wardens would have thought it was Christmas.

'Have you been here before?' I asked Ellrington, to break the silence.

'To Wareham? Yes. I have associate membership of the Yacht Club here.'

'Seems a nice little place. A Saxon walled town I believe.'

He didn't seem either impressed or interested in my fund of local knowledge.

'It's a good, safe harbour,' was all he said.

We walked for about half a mile before we saw the Yacht Club building with its pennants hanging limply in the warm morning air. I wondered idly if the bar would be open yet, took off my jacket and slung it over my shoulder as we marched on.

Here the river did a wide meander and became noticeably wider. In the distance there was a much larger expanse of water.

'Is that Poole Harbour?' I asked Ellrington, trying to remember the map I had left back in the Astra with my luggage.

'Technically, that's the Wareham Channel but it leads round into Poole Harbour,' he answered and then said: 'Here we are.'

'Here' was a boat, tied up to the bank by thick twisted ropes at the front and rear ends with four large orange buoys a bit like the old-fashioned space-hoppers hung from the side to fend off scrapes and collisions. It was over thirty feet long and had a cabin with windows and curtains, and was painted white with a single horizontal red line to mark the deck. It stood about nine feet out of the water and there was a plank leading from the riverbank to the stern and the cabin doors.

The last boat I had been on had been big enough to drive cars around the deck. This one looked safer and the water wasn't anywhere near as deep here, but I had no particular desire to go sailing again.

'The *Margaret Anne*,' I read aloud from where the name was painted on the prow, just as I'd seen it in the photograph at Ellrington's house, when he had posed with his wife.

Had she ever known?

'I renamed her when I bought her,' Ellrington said, indicating that I should walk the plank. 'Please, go aboard.'

I stepped gingerly on to the plank, feeling it bend but not break under my weight. Two steps and I was on board, with Ellrington standing behind me breathing on my neck.

'Go down into the cabin,' he said, 'but mind your head.'

There were two louvred doors which opened on to three steep steps down into a gloomy interior and there was a faint aroma of something I couldn't quite place.

'This looks quite snug,' I said. 'Do you have all the comforts of home in here?'

'Most of them,' said a voice.

I got to the bottom step and raised my head.

There was an upholstered bunk running the length of one side of the cabin to butt up against a small sink unit and gas cooker.

Sitting on the bunk, looking up at me, was Peter Ellrington.

To say I was quite surprised to see him there would be putting it mildly.

And I found the fact that he was pointing a gun at me really quite disturbing.

Chapter Twenty

'That's him. That's the one who came snooping round the house.'

He waved the gun around like a conductor's baton. If he was trying to hypnotise me, he was succeeding.

'His name is Angel,' said Ellrington Senior from somewhere behind me. 'He's my pet detective.'

'So you got an Angel to get you your Angel's Share. That's really rather sweet, isn't it?'

The gun was a large, black metal service revolver of the sort you see British army officers holding in movies all the way from *Zulu* to *The Third Man*. It was probably called a Webley or an Enfield or something, and it could have had a distinguished military career going back a hundred years. Then again, it could be a prop from a movie set. I wasn't inclined to ask for a closer look.

Peter Ellrington read my mind.

'It's real enough,' he said, waving it some more. 'Made in 1947 if you're wondering.'

'I wasn't.'

'Still in perfect working order and there's absolutely no problem getting .38 calibre ammunition to fit it.'

'Pity.'

'I bought the bullets over the Internet,' he said with a hint of pride.

'Bloody eBay has a lot to answer for,' I said. 'That where you buy your skunk as well?'

I had placed the smell I had noticed when I came aboard: skunk, marijuana's stronger, smellier, in-bred cousin. They'd never get the smell out of those curtains.

I felt a push in the small of my back and James Ellrington said:

'Please sit down, Mr Angel, and try not to bicker with Peter. You two will have to get along together for several hours and, as you can see, space is at a premium.'

'What do you mean "several hours"? What the fuck is going on?'

Reluctantly I sat on the bunk next to Peter, as far away from him as was possible but still close enough to get an excellent view down the barrel of the revolver and to be able to smell the T-shirt he was wearing, the same black one advertising Jack Daniels he had been wearing in Merton Park last week. It and he reeked of stale sweat, smoke and dope. Back at his house I was sure I had detected the smell of sherry about him, which made sense. Sweet sherry was one of the few things which masked the smell of skunk. Curry was another – so I'd heard.

'You'll be part of our little crew for a while,' the father was saying, 'just until tomorrow and, believe me, the prospect appeals to us as little as it does to you.'

'Why the need to point that cannon at me? Technically, I'm still working for you. Or is this the equivalent of you legging it out of the restaurant without paying the bill?'

'Please don't be rude. If you must know I have already paid Rudgard & Blugden for your services up to the end of this week, with a generous allowance for your expenses. I doubt there will be any quibbles from your firm's accountants. The cheque should have cleared yesterday.'

Well thank you, someone at the office, for not bothering to pass on that little titbit.

He moved to the end of the cabin and pulled a towelling

curtain aside to reveal a wardrobe no bigger than the inside of a grandfather clock in which were piled five or six old-fashioned flight bags with shoulder straps. He selected a dark blue one and sat down on the bunk opposite us with it on his knees; his knees being no more than an inch away from mine. He pulled back the zipper on the bag and put his hand inside; when he pulled it out it was holding a pistol which could have been the twin of the one his son was pointing at my kidneys.

'What was it? A Buy One Get One Free offer?'

Ellrington *père* snorted at that.

'Actually, the man who obtained these for us would be very amused by that, but you, Mr Angel, I think you should take us more seriously.'

Then he pointed his gun at me too. I was surrounded.

'Hey, I do, I do. Really seriously. You do know that there's a mandatory five-year sentence for anyone using firearms in the commission of a crime, don't you?'

I thought that might strike a chord with the son, Peter, but it was James who took it in his stride.

'Yes, as a matter of fact, I *do* know that, but what crime? You've already said you're still technically working for me.'

It was a fair point and a stupid one under the circumstances.

'I think in this situation we have moved from overtime into kidnapping, or have I missed something here?'

'We're not kidnapping anybody!' he laughed and young Peter laughed too.

'Then why the artillery?'

'We need to keep an eye on you, because you're a sneaky little sod,' said Peter, tapping me on the knee with his pistol.

'Moi? Sneaky?'

'It appears so, Mr Angel. Why did you come snooping around my house?' This time it was James tapping me on the knee in case I'd forgotten he had a gun too. 'If you hadn't given yourself away, I might not have suspected you. Peter said somebody had called but, to be honest, Peter's memory is not what it should be and he couldn't really describe you.'

'The skunk gets you that way, doesn't it?' I said to Peter with as much concern as I could muster. 'But what do you mean I gave myself away?'

'Yesterday, when I turned up at your hotel unannounced, you said straight away that I must have come by boat. How did you know I had a boat? The only way I could think of was if you had been to my house and seen the picture of Cheryl and me at the renaming ceremony. Why were you snooping around?'

'Sneaking,' said Peter, doing a pretty fair Gollum impersonation from *Lord of the Rings*.

'I was just trying to get a handle on you, that was all. I knew you had been holding things back from us, not being straight.'

'I did not lie to you!' he snapped indignantly and when an indignant man has a loaded pistol on you, antique or not, it's best to humour him.

'There were things in your story that didn't quite add up from the start. Like when you said your song, you know, your special song, was *Let It Be*, which came out in 1970, yet in the same breath you said you hadn't seen Mrs Pennington since 1963. You should have gone with *I Wanna Hold Your Hand* or one of the other early singles. Not as iconic, I admit, but less suspicious.'

To my left, Peter Ellrington became quite agitated, the gun shaking in his hand.

'How about that, Dad? You slipped up there, didn't you? But you could never forget 1970, could you?'

'Shut up, Peter. And you, Angel,' he pointed his gun at my face so I would know who he meant. 'Don't make the next twenty-four hours any more unpleasant than they have to be.'

'Why twenty-four hours? I'm due back at my office, I'll be missed.'

'I've told you, I've bought you for the rest of the week, paid in advance, and from talking to some of your professional colleagues, I'm not sure you'll be missed at all.'

I didn't like the way he smiled when he said that. I hadn't liked him much to begin with and since he'd pulled a gun on me, I'd definitely started to take against him.

'So I'm your bitch for the week,' I said and I noticed young Peter flinched at that, 'but why the twenty-four hours?'

Ellrington looked at his wristwatch, a big, thick diver's watch which I'd never noticed before.

'Actually less than that. In about twenty hours we'll be out of your hair and you'll never see us again, but until then, I'm afraid you have to crew with us.'

Crew with him? All of a sudden he was Captain Bligh and I'd been press-ganged to serve on board the *Margaret Anne.*

Margaret Anne.

Twenty hours from now would be roughly the time she would be taking her poodles for their morning walk down to Tyneham and Worbarrow, where the sea came up so close it was possible to land there if you had a boat. A boat like the one I was sitting in. He knew where Worbarrow was, he'd said so. He must have been studying his coastal charts carefully, planning this.

'Bloody hell, it's not me who is being Shanghaied, is it? You're going to kidnap Mrs Pennington!'

'Her name is Margaret Anne!' Ellrington shouted, but the anger flared and died instantly. 'And don't be ridiculous. I'm not kidnapping her.'

And then he smiled a beaming smile of genuine happiness.

'We're eloping.'

The *Margaret Anne* set sail midway through the afternoon.

Of course it didn't actually set sail; it didn't have any sails. James Ellrington started up the twin diesel engines and spun the steering wheel thing full right-hand down. Peter Ellrington untied the ropes that connected us to dry land and jumped back on board while his father executed a nifty U-turn in the river, considering the boat was over thirty feet long, and when we were heading roughly due east, he gunned the throttle and we pushed through the water at a steady, stately pace. We probably cut an impressive profile to anyone watching from the riverbanks, not that there was a house or a human being in sight, as the *Margaret Anne* was a fine motor cruiser, lovingly maintained since she was launched in 1972 as the *Osea Island Maid*.

Below decks, so to speak, she was comfortably furnished with four berths, a shower, a 'sea toilet' and a galley which included a gas cooker and a gas fridge. Technically she came equipped with GPS, Speed Log, NavTex, Radar, Forward Looking Sonar and a fish/depth finder. She had a displacement of just over five tons and her fuel tanks carried 75 gallons of diesel.

Even though I didn't know what most of that meant, I was impressed, but then I was a captive audience. While the father and son crew had got us underway, I had been left in the cabin with only an old sales brochure describing the *Margaret Anne* to read. There were a few tattered paperbacks on a shelf above the bunk opposite, but I couldn't reach them as James Ellrington had handcuffed me to the metal safety rail which ran round the top of the gas cooker, presumably to prevent boiling pans of ship's gruel from sliding off in a storm.

He had produced the handcuffs from the same flight bag he had pulled the pistol from.

'I'm afraid we can't have you jumping ashore, so I'm going to have to restrain you until we get out to sea, then you can take your chances with the currents if you want, but I wouldn't advise it,' he said almost as if he cared for my welfare.

'Please put these on one wrist and then clip the other end on that rail.'

He dropped the cuffs next to me on the bunk mattress and waved the big pistol in front of my nose. I didn't really think he was going to shoot me, but having a gun up so close and personal that you can see the tips of the bullets in the cylinder chamber takes away the urge to argue, so I did as I was told.

'Why are you doing this?' I asked as the ratchets on the cuffs clicked into place.

'I told you, we don't want you jumping ashore while we're in the river or causing a disturbance as we go through Poole Harbour. I'll take them off once we're sea-going.'

'No, I meant why am I here at all?'

'Because I can't afford to let you go.'

'Why on earth not? How am I a threat to you and your little *Love Boat* cruise?'

'If you were at liberty, you could have warned him.'

He reached over and tugged the handcuffs to make sure I'd closed them securely.

'Warned who? Simon Pennington?'

'Yes, him.'

He put quite a lot of feeling and distaste into that 'him'.

'He does have a name, you know. You seem to regard him as He-Who-Must-Not-Be-Named, but that's from another fantasy isn't it?'

'I'm not a fantasist, Mr Angel. I am making my dreams come true.'

'You're claiming your Angel's Share, aren't you?'

'Yes I am, that's exactly what I'm doing. Margaret Anne and I are starting a new life together tomorrow morning. Once we do, you'll be free to go of course.'

'While you sail off into the sunset?'

'Actually we'll be sailing east-south-east, so technically it will still be into the sunrise at that time of day.'

'Is this how you imagined it would be?' I said as gently as I could.

'It has turned out exactly how I dreamed it would,' he answered with a sigh.

'Dreamed, maybe, but you didn't expect it to turn out like this, did you? Otherwise why the handcuffs? Why the *suede-lined* handcuffs? They were for Maggie Pennington, weren't they? If she hadn't agreed to go with you, you were just going to take her, weren't you?'

It was then he whipped the long barrel of the pistol across my cheek. He didn't get much of a swing on it, which was just as well as he could have broken my jaw, but it still hurt like hell and persuaded me it would be a good thing to let him have the last word.

He put his angry face about four inches from mine and I tried to focus through the tears.

'Her name is Margaret Anne,' he said slowly, and I realised he was as mad as a hatter.

On the whole, I reckon Captain William Bligh got a bad press and those mutineers on the *Bounty* didn't have that much to complain about. There was probably not enough rum to go round and a bit too much sodomy and the lash, but then they weren't chained to a stove having to listen to the delusional ramblings of Peter Ellrington. He was almost as irrational as his father, though in his case I suspected the dementia to have been chemically-induced over far too many years smoking too much dope.

Once we were chugging down river, he came and joined me in the cabin. He put his pistol down carefully on the bunk opposite before making himself comfortable. He was nursing an old square tobacco tin which had been fondled so much the metal shone. As the scenery out of the cabin window seemed to be an expanse of mudflat and marsh grass I decided to watch Peter instead, especially when he began the ritual of rolling a joint. From the skill with which his long, thin fingers manipulated the tin, the loose tobacco, the papers and the dope, I surmised that he'd done this before.

'What are you doing here, Peter?' I asked, trying to establish diplomatic relations.

'Dad doesn't like me smoking weed in public.'

'Public?' I looked out of the window and still saw only mud and marsh.

'There'll be more traffic in the Wareham Channel and around Brownsea,' he said, tearing a piece off a strip of cardboard to make a crude filter, then rolling up a neat and incredibly thin cigarette. The only people I knew who could roll a joint that thin were those who had learned the technique in prison where raw materials were at a premium.

'I didn't mean here in this cabin, I meant here on this whole voyage of the damned escapade.'

'I'm helping my father sort out his love life,' he said without a smile, lighting the joint with a cheap Bic disposable lighter which he kept in a small pouch slung around his neck by a shoelace and tucked down the front of his T-shirt.

'Hell of a way to go eloping, isn't it? Carrying guns, I mean.'

'Dad's not going to take "no" for an answer this time.'

'So you know about the other times, then?'

He blew a stream of pungent smoke down his nose.

'Of course I knew. I've lived with his broken heart since the day I was born. In fact, it's probably the reason I was born.'

He sucked hard on the joint until the end glowed and tiny fragments of burning paper floated off like grey snowflakes. The cabin was already beginning to shimmer with a thin blue fog and I wondered how long it would be before I started getting a high from passive toking.

I suspected Peter Ellrington's system was pretty hardened to the effects of the dope and if he was a regular skunk smoker, I was far more likely to be floating with the fairies than he was or, rather, experiencing 'cognitive imbalance' as you were supposed to say these days.

Skunk No. 1 or Super Skunk are basically hybrid strains of cannabis with a much a higher level of THC – tetrahydrocannabinol – the component which gives you the 'high'. Someone, somewhere had the bright idea of crossing Afghani, Mexican and Thai varieties of standard cannabis plants. The Thai varieties provided the high THC levels; the Mexican plants were quicker growing and needed less light (and were therefore ideal for undercover cultivation in artificial light); and the Afghan strains tended to mature early and required a shorter growing season. If you were a grower, you won on all counts. If you were a customer, you got more bangs for your buck.

And it had proved popular with the consumer. Rumour was that skunk had all but replaced the aromatic Moroccan Blacks and Lebanese Reds that second-generation hippies like me had been brought up on.

'So your Dad's been planning this for some time?' I pressed him gently.

He seemed to have relaxed, had his head down looking at the deck and his elbows on his knees. He had placed the pistol to his left, the furthest point away from me and I wouldn't have been able to grab for it even without the handcuffs.

'Since I was born, I told you.'

'What?' I said, genuinely puzzled.

'You're supposed to be the detective, haven't you worked it out?'

'Worked what out?'

'He lost her once, back in 1963. When things weren't working out between him and my mother, when he was seconded up to Yorkshire, he went looking for her. They almost went off together then, but then mum announced she was pregnant and that was it, wasn't it? He had to stay with her and the saintly Margaret Anne didn't want to push it and break up the happy family.'

He snorted more smoke and then leaned across me to reach under the sink, pulling aside the small curtain which acted as a cupboard door. He fumbled around and produced an empty soup can, then settled himself back on the bunk with the can between his feet to use as an ashtray.

'Got to keep the boat clean for Princess Perfect when she comes aboard,' he said with a lopsided grin. 'After all, it is named after her.'

He stubbed the remaining quarter-inch of his joint out in the soup can and reached for his tobacco tin to roll another. The man was a dedicated reefer-head.

'That picture in the house; that was your mother, right? Standing on the boat.'

'Yes, that was her at the renaming launch. Dad insisted that they had their picture taken together.'

'On a boat he'd named after his mistress?'

'You'd better not use that word in front of him. Margaret Anne was always his one true love. "Mistress" is a dirty word for a relationship so holy.'

'Didn't your mother ever guess?'

'She didn't have to. *He told her*. Time and time again. Told her he was naming the boat after her and that once he was free and clear, he would be making a present of it to her.'

He had skinned up a second joint and was flicking the lighter.

'When did he tell her that?'

'Soon after I was born I think, certainly he never made a secret of the fact that he thought my mum was always second choice.'

'That's harsh, that's really harsh,' I said. 'But she still stuck by him?'

'Oh, he treated her all right. I mean, he didn't beat her up or anything and as far as I know, since I was born, he was faithful to her. He just didn't love her, and he told her so. Told her he was just waiting to be free and clear.'

'Told her he was waiting for her to die?'

'I don't think he ever said that in so many words, but she got the message. It was only a matter of time before the cancer took her; there was nothing anyone could do for her and she was probably relieved when the end came.'

I'll bet she was.

Peter was halfway through the next spliff and I was sure I was becoming light-headed. If the atmosphere in the confined cabin became too thick, we could always open a window but there seemed no point in risking a draught just yet.

I was almost beginning to feel sorry for Peter Ellrington. He was one of those people who permanently had the look of having just got up and he'd not had the easiest of lives.

'That was two years ago, wasn't it?'

'Yes, just a bit over – since mum died.'

'So why didn't he start looking for Margaret Anne then, if he was free and clear?'

Peter tried blowing a smoke ring which only emphasised how sunken his cheeks were.

'He wasn't free and clear of all family ties, though. He had to wait for me.'

'To get out of prison,' I completed for him and he nodded slowly. 'What were you doing?'

'Eighteen months for dealing.'

'Whereabouts?'

'Forest Bank up in Manchester.'

'That's a private sector prison isn't it?'

'Yes, thank God. I wasn't potted once.'

'But you were the other times you were inside?'

He turned his head away so I couldn't see his face.

'Three, sometimes four times a day.'

'Potting' is the quaint ritual of throwing the contents of your overnight chamber pot over a suitably deserving fellow inmate, an honour usually reserved for child molesters.

'But you didn't get potted in Forest Bank?'

'It was private sector, they didn't know what my dad did for a living.'

'Your dad's a retired civil servant, isn't he?'

'Yeah, that's right, retired after forty-one years in Her Majesty's Prison Service. For a time, he was a prison governor. That's why I was so popular inside.'

I didn't know what to say to that. When he turned his head to look at me I pointed to the joint he was holding.

'Could you spare some of that?'

Chapter Twenty-One

I was restricted to watching Poole Harbour go by through the cabin windows. They were proper windows, not portholes, and it was rather like watching television with the sound turned down. Yachts and small sailing dinghies zipped by frighteningly close. In the distance a large French cross-Channel ferry was either docking or departing. I noted the 10-knot speed limit signs and the signs saying we were entering Quiet Areas, so naturally I put a finger to my lips and went 'Shh!' to the passing yachts, which I found a quite amusing thing to do. By the time we were passing Brownsea Island, which was famous for something to do with the early Boy Scout movement though I couldn't remember what, I was feeling positively mellow.

Peter Ellrington was, amazingly, still rolling and smoking steadily and continuously. I had never seen anyone virtually chain-smoke joints of skunk like that and still retain their manual dexterity.

When I began to see a wide expanse of open sea stretching in front of us and there was a noticeable roll to the motion of the boat which had not been there before, even a landlubber like me could guess that we were exchanging the shelter of Poole harbour for the ocean wide.

'What'll be our course, Mr Christian?' somebody said loudly in a bad Long John Silver/Robert Newton impersonation. When I realised it had been me, I started giggling.

'You can work it out for yourself,' said Ellrington, reaching into a cubby hole near the cabin doors and producing a huge book the size of two Yellow Pages directories (London Business).

He dropped it in my lap and the impact almost winded me. I focused on the title, *Macmillan Reed's Nautical Almanac*, and tried to lift it with my one free hand. If it floated I could use it as a life raft in the event of us sinking, for at 1,136 pages, it didn't qualify as light reading.

'The Almanac goes west-to-east,' Peter was saying, 'but we'll be cruising mostly east-to-west, so you need to find the right section and then work backwards.'

I wasn't sure I understood any of that, but I started flipping through the book and quickly got distracted by a very pretty chapter on navigation lights and then a colourful section on code flags and what they could mean. For some reason I found it very amusing that the flag for the letter U (Uniform) could also mean 'You are running into danger' but the one I found positively hysterical was that the D (Delta) flag also meant, very aptly, 'I am manoeuvring with difficulty'.

I passed the latest joint back to Peter and opened the almanac randomly near the back, at page 1016 to be precise. I concentrated hard and began to learn more than anyone reasonably wanted to know about a place called Borkum in the East Friesian Islands.

I had no idea where the fuck Borkum was other than the fact that the book – *The Yachthiker's Guide To The Galaxy* – told me it was 53 degrees 33 minutes north and 0 degrees 45 minutes east; presumably of Greenwich, which put it somewhere over in Europe. Be honest, though, who has given a stuff for the East Friesian Islands since Erskine Childers wrote *Riddle of the Sands*?

'Try and find the south-west England section,' Ellrington advised, but when he saw I was having trouble with all those pages, he took the book from me and held it up to his face, with the smoking joint clamped between his lips.

'Here it is,' he read, even though his eyes were watering.

'Poole Harbour and Wareham. Sandbanks, the Studland – that's a nudist beach, isn't it?'

'The things they mark on nautical maps,' I agreed.

'Old Harry and then Ballard Point and in to Swanage Bay.'

'Ah, Swanage, the nightlife capital of the south coast.'

He ignored me.

'Then Durlston Head. Up to this point it's been mostly a southerly heading, but then we turn west for St Aldheim's Head and round by the Kimmeridge Ledges, across Kimmeridge Bay, around Broad Bench and across Brandy Bay and there we are, Worbarrow Tout. Fifty degrees, thirty-seven minutes north, two degrees, twelve minutes west.'

'What the hell was all that, Peter? You lost me somewhere around Swanage.'

'They're landfalls around the coast; navigation aids for the sailor. You'll see them to starboard as we pass them.'

As he had been following the map in the almanac with his index finger, I got the impression he wasn't the skilled navigator he liked to think he was.

'And so they'll be on the port side on the way back?' I asked, thinking it a perfectly reasonable question.

Peter took the joint out of his mouth and blew on the end to make sure it hadn't gone out.

'Oh no,' he said, 'we're not coming back.'

When we were opposite Studland's famous naturist beach, I was allowed on deck to find we were so far out in the bay there was nothing untoward to be seen.

I hadn't been uncuffed and allowed out of the cabin to play the voyeur, though. Once we had cleared Poole Harbour, the water was deeper, the currents stronger and the only other vessels around were large tankers out on the horizon, or flashy yachts under full sail, tacking and weaving and generally showing off and keeping their distance. None were near enough to shout to for help and when I waved frantically at one yacht, the crew simply waved back. Well it was a pleasant sunny afternoon and, relaxed as I was, I couldn't blame them.

James Ellrington had burst into the cabin and waved his hand in front of his nose. He had put on a yellow oilskin jacket and the right hand pocket sagged and bulged with the weight of the revolver in there.

'Christ, but it stinks like a Turkish brothel in here.'

It didn't seem a good idea to tell him that I'd heard they were mostly air-conditioned these days, and anyway I was having a slight difficulty forming words.

'Get up on deck and clear your heads and get the windows open to fumigate this place,' he ordered. 'And no more smoking down here; do it on deck if you have to. I'll want this place cleaned by tonight.'

'Of course, everything must be *perfect* for our guest,' Peter said sarcastically.

I assumed he meant the guest they were expecting but I deliberately took it the wrong way to wind them up.

'I'm sure I'll be perfectly comfortable,' I said with a grin, 'though I am getting a bit hungry. When's lunch?'

Even psychopathic pirates engaged in kidnapping and abduction, not to mention elopement, had to eat.

Ellrington Senior unlocked the handcuffs to free me, only after telling his son not to be so stupid as to leave his gun lying on the bunk opposite me, though I had quite forgotten it was there. Peter picked it up sulkily and raising his T-shirt, stuck it down the front of his trousers. Those old-fashioned British revolvers have very big, fixed front sights known as the 'blade' design and if he tried a quick draw from there, it could have nasty consequences.

James then escorted me up the steps out on to the deck, whilst Peter was told to open some tins of soup and bring it up to us.

The boat's wheelhouse, as such, was a sort of pulpit with a Perspex canopy where, despite an impressive array of electronic

equipment, the autopilot seemed to consist of a leather thong
tying the large steering wheel in place. Ellrington didn't leave it
unattended for long and smartly took his place at the helm and
ignored me.

There was a grey rubber dinghy lashed flat against the stern
of the boat. I hadn't noticed it when I came aboard as, judging
from the dangling hawser, it had been floating in the river. I
didn't give much on my chances of getting launched before I
was shot by one of the Ellringtons, and it did look an awfully
long row back to land, even if I could find where they kept the
oars or paddles or whatever they called them. In any case, they
hadn't provided lunch yet and the fresh air was definitely giving
me the munchies.

The roof of the cabin seemed the logical place for sunbathing
or a maritime picnic, so I fished my sunglasses out of my jacket,
then made a pillow of it and lay down in order to take advantage
of the afternoon sun and let the sea breeze clear my head.

When Peter came from below carrying a tray on which were
three large white mugs, I could see the fresh air take him by
surprise and he blinked violently in reaction to the sunlight. He
gave his father one of the mugs, then, rather unsteadily,
mounted the cabin roof and came towards me.

'Soup,' he said, in a voice which brooked no argument.

It certainly was, though what flavour I wasn't sure. And I
must have wrinkled my nose in suspicion.

'It's a cocktail,' he said, sitting down next to me. 'The cans
got mixed up. It was supposed to be all tomato but one of the
tins turned out to be oxtail and I only realised afterwards that
one was mulligatawny. Sorry.'

'In a curious way, it works,' I said graciously.

'There's cheese and biscuits to follow,' he said, almost
apologetically.

'If there are weevils in the hard tack, it'll be mutiny before
dawn for sure, Mr Queeg.'

'Was that funny?' he asked in the genuine sort of enquiry

only the totally innocent or the very stoned make without expecting a smack in the teeth.

'Not really,' I admitted between sips of soup. 'So you're not going back then?'

'Huh?'

'You said you weren't coming back this way.'

'Nothing to go back for. We're free and clear, or we will be this time tomorrow.'

'So what happens tomorrow then? Like I'm only asking 'cos I've got a vested interest in all this, seeing as how I'm being held against my will.'

'Join the club,' he said quietly. 'Plan is that we meet Princess Perfect at the Worbarrow place or Tyneham – wherever – and she sees that she has a boat named after her, and she already has her suitcase packed, so we sweep her on board and sail off to Happily Ever After.'

'Surely there's an easier way? I mean, I could call them a cab.'

Well, I could have if I hadn't left my phone in my hired car which was probably being impounded by the Community Street Wardens of Wareham as we spoke.

'No, you don't get it, do you? Dad has been planning this for thirty-five years. He's dreamed the way it's going to be. When he got into boating and first joined a sailing club, years ago, that's when he got this idea of coming to get her by boat and sailing off with her. That's why he sold the house. Let's face it, if you're going to whisk your child bride off to somewhere romantic, it's not going to be Merton Park is it?'

He had a point.

'So where then, a castle in Spain?'

'Place in Brittany actually. The house is sold subject to actually getting the money and he bought a place down near Quimper about five years ago. It's all set up and waiting as the honeymoon home.'

'Boats and second homes in France don't come cheap; he must have been on a fair salary.'

'You can say that again. He was one of the top men in the prison service as people always kept reminding me. But this has been a long game for him. When I was a kid, we never had a new car, they were always second-hand and we never went on family holidays, not even a day trip to the seaside. Of course we didn't know he was saving up for a second life with a second wife.'

'That's terrible, man. That's truly cold-hearted. That's ice that is. Did you say there was cheese and biscuits?'

I'd had better two-course lunches. Peter Ellrington had probably had better in prison.

'So you won't be joining the happy couple in their honeymoon hideaway?'

I kept an eye on James Ellrington, but he couldn't possibly hear what we were saying above the steady throb of the engines and anyway, he was concentrating on steering the boat and relishing how every nautical mile brought him closer to his true love.

'I don't think I'd be exactly welcome,' Peter said. 'I don't like France and the sound of all that creaking and groaning as they mashed the mattress would turn my stomach. Anyway, I'm too old to start bonding with a stepmother.'

'I know that feeling,' I agreed, but he wasn't interested in my parental problems. To be fair, if it wasn't for the guns and a lengthy swim to dry land, I wouldn't be the slightest bit interested in the Ellringtons' domestic arrangements.

'I'm taking my share and I'm off. If I never see my father again, it'll be too soon.'

'Your share? I thought Daddy was the one looking for his lost "Angel's Share".'

'Is your name really Angel?'

'Yes it is,' I admitted.

'Funny that; him getting an Angel to help him find his Angel's Share.'

The thought amused him so much he opened his magic tin

and began to put together the makings of another spliff.

'So what is it you've got a share of?'

'I get the proceeds from the sale of the house in Merton Park, paid into a bank account of my choice. He gets the boat, the place in France, his pension and the end of a loveless life.'

'*With dreamless dreams and schemeless schemes, we wreck our love boats on the shore,*' I mused.

'Is that poetry?'

'Yes it is, but it's also a song, a famous song called *Loveless Love.*'

'Who's it by?'

'WC Handy.'

'Never heard of them. D'you want to roll one?'

He offered me the tobacco tin but I waved it away. The sea breeze was gradually clearing my head and I thought it might be a good idea to keep it clear.

'Fancy a drink instead?'

'Now you're talking.'

When Peter Ellrington emerged from the cabin with a white mug in each hand, the *Margaret Anne* was turning west around Durlston Head, the impressive if crumbly limestone cliffs on the top of which ran the Dorset coastal path. The swell under the boat moved up a couple of notches in strength and Peter picked his way over the cabin roof, balancing his weight carefully before moving his feet. It meant he was either an experienced sailor or a hardened drinker used to moving through crowded bars carrying two drinks.

Taking a proffered mug I sniffed my drink delicately. It had the right sort of smell, but I watched him drink some of his before I swallowed.

'It's cider brandy from France,' he said with relish.

'So it is,' I squeaked, my throat on fire. The mug contained about a third of a pint of muddy brown liquid. 'It could come in useful if we run out of diesel.'

'This is nothing to the stuff we used to make inside,' said Peter.

'Inside, as in prison?'

'Yeah, every nick I've been in had a still. Apples were really good, but we used anything we could get our hands on. You could always get fruit brought in by visitors or persuade the Medical Officer that you needed more fruit in your diet.'

'What about dope?'

'Never had any problem getting dope inside.'

'So I've heard. How does it get in there?'

'Most of it's brought in by lawyers, or sometimes screws. The people who don't normally get searched thoroughly or even at all.'

'Crazy world.'

'One I'm not going back to,' he said.

'You were never in one where he was…?'

'Oh no, that never happened. That would have been just *too* embarrassing, but most of the cons I was with knew what he did for a living, or if they didn't, then some bastard screw told them just to make life uncomfortable – for me, that is, not for him. Funnily enough, most of the cons I met inside who'd been inmates at one my Dad's gaffs, they said he was a decent Governor. Strict but fair, with a sense of honour.

'You know, he would get mentioned in the wills of some of the older lags, they thought that much of him. That's where he got those pistols. Some old con left them to him. He did a ten stretch for armed robbery and then snuffed it within a year of coming out, aged about sixty. Left Dad a note saying they were family heirlooms from *his* father's time in the Army and said he would swear on a stack of Bibles that they'd never been used in the commission of a crime.

'They were a bit rusty, but they cleaned up and they still worked. I helped Dad get some ammo that fitted and he's been practising with them for the last five years. He's not a bad shot now.'

I gulped down some more Calvados. Suddenly it didn't seem strong enough.

'He's been planning this for five years?'

'Longer than that, haven't you heard what I've been saying? When Mum had me, he had to stick by her; that was the honourable thing to do. But when she was diagnosed with the cancer, he knew he'd be free...'

'...and clear, yes, I remember that bit.'

'Me being inside delayed things a bit, but once Mum had gone and he was coming up to retirement, the timing came right, but he's been dreaming about it for years. He knew he might need the guns in his master plan, so he never handed them in or reported them like he should have done.'

'Exactly why would he need the guns, Peter?' I asked cautiously.

He looked at me pityingly for not knowing.

'He was free and clear, but that didn't mean that Margaret Anne was. She might still be married...'

'So if she'd said she wouldn't come with him, he was going to murder Simon Pennington?'

'Not murder him – not as such. He was going to challenge him to a duel. That's why he brought along both the revolvers. It's kind of a romantic notion when you think about it, isn't it?'

Chapter Twenty-Two

James Ellrington asked me politely to go below into the cabin where he would handcuff me once again to the gas cooker. We were getting near Worbarrow Bay and there might be some tourists still enjoying an early evening stroll on Worbarrow Tout. It was his intention to anchor overnight in the bay itself. It was unlikely there would be any other craft there, despite it being the height of the summer season, as there were no facilities at all at Worbarrow and just around the next headland was Lulworth Cove which was far more picturesque.

We had seen considerable nautical traffic on our cruise that afternoon, mostly small sailing craft but also the occasional fishing boat probably heading for Weymouth, but nothing had come near enough for me to yell 'Help, I've been kidnapped!' or even run up the appropriate distress code flag, if there was one for such a contingency. There were hundreds of fossil-hunting tourists on the beaches around Kimmeridge Bay, but they were too busy and too far away to have noticed if the Ellringtons had suddenly decided to keelhaul me, even if I wasn't altogether sure what that would have involved.

Worbarrow Bay, though, was deserted and the nearest village, Tyneham, had been officially deserted in 1943, so there wasn't really any need for the handcuffs. I wasn't going anywhere.

For some reason they didn't see it that way and I had my left hand cuffed to the stove except when I demanded to use the 'sea-toilet'.

I watched the sun go down across the mile and a half expanse of Worbarrow Bay through the cabin windows as we gently bobbed at anchor in about two metres of water. I didn't know if the tide was going out, or coming in, but I probably wouldn't notice as there was very little tide fall in the bay. I knew all this because the only thing I had to read was that huge and heavy almanac. I supposed I could always hit one of them with it.

There was even a section in there covering disasters at sea and the reassuring discovery that the most common cause of death, disaster and injury on small pleasure craft came from the gas cylinders used in the cookers, just like the one I was attached to.

Naturally, I got worried when James Ellrington said we should eat 'before turning in' and Peter offered to cook dinner. Fortunately this involved nothing more dangerous than opening tins of corned beef and packets of crisps, which we ate off paper plates.

'He's saving the posh dinner service for you know who,' said Peter, which produced a grunt and a look of distaste from his father.

As it grew dark, James turned on a single electric light and unpacked three sleeping bags from a locker at the rear of the cabin.

It was clear they expected me to sleep still handcuffed to the stove and I was not even allowed to join Peter on deck for one last smoke, or three. If it hadn't been for the bottle of Calvados he had left within reach, I wouldn't have slept a wink.

It felt as if I hadn't, but it was light and somebody was prodding me awake and I could hear water running in the shower.

I almost broke my wrist trying to check the time on my watch; and when I saw it was 5.10 a.m., I wished I hadn't bothered.

'Come on, get up,' said Peter Ellrington. 'Let's get this over with.'

'Take him on deck and keep an eye on him,' said his father, handing him the key to the handcuffs. 'Fasten his wrists behind his back.'

I was impressed by that touch. Very few people would fancy diving into the sea with their hands tied behind their back no matter how good a swimmer they were. All his years in the restraining people industry were finally paying off.

The morning mist was thick and damp and the shore only just visible even though it was no more than thirty yards away.

'So what's the plan?' I asked, shaking my head to try and clear it. Being kidnapped and shackled and woken up at dawn was one thing; not being provided with coffee was cruel and unusual punishment.

'Margaret Anne is meeting us in Tyneham at six o'clock. By seven, if this mist has cleared, she and I and Peter will be out to sea and you'll be free to go.'

James had showered and shaved and was dressed in clean khaki slacks and a check shirt with a plain blue tie under his green blazer. He had scrubbed up well and even exchanged his canvas deck shoes for a pair of highly polished brown brogues. Peter Ellrington and I were unshaven, unwashed and looked as if we had slept in our clothes, which we had.

'Can I ask you something?'

'If you must,' he said coldly, as if he had just realised I was still there as a temporary and very minor obstacle in the path of his master plan.

'How did you persuade her to leave her husband? You were only with her for about an hour yesterday.'

James Ellrington squared up to me and looked me straight in the eyes. When he spoke it was as if he was talking to a particularly stubborn and stupid child.

'We love each other. We always have.'

And then he turned away and ordered Peter to unlash the rubber dinghy and get it in the water.

Before we transferred to the dinghy, James bobbed back down into the cabin to straighten the bunks, neaten the curtains and bring out the trash in a black bin liner. His last act, rather touchingly, as he climbed the steps, was to spray the cabin with air-freshener from an aerosol can.

From the tiny wheelhouse, he picked up his flight bag, unzipped it and placed it on the deck at his feet. Bending down, he took out first one revolver, then the other, broke them open and satisfied himself they were loaded. From where I was standing it looked as if they were.

'Those things don't have safety catches, do they?' I said, thinking aloud.

Ellrington glared at me, then zipped up the bag and slung it over his shoulder just as the dinghy splashed into the sea and I felt salt water spray on my face and lips.

'Let's go,' he said, straightening his tie.

'Wait. I'll just get my jacket,' I said, sidling towards the cabin doors.

Peter was tying a long thin line to secure the dinghy to the boat; James didn't seem inclined to help me or even acknowledge my presence anymore, which suited me fine.

Clumsily I got the cabin doors open and jumped down the steps. I fumbled in my jacket to make sure my wallet and hire-car keys were still there. It wasn't that I thought the Ellringtons might have taken them, it was that I didn't want to leave any evidence that I had been on the boat that night.

The air in the cabin was thick with pine-scented air freshener, which was perfect for what I had in mind even though I didn't know if the cylinder gas powering the cooker had its own smell or not.

Even with my hands tied behind me, it was easy enough to turn all the burner gas taps on full. Then I climbed up on deck, dragging my jacket behind me, and closed the cabin doors with my foot.

* * *

I got ashore getting only one foot wet in the process and stumbled up the shingle beach, the crunch of pebbles sounding extremely loud, echoing off the surrounding hills. If I had been the invading Nazi hordes back in 1940, then Allan Farrell, waiting up the path in his ironclad turret armed with a tommy-gun, would have heard me coming.

James Ellrington set off at a brisk military pace up the path towards Tyneham. I stumbled along behind him hoping the mist would get thicker and I could do a runner into the wood to our left. But even if I avoided Peter Ellrington, bringing up the rear, I wasn't sure how it would help. I would still be handcuffed and still miles from anywhere. James would probably not have noticed if I had gone walkabout, and neither would Peter. When I turned around to check, he was sitting on the foundation stones of a ruined cottage rolling a joint.

It took us a good ten minutes to reach the car park, empty of humans at that time of the morning but crawling with rabbits who showed a conspicuous lack of interest in us, although Peter seemed to find them amusing.

We marched on across the damp grass heading for the village pond and the skeleton of Post Office Row.

'So where is she then?' Peter said loudly from behind me and then burst into manic laughter. 'Sure she's coming?'

Although I knew it wasn't possible, I thought James hadn't heard him. He didn't slow his pace, but he hitched the shoulder bag round in front of his body. I could not see what he was doing but I had a damn good idea and when he swung round holding one of the revolvers, I stopped in my tracks and went down on my knees.

I need not have bothered; I might as well have not been there. James Ellrington only had eyes for his son and one of them was peering down the back-sight of a pistol.

'I told you to behave,' he growled. 'I will not have my actions questioned by a sorry piece of shit like you.'

Peter just stood there, smoking calmly and smiling, not

believing for a second that his father would shoot him. I was convinced he was crazy enough to do just that and, if he did, he wouldn't want any witnesses around.

'Have I been a disappointment to you, father dear? Ever considered what you put me and Mum through?'

'I stood by your mother; don't you dare say I didn't.'

'Stood by her? She was not some simple barmaid you got knocked up. She was your wife.'

'And I did the honourable thing!' James roared, going purple in the face. 'I made it quite clear I did not love her.'

'Oh yes, you did that all right!' Peter shouted back.

I looked between the two of them as if I was watching a tennis match. Peter was clearly out of his mind on too much skunk. James was simply out of his mind. I was kneeling in the grass, my hands locked behind my back, slap bang in the middle.

Then we all heard the sound of a car engine coming down the hill through the mist.

'She's here!' James exclaimed, his scowl changing into an expression of almost childish glee in the blink of an eye.

'Fuck me, she actually came,' said Peter.

I was quite surprised myself.

In my brief acquaintance with Margaret Anne Hayes-Pennington, she had struck me as an intelligent, attractive, confident and eminently sensible woman. She had enjoyed a forty-year marriage with only one blip (as far as I knew) and seemed set for a comfortable retirement in a beautiful part of the country, keeping active with a responsible job and the added bonus of no troublesome children to worry about.

So there was the element of romance, which you can never be sure of, and she was probably flattered when James offered to take her away from the horror of her humdrum existence, or whatever it was he said. But to actually go along with it? To just up sticks at less than twenty-four hours' notice, leave her loyal husband, her house and her dogs and, at the age of 62, opt for a life in a foreign country with an old boyfriend she hadn't seen since 1970? What sort of a woman would do that?

Actually, my mother probably would. Perhaps it was thinking that which made me want to give Margaret Anne a slap and say 'Just grow up, will you?'

Instead I got to my feet and stood in front of James Ellrington's gun, then turned so I was sideways on and jerked my head backwards.

'How are you going to explain the handcuffs?'

'Yes, there seems no need for those now,' he said calmly, returning to Planet Normal. 'Peter, bring the key.'

They unlocked me and while I rubbed my arms to get the circulation going again, James packed the handcuffs and his gun back in his shoulder bag. Peter said nothing; at least nothing aloud, though he was having a whispered conversation with himself.

And then through the mist appeared Margaret Anne's BMW estate car and before she'd applied the handbrake, James was running to meet it. He had the driver's door open and was helping her out almost as if she was an invalid. She didn't seem to mind. In fact, she was beaming and breathless and laughing and excited all at once.

James threw his arms around her and she grabbed him back with equal fervour, then they kissed long and hard and I suspect tongues were involved. When they came up for air she was still smiling and her face was flushed and then she looked towards me and said:

'What's he doing here?'

'I had to bring him,' James said to her. 'He won't be with us long. We can drop him off in Bournemouth or Christchurch before...'

And by then I realised they were talking about Peter, not me.

'But you never said...I never expected I would have to see him...'

'Bitch!' said Peter under his breath.

'I think you've managed to spoil the fairy tale ending,' I said to him out of the corner of my mouth.

'Good.'

But his satisfaction was short-lived.

The real party-pooper was coming down the hill in a Land Rover.

'It's my husband!' screamed Mrs Pennington, hearing the familiar engine. 'We have to hide!'

I had to laugh; they were behaving like big kids.

Margaret Anne grabbed James by the hand and they ran into the village, or what remained of it, taking shelter in the last derelict cottage in Post Office Row just as the Lulworth Rangers' Land Rover turned into the car park.

Suddenly I realised Peter Ellrington seemed to have disappeared and it was left to me to hold my hands up in a Stop gesture to the Land Rover.

Simon Pennington climbed out of the driver's side and furrowed his brow in my general direction.

'Who the hell are you?'

'We sort of met yesterday,' I said.

'We did? Oh yes, you were a visitor here, weren't you? What the hell are you doing here at this time of the morning?'

'I'm here with a client...'

'You haven't seen my wife Maggie have you? That's her car there, but...just a minute, you're not that bastard Ellrington are you? No, of course you can't be. You're not his idiot son are you? The one with drug problems?'

'Listen, Mr Pennington, I think we should try and keep calm...'

'Don't worry, the girls will find her.'

He walked around the Land Rover and opened the rear door, releasing Sheba and Jezebel.

'Go on, girls, find her! Go find Mummy!'

This was getting to be far more than I could handle this early and without caffeine.

The two poodles leapt to the ground, yapped at his feet and circled each other then ran towards the BMW. As tracker dogs, they weren't impressing anyone, but Mr Pennington didn't seem to notice. He was still shouting instructions whilst busying himself with something inside the Land Rover.

'Come on you dogs, go fetch! Find her! Find Mummy. Show me where the lying whore is hiding.'

I was taken aback by that outburst and even further shocked when he stepped away from the Land Rover. He was stuffing cartridges from a box into the breast pocket of his Lulworth Rangers overalls and in the crook of his arm he held a broken-open double barrelled shotgun.

My morning just got better and better.

'Maggie! Show yourself! Come on, dear, you owe me that.'

Simon Pennington was stalking his wife through a ruined village armed with a shotgun and I was following along behind him. The two poodles had decided to stay behind me for health and safety reasons.

'Mr Pennington, if you'd just give me a minute to explain…' I tried.

'Nothing to explain. The wife left me a note on the kitchen table. After forty-two bloody years, I get left a note on the kitchen table saying that out of the blue, she's pissing off with her old boyfriend Ellrington.'

'You knew about him?'

'Of course I did. She couldn't resist telling me about their sordid little affair back in 1970. Well, I might forgive, but I don't forget. I'm 74 years old and I haven't many illusions left, but I still have my pride.'

'Think about it, Mr Pennington, think what you're doing. Going after him with a shotgun is not going to solve anything.'

The old man stopped in his tracks and turned on me the shotgun pointed loosely at my stomach.

'What do you mean *him*? The shotgun's for that bitch of a wife of mine – and just who the fucking hell did you say you were, anyway?'

I needed caffeine so badly it hurt.

The three of them were waiting for us in the middle of the road between the church and the tiny schoolhouse. James Ellrington had an arm around Margaret Anne's shoulder and Peter was skulking off to one side.

When the poodles saw her, they ran to greet her but she held up a hand in a command which obviously meant 'don't jump up' and they took a perfunctory sniff at the hem of her Barbour coat before racing off snapping at each other into the trees and long grass behind the school.

'You forgot about the girls, Maggie,' Simon announced, advancing on them with me tagging along behind. 'When they thought you'd gone for their morning walk without them, they came and woke me up. I found your note a bit earlier than I was supposed to, didn't I?'

'I suppose you did, Simon. I'm sorry.'

She didn't sound very sorry and I thought it odd that a dog person like Margaret Anne would have forgotten about the morning rituals of her 'girls'.

'I'm taking her away from you, Simon,' declared James Ellrington, one hand on her shoulder, the other clutching the strap of his flight bag.

'Oh you are, are you? What if I don't want her to go with you?'

'Oh for God's sake,' I interrupted the negotiations. 'A minute ago you wanted to kill her. Look, all of you – just GROW UP! Can we not sort this out like adults?'

'Yes we can,' said James Ellrington, throwing his flight bag on to the ground in front of Margaret Anne's husband.

'What's that supposed to mean?' Simon demanded. 'What's in the bag?'

'The only honourable solution,' said James Ellrington.

And even then, I knew Simon Pennington would go for it. They were both as mad as each other.

Simon waved us all away with the shotgun while he knelt down and examined the contents of the flight bag.

He looked up at James.

'What are you proposing?'

'I'm proposing that I don't leave this place without Margaret Anne,' Ellrington said grandly, like he'd rehearsed it, which he probably had. 'Both pistols are in full working order and both are fully loaded. Winner takes all, simple as that.'

Now this was where any sane person, especially one holding a loaded shotgun and theoretically in charge of the situation, would have behaved like a responsible adult and told everybody not to be so silly.

'So what do we do? Stand back to back, take ten paces, turn and fire?'

'I believe that's traditional.'

'HELLO! Reality check!' I shouted at them. 'Is there anyone else here who believes this is actually happening?'

'Be quiet.' Simon turned the shotgun on me again but I was used to having guns pointed at me by now. 'Whoever you are.'

'Mr Angel is an innocent party in all this, Simon,' his wife said, finding her voice at last. 'If you have to blame someone, blame me.'

'Oh I do, Maggie, I do, but it's your boyfriend here who's the problem. He just can't stand losing, can you, James? You lost her in 1963 and then you lost her again in 1970 and now you're going to lose her again.'

'Oh shit, they're going to kill each other,' I said, appealing to Margaret Anne. 'Can't you do anything to stop it?'

I hadn't been paying enough attention to her, otherwise I

would have noticed earlier that her eyes had glazed and that she was quivering not with fear, but excitement.

'They're fighting – over me!' she said softly so that only I could hear.

Pennington placed the shotgun down on the road and armed himself with both revolvers from the flight bag. He ordered his wife, Peter and me to stand up against the schoolhouse and then he approached James Ellrington, who was standing where the road gave way to long grass and the overhanging trees in front of the shell of Rectory Cottages, the ruin with the same outline as the Alamo.

Maybe Simon Pennington had seen too many old westerns, though of course they would have been new when he saw them.

'You're younger than me, so I will pick the ground,' he told James, their faces a foot apart. 'Are you ready?'

Ellrington turned around and stood ramrod straight, facing down the little road towards the church. What should have happened was that Simon Pennington should have taken up a back-to-back position so that he would be facing the ruins of Rectory Cottages, then they could have asked one of us to count out ten paces or something. But it didn't work out like that.

For a start, Simon still held both guns.

But not for long. He stuck the one in his right hand into his left armpit, then took the one in his left hand by the barrel and threw it as hard and far as he could into the churchyard where it bounced off a gravestone and disappeared from sight.

Then he was waving the second revolver under James's nose and James was looking decidedly worried as this wasn't in his script at all.

'I would have handed you yours,' Ellrington said to his opponent who had just declared war.

'That's because you like me more than I like you,' said Simon.

I knew I was right about one thing, he had seen a lot of old westerns.

Chapter Twenty-Three

For two old men, they moved fast when they wanted to.

Before Ellrington had even got into the churchyard, Pennington had disappeared into the greenery surrounding Rectory Cottages so that when James straightened up, gun in hand, Simon was nowhere to be seen. For a second or two he just stood there looking totally perplexed. Then the first shot rang out and took fragments off the gravestone about a foot to his left. He fired a snapshot response in the general direction of Rectory Cottages and ducked down behind another headstone.

Matters were clearly out of hand now and there was only one sensible thing to do.

'Come on, we're making a run for it,' I said, grabbing Mrs Pennington by the arm.

She resisted. She actually dug her heels in and pulled against me.

'No! Let me go! I have to see this.'

'Somebody's going to die for you and you want to watch? What does that feel like? Good? Satisfying? Sexy, even? Come on lady, they're dumb, but you're sick.'

Reluctantly she let me pull her by the arm and as another exchange of gunfire rang out we ran around the bend in the road towards Post Office Row and the car park. I was banking on the probability that with her in tow, no one would be shooting at me.

There were more shots and I knew I ought to be keeping count. They only had six bullets each as far as I knew. Each time we heard a bang, Margaret Anne stopped in her tracks and I had to keep jerking her off her feet to keep her moving.

'What have I done?' she said.

'Nothing you could have avoided, short of joining a nunnery,' I told her breathlessly. 'You just had that effect on the men in your life.'

Pity they were both psychos.

Then we were round by Post Office Row and the quaint white phone box and the Lulworth Rangers' Land Rover and just beyond was her BMW.

'Have you got your car keys?' I shouted at her.

She fumbled in her pocket as we ran, then flinched as another shot rang out in the distance, but her hand came up waving a set of keys.

I was distracted by the movement of her hand so I never really saw Peter Ellrington step out from behind the Land Rover and swing the butt of Simon Pennington's shotgun at my head.

Whenever you've fainted or been knocked out, the first thing you are always asked as you come round is 'How long have you been unconscious?' as if you have been timing things. It happens at road accidents or when you wake up in a cell wearing a paper suit.

I had little idea of where I was let alone how long I had been unconscious. My most immediate concern was why someone was trying to revive me by wiping my face and neck with a rancid piece of liver and then I opened one eye enough to realise I was nose to snout with one of Maggie Pennington's poodles. I didn't know which one and didn't much care.

'Piss off,' I hissed, flapping at the dog's muzzle, and with a huge effort, I managed to sit up.

The Lulworth Rangers' Land Rover was still there but there was nobody hiding behind it this time. I know, because I was in the perfect position to look under the wheel-base. Maggie Pennington's BMW was still parked on the other side of the village pond, but of her, and Peter Ellrington, there was no sign. The white telephone box was still there on the other side of the stone wall and I found that oddly comforting even though I knew it didn't work.

I could taste blood in my mouth and reasoned that I must have bitten my tongue. The whole left side of my face hurt and with a very tentative fingertip examination I found a swelling the size of a small melon, but at least my nose seemed to be intact and all my teeth were present and correct.

I hung on to the ladder at the rear of the Land Rover to haul myself upright, the first time I had ever found a use for one of them, and slowly edged my way along the side towards the driver's door and the wing mirror so I could assess the damage. In gruesome close-up, I could see my cheek already turning purple with what had the makings of a spectacular multi-coloured bruise.

Then my gaze strayed above the rim of the circular mirror and I automatically shrank against the metal of the vehicle as James Ellrington came marching round the corner from the church like a zombie, holding the old Webley revolver down by his leg. His trousers were green with grass stains and there was dirt down the front of his blazer, but I couldn't see any blood or obvious injury.

I could hear his footsteps on the concrete track and I could see the glazed look in his eye, but he didn't seem to register that I was there, directly in his path and in no shape to get out of his way.

'James, what have you done? What happened back there?'

He was almost level with me, no more than six feet away, when he finally noticed I was there. His first reaction was to raise the pistol, point it right into my face and pull the trigger.

If I hadn't already been in shock, I might well have thrown a wobbler at that point.

Instead, I calmly watched the gun's cylinder rotate and heard the hammer snap down with a loud click rather than an explosion. It was James Ellrington's rather dramatic way of telling me he had run out of ammunition. And that appeared to be all he had to say on the subject of the great Tyneham gunfight. He let the pistol fall from his hand to clatter on the road and then he was off again, stepping out at a brisker pace, arms swinging, towards the path down to Worbarrow.

As he passed the village pond, the two poodles, Jezebel and Sheba, bounded around his legs, having abandoned me as too boring, fickle bitches that they were. Ellrington said something to them which I couldn't make out and waved them away with both hands. The dogs yapped, bounced up and down a couple of times and then set off at a gallop towards Worbarrow and the sea.

I pushed off from the Land Rover and staggered up the road round to the church, weaving like a Saturday night drunk avoiding the CCTV cameras.

Ellrington's flight bag was still in the middle of the street but Simon Pennington's shotgun had gone, as I knew to my cost. I checked the bag but apart from the handcuffs I had worn, it was empty. James Ellrington had brought enough bullets for a duel, he hadn't bargained on it turning into a war.

'Simon! Mr Pennington, are you all right?' I shouted, but I got no reply.

I made a quick detour into the churchyard and found the gravestones behind which I had seen James take cover. There were three bullet marks I could identify and taking a general bearing on the 'incoming' and given that I knew, roughly, the range of such guns, that put Simon Pennington somewhere in or around Rectory Cottages when he'd started firing.

He was still there. Fittingly, for a ruin that looked like the Alamo, he had chosen to make his last stand there.

I found out by poking my head through one of the holes which had once held a window and coming face-to-face, for the

second time in less than ten minutes, with the business end of
an old Army revolver.

'Jesus! Steady on, Simon, I'm not the enemy.'

He was lying on his back on a pile of fallen bricks and
masonry which looked painful enough even before I noticed
that his right ankle was twisted at a nauseatingly unnatural
angle. If he was feeling it, he didn't show it and the gun
remained steady and levelled at my face.

'Where is the bastard?' he spluttered, having realised I wasn't
worth shooting. 'And just who are you?'

'He's gone and I'm just an innocent and very nervous
bystander. Would you mind pointing that somewhere else?'

He tossed the pistol to one side quite casually and I flinched,
half expecting it to go off.

'I ran out of bullets about fifteen minutes ago,' said
Pennington, trying to sit up and wincing at the effort.

'So did he,' I said. 'I'll come round and give you a hand.'

With considerable effort and some harsh language on both
our parts, I got him on his feet and helped him hobble out of
the Rectory Cottages doorway, propping him against the wall
while I nipped back inside to pick up his empty gun.

'Were you hit?'

'Not by him. I was trying to climb up higher, get a better
shot. Stupid old git that I am, I fell and did my ankle in. Did I
get him?'

'No, you missed.'

'Fuck it. Who got you?'

'His son ambushed me. Have you got the keys to that Land
Rover?'

'Breast pocket,' he grunted. 'Where's my shotgun?'

'Ellrington's son's got it.'

'Where's my bloody wife?' he said, like he'd just remembered
he had one.

'I think he's got her too,' I said.

'Then we've got to get after them.'

I was in Pennington's face, quite literally, and supporting the bulk of his weight, yet I felt as if I was on another planet looking down.

'You want her back?'

'I'm not letting that swine Ellrington have her.'

I'll never understand the older generation.

When we got to the Land Rover, Simon produced the keys and handed them over when I insisted on driving. Once I had him comfortable in the front passenger seat, I staggered back around the vehicle and picked up Ellrington's pistol from the road. Now I had both empty guns.

I jogged the few yards to the murky village pond and both of them made satisfying plops as I threw them in. I didn't know how often they dredged the pond but if they ever did there was a good chance their presence would be put down to a careless British army on manoeuvres.

As I was walking round to the driver's door of the Land Rover, I heard first one, then a second, distant shot.

Simon Pennington was still screaming 'Maaaaggie!' as I fired up the engine and jammed home first gear.

The Land Rover was just about the only vehicle I would have tackled the Worbarrow path in but it was still a bumpy ride and my concentration was not helped by Simon howling at the pain in his ankle every time we hit a pothole or ran across a tank track.

Even with the engine screaming, I think we saw them before they saw us.

The tableau ahead of me was made even stranger by my seeing it through a bouncing windscreen which framed them as if they were on television.

Margaret Anne was kneeling in the middle of the path and James Ellrington was kneeling at her side, his arms around her. Behind them, some yards away, was Peter, moving away as if backing off. Behind him I could see the sea and Worbarrow Bay and the *Margaret Anne* sitting motionless on the glassy water. There was no sign of a shotgun anywhere.

'The girls...' Simon Pennington said at my side and I shook my head to refocus my vision.

It was only then I noticed the two dead poodles, which Margaret Anne and James appeared to be praying over.

I stood on the brakes and heard Simon's inertia-reel seat-belt snap into place, then I turned off the ignition and was out of the door and running towards them, ignoring Pennington's shouts for help.

I wasn't sure what I could or should do to resolve the situation but I knew that putting him and James Ellrington within punching distance of each other was probably not a good idea. Before I got to them, though, the violence started and to my amazement, it was Margaret Anne who took the first swing.

It was a beauty, too.

From a kneeling position, and whilst sobbing hysterically, she delivered a right upper-cut to her old boyfriend's jaw. Before James Ellrington had toppled sideways, she was on her feet and kicking him in the ribs.

Instinctively, I slowed to a walk as I approached them. Walking into the middle of a gunfight was one thing, facing up to a woman intent on giving her lover a good kicking was quite another.

'You stupid, stupid sod!' she was shouting. 'Why did you have to bring your moronic offspring along with you? Did you want to spoil it all? Look what he's done to my beautiful girls. He's a maniac, a psycho. Why would I want anything to do with that bastard or the bastard who fathered him?'

Ellrington finally managed to roll clear of her flying foot and when her kick missed, she seemed to compose herself for a second, but only long enough to glance down at the hairy, bloody mess of torn dog flesh.

She collapsed on to her knees again, reached out and stroked the nearest body and then threw back her head and wailed her heart out. It was a primal scream of Biblical proportions and it bounced off Worbarrow Tout and echoed across the bay.

James Ellrington had made it to his feet and was looking down at Margaret Anne as if he'd only just seen her for the first time.

I thought he was going to plead with her but then I saw him shaking with rage, his fists clenching and unclenching, and I thought he might hit her.

I was now close enough to see Margaret Anne's tears running down her cheeks although, once again, no one seemed to notice I was there. It must be an age thing. Once you're over sixty you don't have to see anything you don't want to.

She was looking straight at me, but *through* me rather than at me, when she filled her lungs and yelled: 'Simon! Look what they've done to our girls!'

From behind me I heard his reply: 'I'm coming Maggie, I'm coming.'

It was almost joyous.

James Ellrington let out a hiss, there was no other way to describe it, and he turned on his son who was still backing sheepishly away towards the beach.

'This is your fault!' he screamed at him. 'You've lost her for me. I had her and you pushed her away.'

Peter Ellrington wasn't going to argue the point. He turned on his heels and ran for the beach and his father followed in hot pursuit.

'Are you all right, Mrs Pennington?' I asked, helping her to her feet whilst trying not to look at the dogs.

'He shot them. Peter, James's son, he shot my girls for no reason, then he threw the gun over there.'

She gestured towards a clump of long grass to the side of the path.

'Maggie!'

We both looked towards the Land Rover and Simon

Pennington who was limping towards us obviously in considerable distress.

'Simon!' she shouted, and pulling herself free of my hand stumbled towards him.

They met and the impact almost knocked him over. Then she had him in a bear hug and was burying her head in his chest.

It was suddenly very quiet, the only sound being a distant one of crunching pebbles, and I guessed Peter had made the beach and was going for the dinghy.

As far as I was concerned, the Ellringtons were out of sight and out of mind and I could concentrate on the happily reunited couple who might perhaps invite me home for some coffee.

Except the Penningtons weren't kissing and cuddling and making up, they were wrestling.

'No, leave it, let him go!' Simon was saying angrily, holding his wriggling wife by the wrists.

'No, I won't,' she was shouting back in his face and then she did what every woman should do when struggling with a man with a height and weight advantage, she fought dirty.

She kicked him quite deliberately on his twisted ankle. He howled and went over like a felled tree.

I was shocked. What was it with these affluent, middle-class pensioners? Were they all violent loonies at heart?

Before I could move to help, Margaret Anne was crouched over her howling husband and I assumed she was going into instant remorse overdrive and demanding to kiss better the hurt she had caused. But that wasn't it; she was picking his pockets, ripping open the flaps on the chest pockets of his Lulworth Ranger overalls.

She grabbed at something and then she was up and running away into the long grass. It took me several seconds of stupidity before I realised that she was clutching a pair of 12-bore shotgun shells in her hand.

She found the shotgun where Peter Ellrington had thrown it and had scooped it up before I had even started moving.

Holding the spare shells between her teeth, she broke the gun whilst on the run, ejecting the spent cartridges. But she had to slow down to reload and I caught her right on the edge of the beach.

I should have had a line prepared like 'Let 'em go, Maggie, they're not worth it' but I was too out of breath and too annoyed and I hadn't had any coffee that morning. So when I was close enough, I just put my head down and shoulder-charged her in the back, knocking her off her feet. She landed face down on the shingles, the shotgun landing about six feet away and fortunately not going off as the barrels, as usual, were pointing up the slope of the beach straight at me.

'For God's sake, can't you people act your age before someone gets killed?' I shouted at her prone figure.

She was winded but not hurt and she raised herself on her hands and knees. She wasn't interested in me, or the shotgun or the pebbles she was lying on, which must have been uncomfortable. She only had eyes for the waterline.

I had almost forgotten the Ellringtons.

Peter had outpaced his father and taken the rubber dinghy and was now swinging his legs aboard the motor-cruiser. James, undaunted, had ploughed into the water and was swimming strongly, only feet away from the stern.

I watched in silent horror as Peter clambered on deck and staggered to the wheelhouse. He must have pressed the starter for the engines at exactly the moment his father swung an arm out of the water and grabbed the stern rail in order to pull himself aboard.

'Is that the boat he named after me?' said a child-like voice in my head and then I realised it was Mrs Pennington and I sensed another major mood-swing coming on.

'Oh, grow up, woman. It's over,' I said.

She was still on her hands and knees, staring moon-faced at the *Margaret Anne* when it exploded and showered Worbarrow Bay with about a million pieces of debris.

The blast knocked me off my feet and I was right about the shingle beach being a really uncomfortable place to relax on. The noise of the explosion had set my ears ringing and I wasn't really conscious of anything much until I saw Simon Pennington limping over the stones to get to his wife.

'Did you do that, Maggie? Jolly good shot, my dear.'

His voice seemed to come to me from a long way off, over a hill, through a thick silent growth of trees.

Old people were certainly resilient.

Epilogue

I had no idea what had actually happened. I had read that the most common cause of accidents on small boats was where gas leaked (or gas taps were turned on) and filled the well of a cabin or below-decks space. Inadvertently, yachtsmen or women would succumb to the gas or simply turn in for the night and breathe it in as they lay on their bunks as the gas, heavier than air, waited to ambush them.

Of course there had always been the risk of an electrical spark, or maybe even someone lighting up a joint, which would trigger off an explosion. You can never be too careful when messing around in boats.

I didn't know how much anyone would be able to piece together – if anyone ever bothered to look at all. Certainly there was no sign of James or Peter Ellrington and their fate now rested with the tide and the fishes.

There was a lot of debris scattered over the water, but the bulk of the *Margaret Anne*'s fibre glass hull had sunk from sight in about four metres of water.

'It was a boating accident,' I said to the Penningtons individually, squaring up to them and wagging a finger in each of their faces. 'None of us were ever here.'

'But we're Rangers, wardens, we'll have to report it,' said Simon.

'Then report that you've spotted debris on the shore. No one saw what happened.'

I looked at my watch and was quite surprised to find it was only just 7 a.m.

'What do we do about the dogs?' I asked, at which Margaret Anne burst into tears.

I had to ask. The great British holiday-making public wouldn't give a flying fig for an exploding boat, but find a pair of shot dogs and they'd call out Scotland Yard.

'I want the girls buried at home in Upwalters,' she said tearfully.

Her husband put his arm around her waist and pulled her in close. For once, she didn't kick him.

'Come on, let's move it,' I urged, anxious to get out of there.

I collected the shotgun from the beach and unloaded it, putting the shells in my jacket pocket. Then I turned the Land Rover around and reversed up to the bodies of Jezebel and Sheba.

There was a length of old tarpaulin in the back of the Land Rover which served as a shroud for one of them. Simon sacrificed his jacket for the other. Mrs Pennington insisted on lifting both dogs into the back and laying them carefully down.

I drove us down the track and, on the edge of Tyneham, she transferred to the BMW. I kept my eye on her in the rear view mirror all the way back to Upwalters where I parked the Land Rover behind their cottage and we all climbed into her Beamer.

Simon needed a doctor to look at his ankle and she had decided that hospital in Bournemouth was preferable to a nosy local GP. That suited me as they could drop me off in Wareham on the way and I could pick up my hired Astra.

We didn't actually say goodbye, simply exchanged nods.

I didn't expect to see them or hear of them again. In just the short distance from Upwalters to Wareham I could tell they had bonded again and were even holding hands, probably convincing themselves that it had all been just a very bad shared nightmare.

They would get over it together. Perhaps they already had.

It was a thought I carried with me on the drive back to London, or at least until I found the first place that served decent coffee.

I didn't go into the office; instead I rang them from a motorway service station where I knew they did double espresso, and was a little put out to find they hadn't missed me. For that matter, they hadn't even noticed I'd been absent without leave for 24 hours.

I told them everything was fine; case closed; job done; and the client wouldn't be requiring a final report. Even better, Laura told me, the client's cheque had already cleared and he'd even given the firm a bit of a bonus.

So that was all right then.

On the way back through Hampshire, I kept the radio tuned to local stations but there was no mention of anything untoward happening in Dorset that morning.

Once on the M25 I stopped at another service station for a cheeseburger and a thick vanilla shake. It was comfort food to ward off the effects of delayed shock and the caffeine injections I had been getting on an empty stomach every forty miles. For dessert I had a piece of nicotine gum and did some deep breathing.

It was early afternoon and I was shattered as I drove into Toft End and pulled up outside the Old Rosemary Branch.

Home sweet home.

Amy's car was the only one in sight, so she was at home and maybe had missed me. I began to feel guilty about not calling her.

But not for long. My unexpected return had caught her red-handed and looking, for once, guilty.

Still, she tried to brazen it out and as I came in the front door she rushed towards me, throwing her arms around me.

'Honey! You're home!' she squealed. It was one of her favourite lines.

I pressed my lips against her cheek and got a mouthful of hair.

'What happened to your face?' she said. 'Does it hurt? Oh, my poor darling.'

Then she wrinkled her nose.

'Have you been smoking? Never mind, I forgive you.'

It was a good act and she was good at it, but I wasn't going to be put on the back foot.

Over her shoulder, through her hair, I saw an all too familiar figure standing in the kitchen doorway, leaning against the door jamb nursing, in one hand, what looked to be a flower vase half full of a pale brown, and I suspected Scottish, liquid.

'Mother, what are you doing here?' I said and I felt Amy go taut as I squeezed her.

'I'm so very, very sorry,' she whispered in a small voice into my ear.

'I want to make sure that my first grandchild enters this hard, hard world safely,' Mother said imperiously.

'You're kidding.'

I felt Amy's fingernails dig into my flesh.

'Never been more serious, Fitzroy. If I'm going to be a grandmother, I'm going to make sure everyone knows that that slimy ex-husband of mine, who is about to marry a girl of indecent youth, is going to be a grandfather. Let's see how that goes down with the gossip columnists.'

'Oh mother, grow up, can't you? Just act your age for once.'

My mother took a sip of Scotch and fixed me with the Mother Look you don't argue with.

'I am not,' she said slowly and deliberately, 'my fucking age.'

I let her have that one. It wasn't worth topping.

Author's Note

As Fitzroy Maclean Angel now seems to be an established private eye, readers with too much time on their hands will have noticed that there is a tiny homage to the great Raymond Chandler in every chapter. Most are taken from his well-known novels, but some are from his earlier short stories such as *Mandarin's Jade*, *Bay City Blues* and *Try The Girl*, which was the prototype for *Farewell, My Lovely*, where Velma was originally called Beulah. There are no prizes for identifying all the references, but I can guarantee fun trying.